Family.....
Secrets, Lies and
Alibis

A Novel By
Nanette M. Buchanan

D0886026

Type of Work: Text
Creation Date: 2006
Second Edition: March 2010
ISBN-13 978-0-979-3883-0-9
ISBN-10 0-9793883-0-9
Cover Design: Bradford Brown, Bradford Brown Art Gallery
              East Orange, New Jersey

I Pen Books
www.ipendesigns.net

Acknowledgements

To my family, husband James, children; Tynicia, Katia and Aaron, thank you for your support and faith. It is not easy to stumble, fall, brush yourself off and start all over. Thank you for telling me to keep my eyes open and always look up. To Ty, you are my lead in this dance, may we always be able to keep up with the beat. Bradford you are the exclamation point at the end of this fantastic work. It is for you all that I am proud to say
I will always pen.

To the family I never knew.

You are the best kept secret.

Chapter 1

The phone rang. It was early. The April mornings were still chilly and the phone beside the bed roused Darrell Mince from his deep slumber. He had slept under the quilt and left the windows open. The street was quiet, he noted, the dawn's light was making only a bleak attempt to crowd in through his blinds. It was not the time for phone calls, at least not as a start for a Saturday morning. On weekends, away from his desk, the crunching numbers for faceless clients, the constant conference calls allotted to his position as a top CPA at Sheldon Finance, sleep was sacred. Even so, the ringing was insistent, and Rell lunged at the receiver, exposing only his arm to the chilled air.

"Yes." he croaked.

"Mr. Darrell Quincy Mince?"

The voice had a professional quality, detached, impersonal, and no one had called him Darrell, since he was six-years-old.

"Who is this?" he asked.

"Good morning Mr. Mince. My name is Stan Simpson. I apologize for calling you so early on a Saturday. Did I wake you?"

"You did, in fact", he said, sorting it out. "Whatever you're selling, I don't want it."

Ignoring the man's protests, Rell slammed the receiver back in the cradle. His arm was just getting

1

warm under the quilt when the phone rang again. He swore and picked it up on the first ring.

"Hello." Darrell answered questioning himself about who could be calling.

"Mr. Mince, it's Stan Simpson again. Please don't hang up. I'm not a salesman. I'm an attorney."

Rell turned over; the remnants of his dreams lifting like fog.

"Ok, you've got my attention. What do you want?"

"Well sir, we haven't heard from you regarding your father's requests, and I'm simply calling to make sure you sign and return the paperwork we sent you. No later than Wednesday if possible."

He paused and drew a rehearsed breath to signal concern.

"And. Mr. Mince, I'm quite sorry for your loss."

Rell struggled to sit up fully, the importance of the words weighing him down.

"What loss, Mr. Simpson?"

There was a long silence.

"Didn't you get our certified mail?"

"I was away."

There was a stack of mail on his kitchen table, left there after he'd come in late the night before from the airport, bills unopened, personal letters unread. He'd planned on making a morning of it over breakfast.

"And has no one told you?"

Mr. Simpson spoke slowly, tentatively. The way one would speak to a child who had just lost his dog.

"Look, I haven't talked to my father in quite some time," replied Rell. "Can we get on with it?"

"Mr. Mince, I'm sorry to be the one to tell you this, but your father passed away last week."

Rell was more than stunned. He hadn't heard from any family members in the past week. He had let them know he would be away on business, but they could have contacted him by phone. Mr. Simpson allowed the pause in the conversation realizing the news had left Rell at a lost for words.

"Mr. Simpson, I must apologize for my rudeness when you called. I had no idea of the importance of the call."

"No need to apologize Mr. Mince. However, I must repeat the importance of you reviewing the papers that were mailed to you."

"Mr. Simpson, if it is not asking too much may I have your number to return your call. I have not had a chance to go through my mail, as I mentioned I was out of town."

"Certainly, the number is on the letter introducing myself and the need for your attention to the enclosed papers. I will wait to hear from you."

"Sir, I will definitely call you. I will need time to confer with my family."

"Of course, shall we say we will speak shortly after the funeral?"

"Yes, unless of course I have questions before hand."

"Yes, that is understood. Again, Mr. Mince I'm sorry for your loss, your father was a good friend of mine. I hope to speak with you soon."

"You will, Mr. Simpson. Thank you for the call."

Rell got out of bed, now fully awake he noticed the chilled air more. He pulled down the bedroom windows and put his bare feet into his slippers. The bathroom was calling delaying his intentions of opening the mail right away. Rell paused while in the bathroom. He reflected on what he was sure had been his father's last thoughts of his son not visiting him at the hospital. Rell washed the morning sleep from his eyes and rinsed his mouth with mouthwash. He realized he was only prolonging opening the mail and wiped the tears that welled in his eyes.

The letter was addressed, "Mr. D. Quincy Mince", knowing what the envelope contained Rell hesitated and took a deep breath before opening it. Rell read the letter over slowly wondering with each word why he hadn't been called. He laid the letter on the kitchen table and held his head between his hands. Rell had never thought about losing either of his parents. The letter gave a few details while mentioning that it was imperative for him to contact the Office of Simpson & Simon, Attorney's At Law. The papers requested his current contact information and explained that he was named in his father's will as the executor of his estate. If Rell had any objections, there were directions and more forms for him to fill out. In reading the papers he realized they were mailed while his father was in his final days. Rell's father, Derek Quinton Mince, better known as D.Q., had always hinted toward Rell taking his place one day, but Rell never thought about his death. Rell realized he needed to talk to his mother, his grandmother, or someone who could explain why no one called him. As he reached for the phone, it rang.

Rell answered, "Hello", trying not to sound as depressed as he felt.

"Baby what's wrong? You must have gotten the news."

It was his mother, Nikki. She sounded as though she had been crying.

"Ma, you knew? You knew dad was sick? You knew he died?"

"Rell I," sobbed his mother. "I got a letter from an attorney today."

Rell cut her off saying, "Dad died from respiratory failure after a long hospital stay. Are you saying you didn't know he was in the hospital?"

Nikki thought it best not to mention that she did go to the hospital two days before D.Q. died. She knew that would only spark an argument with her son, and she wanted him to come home without the bad feelings coming between them again. Since his move to Maryland, they had rekindled the relationship that had been lost. She had hoped D.Q. would have gotten better, and then she would have coaxed Rell into visiting him in the hospital. She couldn't tell him that his father had been sick for at least three months off and on or that this was his second hospital stay.

"Yes, you got the same letter?" Nikki questioned, ignoring his question about D.Q.'s hospital stay.

"What else did your letter say?"

"I guess it's the same as yours." Rell wasn't interested in discussing the attorney's letter. He wanted to know why no one contacted him.

"Why didn't we know he was sick? Why didn't Nana call us? Mama, both you and Nana had my number to call if anything came up. Why didn't you call me?"

Rell was feeling the pain of his father's death fully now. Tears began to run down his cheeks. He didn't know if he could have handled the information being away, but it hurt him deeply that he wasn't by his father's side. It was more than the pain of their distant relationship. Rell hurt more knowing it was a relationship that was permanently lost.

"I don't know baby, but I did call Nana after I got this letter. She said he died three days ago and no arrangements have been made. I guess she is waiting for your Uncle and Aunt to fly in from Detroit to help her with the arrangements. Rell, your grandmother said she wanted you home too."

Nikki hadn't called him sooner because she was in shock. She promised Nana she would call Rell right after she knew of his death. That was yesterday, her letter from the attorney's office brought her to reality. She knew if she didn't call him Nana would.

"So does this lawyer. This letter says nothing from his will or estate can be released without my signature. I was named executor of all his possessions. What was Dad thinking? We haven't talked for at least a year."

Rell let the words fade to a mumble. He regretted having to admit that he and the only man he loved had a wedge between them. Somehow now it seemed as though he built the wedge and his father just gave him the space he needed.

"Rell, Rell", his mother repeated softly, "You are coming home aren't you? I need you by my side for this Rell, come home baby please."

Since Darrell's move to Maryland, Nikki had not seen him long enough to consider it a stay. Even when he visited, he would only stop in for a day, always on his way back home. Darrell's thoughts drifted back two years to what led him to leave the home he knew in Richmond, Virginia. His new home was now in College Park, Maryland.

Chapter 2

here had been an uneasy feeling in the house the entire week. Rell hated that feeling. He and his father walked through the house, as though they were creeping on eggshells. They would ignore the yells and sudden outbursts from his mother as she would explode waiting for responses from Derek. Derek would whisper to Rell that his mother was going through the "change" and sometimes she needed her space. To this comment Nikki would yell, "Yeah things are gonna' change, you can believe that!"

D.Q. and Rell would laugh quietly as D.Q. would shrug his shoulders and slowly shake his head no. Rell enjoyed these moments because he and his father used these times to bond. They would talk about women and their emotions agreeing when it came to his mom's attitude, they just never understood what she was mad about. This day was different.

Their house was beautiful. The five bedrooms, three baths, living room, den, sun parlor and kitchen were decorated with Nikki's talent for color schemes and designs. She took pride in making it cozy. Their home always had a sense of love. Darrell continued to live with them after his graduation from the University of Maryland. They insisted he became stable and save his money for a home. Rell understood that his father worked nights and his moving would leave his mother home alone at night. It was a long debate and although Rell didn't agree he stayed with them promising to move when he felt he needed space. He always had his privacy. If he wanted to entertain, he would use the finished basement that was perfect as a bachelor's hideaway, complete with a wet bar, full bath, living room and bedroom. For special guests, if he needed to, he would make reservations for the entire weekend away from home. Whenever a serious argument erupted between his parents, they agreed to take it to their bedroom or the sun parlor. There was an unspoken rule that Darrell shouldn't be a part of their disputes even as an adult.

On this day Nikki and D.Q. were in the kitchen. Rell heard his father pleading with his mother saying, "Calm down baby." Nikki would yell off and on until she would break into a sobbing cry.

D.Q. was always a soft spoken man, a quality most would describe as sensitive. He explained his character as a direct result of being the baby of his family, raised by a mother while under the watchful eye of an older sister giving him a different perception about females and their emotions. Although his demeanor was quiet, his physical appearance was that of a strong man. This was always an attraction for Nikki. Derek's physique was one to die for. He was not a physical fitness fanatic. For a man, at fifty plus, he held a well developed six pack with the legs and a butt that could compare to the men in any gym. Nikki had a point to make and today's argument would not end with her in his embrace, her melting point. She was angry and this conversation was long past due, even if it did turn sour.

Rell began to enter the kitchen but thought twice when he heard his mother crying. He stopped at the kitchen door. Just his appearance was always enough to stop the argument, so he decided he would not interrupt them. The argument was his mother's emotional release. Rell decided to stand in the living room within a safe distance to hear the cause.

"How long D.Q.? How long? Rell is an adult. We have been together all his life. I've been with you over thirty years. I've been holding on to an empty dream for how long?"

D.Q. rose to his feet and walked slowly back and forth as though in serious thought.

"Baby, I know it's a dream for you, it's a dream for me too. But what can I do? I love you and I have always loved you, isn't that enough? I love Rell, I love you both. We are a family, even if we're not married."

D.Q. started to walk toward Nikki, who was now crying and yelling.

"We should have been married. It's been over thirty years!"

Rell couldn't take it any more. He was definitely his father's child. His emotions quickly flared. Rell busted through the kitchen door.

"You aren't married? Why didn't I know that?" Rell's emotions took over.

"I thought our so called family was a model to follow. Secrets and lies don't stand as a foundation! Dad, what about a man's word? You're, living a lie? I guess the only real thing is I'm a bastard!"

Rell left through the back door, slamming it hard enough to shake the decorative dishes that were arranged on the wall cabinets. Once outside, Rell knew he needed space. He knew it wouldn't be temporary. *"I can't stay here. It's time to move on."*

Rell's thoughts were racing. He jumped in his 2004 silver Accord and decided to ride and get his mind off what was now anger. He didn't know if he was mad because they hadn't told him, or if he was feeling his mother's pain. Rell enjoyed living with his parents because he valued their relationship and the home they had made for him. Since he was a boy, he couldn't remember his father not coming home every day or not being there for him and his mother. *"So why weren't they married? What's that about?"* His mind drifted for a moment from anger and pain to curiosity.

Rell pulled into the parking lot of the Belt Mall. Rell loved walking through the mall. He decided he would clear his mind by shopping for a pair of sneakers. He'd add them to his collection. He kept in shape by playing racquetball with a couple of his co-workers, at the Sheldon Finance Company, after work and on Saturday mornings. Shopping would take his mind temporarily off his parents. He parked his car, checked his wallet for his money and started into the mall. *"Shit! Not married. What is that about?"* Rell couldn't get it off his mind. *"Yeah, I got to move. It's time."*

Rell had been saving his money. He was financially prepared to move. After landing a few jobs before working at Sheldon Finance, he finally secured a good position in the company as a CPA. Sheldon Finance was one of the largest accounting firms in the state. He had become one of the company's top accountants with a decent list of clients. Mitch, a good friend and associate, who worked in the Maryland office, had talked with Mr. Moore, a top executive for the company. Darrell was being considered for a new position. Rell didn't mention it because the job was located in Maryland, and he hadn't anticipated moving. Rell would tell his parents he was taking the offer without mentioning his feelings about the day's revelation. Rell walked slowly toward Footlocker and laughed to himself. His secret about his job didn't compare to theirs.

Rell looked at the window display and noticed the reflection of a female's body that could be a runway model for Victoria's Secrets. She stood 5'9" with incredible beauty. Her features were strong and beautiful. Rell loved the sleek look of tall women. He stood 6'4" and although he would date women of all sizes, taller women turned his head. Rell thought to himself, *"She had to have a beautiful mother because a man who passed off those type genes would definitely be gay."* Her skin was bronze, and he could only imagine how the summer sun would give it a golden glow. Her hair was below her shoulders and was brushed back neatly into a ponytail.

When she noticed Rell was looking at her through the glass she smiled slowly and mouthed, "Hi". Rell turned to speak as she walked to the store next door and pretended to window shop herself. He smiled to himself thinking how the game of cat and mouse could be played, but he really wasn't in the mood. He decided to go in Footlocker and forget the next anticipated move.

Footlocker didn't have his size sneaker in stock. Rell decided to check two other stores before leaving the mall.

As he walked out the door, he heard a voice saying, "Shopping alone?"

Standing at the window where Rell left her was the 5'9" beauty waiting for his move. Her voice matched her beauty, and he felt his nature rising.

"Yeah, I'm shopping alone. What about you?" asked Rell.

"Just looking, I have a habit of window shopping at least once or twice a month. It helps me think," replied the young woman.

"Hmm, I don't mean to sound corny, but me too."

Rell wasn't about to explain what thoughts he had. Especially, the thoughts he had about her.

"I'm shopping for sneakers. If you like, I wouldn't mind you walking and thinking with me." He spoke hoping she would say yes.

Her smile was beautiful. She had deep brown eyes with long lashes. Rell couldn't help but think he had seen her before in a picture somewhere, maybe a dream.

"Maybe, I'll just walk with you, if you window shop with me. I'll hold my thoughts for later." She smiled and looked in the next store window.

"Thanks, what's your name. I'm Darrell, Rell for short."

"My name is Dershai, people call me Shai."

Chapter 3

His mother's voice brought him to the matter at hand, going back to Richmond. "Rell?"

"Yeah Ma, I'm coming home."

Rell said bye and assured Nikki he'd call when he was on his way.

Two years ago, that day was truly filled with new beginnings. He met Dershai and kept in contact, off and on, for two months. He was eagerly waiting for his transfer papers from the Maryland office of Sheldon Finance to go through. They went to dinner once. Rell used their date to tell her if he stayed in Virginia, she would definitely be a reason for his happiness. He didn't tell her of his four year relationship with Monique. Since he was leaving, there was no need. They hadn't gotten any further in their relationship than phone calls, small teasing talks and the one date. Rell was sure things would have heated up if he stayed, but he needed the space from Richmond totally. It wasn't long before Sheldon Finance gave him his requested transfer. The promotion to Regional Executive Officer in Maryland was approved when he asked to relocate.

Now he would be returning to unfinished business. Lately, he called Dershai as much as he called Monique. There was a difference in the relationships. Dershai never pushed to be closer than a good friend. Rell was tempted to invite her to Maryland to see if that was all she wanted, but he couldn't trust himself. No need starting what you can't finish, Nana would say. So Shai got plenty of attention by e-mail and the telephone both on and off his job. She was his tease, foreplay, and she did turn him on. He thought often about taking it further. It would take some arranging to handle her and Monique.

Rell loved Monique, but the distance made the relationship hard to maintain. After all, he was human and Shai was FINE!

"Damn!" Rell jumped to reality. He reached for the phone and dialed Monique.

"Hey Babe, what's up?"

Rell still had Shai on his mind. He was getting a hard on thinking about the "ifs."

"Hi, Sweetie, I just got in. I see your Mom called me. Is she okay?"

Monique kept in touch with his mother. She comforted her on days when she missed Rell the most. She helped his mother through the first few months of Rell's leaving. Nikki had missed him. She cried often and didn't go out much. Monique would invite her shopping, to the movies and dinner. Nikki grew found of her as a friend and prayed she would be Rell's wife.

Monique was pretty, and petite. Everything about her appearance was cute. She was about 5'4", deep dimples, and a dark complexion. Her hair was what most would consider that *good stuff,* and she kept it in a short sharp cut. Rell loved black women because they came in so many shades, shapes and sizes. He wasn't what one would consider a player but Shai could be a temptation. Lately Monique had been questioning Rell about their relationship and what could be done about the distance between them. She felt they should really consider moving closer so they would see each other more often. Rell knew it was a question of trust even if Monique didn't want to say it.

It was Monique's question that brought Rell from his thoughts of Shai. Rell brought his desires and attention to Monique. It had been three weeks since her last visit. It was his turn to visit Richmond. He had planned on it being a weekend of surprises. Now with the news of his father's death it would be business before pleasure.

"Money, I have to come home for awhile, we need to talk before I leave here though."

Monique wanted to comment about him calling her "Money". She hoped he would only call her that between the two of them. Lately, he did it more. She didn't want to be confused with one of the fellas. She started to speak about it but noticed the seriousness in his tone.

"What's up?"

Rell wanted to explain the situation, but decided it would take more time, he needed to go to his job and make arrangements.

"I was thinking about taking a leave of absence. There's some business I need to tend to and it may take longer than my scheduled vacation. Besides, I'd rather travel with you during my vacation like we planned."

He still hadn't come to grips about his dad's death, the letter and his grandmother not calling him, but wanting him home. Rell didn't really want to go home without talking it out with Monique. She had been his support since he left Richmond. Rell had shared his feelings with her and those same feelings were rising **again**. Monique told him that his parents situation wasn't as important as the life he shared with them. He slowly understood, which allowed him to feel different toward his mother, but he hadn't reached that point with his father. Monique sensed there was something brewing. She sighed, praying that he was coming home to stay, and he didn't know how to confront his parents.

"What's the matter Rell? Is it your parents?"

"It's quite a few things. Listen, you just got in, and I have to go by my job to tie up a few things. It's four o'clock and if I leave now I can catch Mr. Moore and Mitch to arrange my leave of absence."

"I thought you needed to talk things through." Now Monique was confused. Obviously, Rell had made up his mind about coming home. She didn't have a clue about what was going on.

"Babe, I have to come home, there's no way around it. I also need for us to talk this mess through. You know you're my balance. Just promise me you won't call my mom or Nana before we talk."

"But she called me, will Nana call me too? Rell, I'm not sure what this mess is. What's wrong? Call me on your cell so we can continue to talk."

"It will only take me a couple of hours to wrap things up here. Please trust me Boo."

"Alright, but what do I say to either of them if they call?"

"You won't have to talk, just listen."

Chapter 4

Monique kicked her shoes off in the living room of her apartment. The weather was beginning to change from spring to summer, and she was glad for the change. She enjoyed wearing shoes of the latest fashion but her feet told a different story. The summer styles allowed her to wear open toe shoes more often. Rell would tease her about buying them the right size, but her foot was smaller than most and hurt just as much. She checked the rest of her messages and turned on the television to catch the local news.

"What could Rell be going through now?" His problems were always deep. He could be the topic on any of the daytime talk shows and keep a captive audience. Monique sat on the couch to gather her thoughts. She allowed old memories to surface as she began to sink into the couch cushions for comfort. She reflected on Rell's, *'I got to leave'*, speech that he gave two years ago in the same serious tone he had today.

Rell came to Monique's apartment the day he found out his parents weren't married. He called saying he was

for this, and he wouldn't hold her responsible for keeping his father and mother's secret.

"It doesn't matter if she knew. It wasn't for her to tell me. That's not why I need my space, I need to move on."

"Where are you going? This discussion wouldn't be about living arrangements would it?"

Monique was always up front with Rell. She had been in relationships where she guessed her way right into quick flings, live in lovers, and heartache. She loved her apartment, her space and Rell understood why.

"No Babe, I'm taking that promotion I told you about in Maryland. I know it will put a strain on our relationship, but I don't need to be where they can pop in anytime trying to repair damage. Right now it can't be smoothed over and the distance will help them understand my pain. I will get over it, but it will be when I feel better about this."

Monique could have argued. What about her feelings for him? What about their plans? She even offered to move with him saying maybe she could find a job in Maryland. Rell told her no and stuck to it. He didn't expect her to move. He promised he would stay in touch and visit often. Since then they communicated by phone, e-mail and monthly dates and long weekends. They alternated on travel and Rell paid the expenses.

Monique checked the clock which now read five-thirty. Rell wouldn't be back until at least six-thirty. She had time to start her dinner and take a shower. She knew it would be late when they got off the phone and this free time shouldn't be wasted. Monique's two bedroom apartment was her haven. She walked into her bedroom undressing as she approached the door to the bathroom of the master bedroom. While running the water she looked for lounge wear and avoided the bed because she knew if she got in the bed, she would indeed miss Rell's call.

After her shower, Monique pampered herself with lotions and body spray. She felt the tension in her body ease her into a more relaxed mode. Monique stretched across the bed, closed her eyes and smiled. She knew it would only be a matter of days before she could release her tension and receive the best sex ever.

Chapter 5

ikki hung the phone up slowly wondering, *"Would Rell come home, could Rell come home?"*

He told her his discomforts but now things were different. D.Q. was gone; Rell wouldn't have to leave. D.Q. and Nikki had not been together since Rell moved out. Nikki lost both of her loves at once. Rell could be stubborn, just like his father.

"D.Q. is gone, gone, I love you so much D.Q.," Nikki began to cry again.

"I need to talk to you D.Q.. What about Rell?"

Nikki hadn't been able to sleep for the past two days after Nana called to say D.Q. didn't make it through the night. Nikki went to the hospital the day before he died. D.Q. had asked the head nurse to call her and tell her he needed to see her before the morning. The nurse waited for his visitors to leave that evening and called Nikki telling her to come to the hospital, D.Q. wanted to see her. D.Q. had purposely pretended to be overly tired so his immediate family would leave.

Nikki had never met his family members other than Nana, his brother Darryl and his wife Francine. Though his sister lived close to their home, Darlene didn't know Nikki. There was a lot Nikki didn't know, and she found out the same day Rell overheard their argument in the kitchen.

After Rell stormed out of the kitchen; Nikki took a moment to prepare for what was to be the worst argument she and D.Q. would have. D.Q. immediately blamed her for pushing things too far.

"Damn Nikki. Did he have to find out this way? You know that I can't marry you until the finances from my business and the properties are straight. Tonya will take me to the cleaners!"

"D.Q. she couldn't take you to the cleaners twenty five years ago. You didn't have shit but a good job and benefits. No, you stayed with her until you gained property and assets. You stayed until you became President and CEO. You stayed because you wanted to!"

"I stayed because of my children!"

"Children, what children? You said Rell was an only child.
You wanted me to have another child, so he wouldn't be an only child. What is this Bullshit Q?"

"We had a son first. He's two years younger than Rell. Our daughter was born two years later. She lied when she said she couldn't bear children. When Rell was born, I thought I would only father the children you, and I could have."

"So you were using me to bear your children? She had a son two years later, and you stayed long enough to have a daughter?"

"She was born after you said you didn't think you wanted more children!"

"You were married with no intentions on leaving. You expected me to keep bearing your children and sharing you with your wife?"

"Nikki, they are grown now, just like Rell. There's nothing to argue about. What's done is done. The important thing is I spent plenty of time with you and Rell. Shit, the boy didn't even suspect that we weren't married."

"That's because I lied for your black ass and told him from the time he was young that 'Daddy works nights'. There were plenty of times that he questioned your whereabouts, but I covered for you. I did a damn good job, I even convinced myself. It seemed to be easier to believe the lies than believe that you stayed with a woman you didn't love. In my heart, I believed it was about the business and there was no way that you would be sexing her and me for all these years. It takes a fool!"

"Baby, you ain't no fool. I am. I know where I should be I'm just scared to make a move and get there. Tonya held our relationship over my head for years."

"She knows about us?"

"Yes, she knows."

"And she stayed with you knowing I had your first born. Shit, that's hard to believe."

"Why? You stayed."

D.Q. knew from that moment that he had hit a major nerve. Nikki shutdown on him. The look she gave was vicious. He grabbed his keys and walked out the door.

Later, that week he tried calling and got her answering machine. After Rell moved, he tried to come over and apologize. The locks had been changed. He called before he drove to the house but the number was changed and unlisted. D.Q. waited until the next day and called Nikki at her job.

"Ms. Nikki Robbins, please."

D.Q. felt as though it was his first time contacting her. He waited so long he thought she was avoiding the call. He almost hung up the phone when he heard her voice.

"This is Ms. Robbins, how may I help you?"

"Nikki, its Q. I was wondering if we could talk later?"

"I would prefer if you didn't call my job again."

"Nikki, I understand. I need to get my belongings. I mean, if we can't resume our relationship, I need to give you your space."

"Fine, meet me at **my house** at six."

She hung up the phone. D.Q. was stunned. She didn't say home, she said her house. The house he had bought. Nikki was serious. He arrived at six as arranged. Nikki wanted to use his body one more time but decided against it. He was dressed from head to toe. D.Q. deliberately took time to make his appearance unforgettable. His thought was he would leave her with a strong memory of what she would miss. Nikki fought her devilish thoughts off and stuck to business. She knew he didn't come to collect his items dressed like he was.

"What belongings are you picking up dressed like that?"

"I have a meeting to attend at eight o'clock and thought maybe we could talk. If we can't come to an agreement about us, I'll come back for my things. Is that fair enough?"

"That's fine with me."

Nikki walked into the living room and turned off the television. She wanted to hear his whining for the last time. She had really thought about this, and she understood now how Rell felt, betrayed. D.Q. was at a lost for words. He loved Nikki, he cared for Tonya, and he loved his children. That was the problem. How could he choose?

"Nikki, I love you. I always have. I know that doesn't change the circumstances, but it is a fact. Tonya is not going to divorce me. She knows I want to be with you and that's why she won't divorce me. This is her way of fucking me over. I don't want you and Rell to become a part of her plans to pay me back. I should have told you all of this sooner in our relationship and given you a choice to stay or leave. I couldn't bear you leaving me or losing what I had with you. I was wrong. I'm not able to sleep or keep a focus on anything but you and Rell. I wanted to talk to you, and I plan on going to see him. I don't know what else to say. I have never been much on long forgive me speeches, but I need you in my life. Even if we can't continue this as a relationship, I need you as a friend."

"Q, I can't continue this lie. We can and should remain friends. There is too much time between us to be anything less than that. We are Rell's parents and always will be but there's nothing else left. You drained me Q. I have to begin to love me a little more than I love you."

During that same week, D.Q. gathered his belongings leaving a few pieces as evidence that a man was in her life. Nikki stored those in a box hidden in her closet. She smiled as she put the box away thinking, *"One never knows when a drop in visit may turn into an all night thing."*

Nikki reread the letter from the lawyer's office. Her letter didn't state any urgency for her to be present, but who else got a letter? During her visit at the hospital, D.Q. told her he loved her and needed her to remember that always. He assured her that Rell would be taken care of in the event of his death. Nikki told him she didn't want to hear anymore and for him to concentrate on getting better. Now that D.Q. was gone, she needed to know what drama would surface after this will was read.

Chapter 6

onya's day began with cleaning the guest rooms. She thought that a lot of the out of town family members would want to stay in her home. The guest rooms hadn't been used for a while, both rooms needed a thorough dusting and vacuuming. Lately, she only entered the rooms to put clothes that she planned on giving to the church on the bed. As she cleaned, she tried to prepare herself for the days ahead. *"A cheating husband's death could only bring drama to his funeral."* Proof of that was the letter from the attorney's office. *"What could be so important that all the family needed to be present? Did that include D.Q.'s tramp and her son? Well, they could bring on the noise."* Once Tonya got over the fact that D.Q. had passed on, she steadied herself, for the after winds. Tonya thought about the thirty years of what she considered *"Mince Bullshit"* and she intended to be rewarded for her tolerance. There was no evidence of her causing any disturbances ever. She kept her indiscretions out of the limelight. She planned on playing the role of the scorned, grieving wife if there was to be any disputes about where D.Q.'s money would go.

Tonya called Nana to see if she too had gotten the mail. Nana was not one to get into family problems, so Tonya was sure she didn't know about Nikki and her "*bastard*" son. Tonya was interested in how Nana's letter read. "*What would he be leaving his mother? After all he gave her all she had. Hell, all her children provided well for her.*"

Nana didn't need anything, at her age, she had it all, health and wealth. Darryl, D.Q.'s brother, helped D.Q. purchase and furnish her home. Darlene, his sister, took care of all her needs. Mrs. Mince was the best dressed senior at the church. Nana no longer drove the Cadillac they all gave her. Darlene or D.Q. picked her up and chauffeured her when needed. Nana told Tonya she got a letter, but she wasn't thinking 'bout no lawyer and no money until she buried her baby. Nana never liked Tonya much. She put up with her for D.Q. Now that he was gone, well, she hung up the phone without a word of goodbye. Tonya looked at the phone and rolled her eyes.

Francine, Darryl's wife, had called to say that she and Darryl were leaving this morning from Detroit and would call when they reached the borderline. If it was early enough they would stop at Nana's first and then head to her house. The phone rang all morning with condolences and "whatever I can do to help" calls. Tonya was expecting her children to call but after the arguing over who, what and when regarding their father constantly when they were younger, she wasn't totally surprised that they hadn't called.

Tonya attempted to give them a warning about Nikki years ago. She didn't get far because they didn't believe their father would cheat on family morals, let alone her. D.Q. did no wrong in their eyes. After D.Q. and Nikki decided their relationship was indeed over, D.Q. moved in with his mother. Tonya tried to persuade him to come home. D.Q. refused. She attempted to explain the problem to her children again. They didn't accept her excuses calling them lies. They were hurt by his leaving home, and she was hurting them more by bad mouthing the marriage. Now that he was dead; they didn't want to talk to her at all. Tonya decided the meeting with the lawyer would tear down their everlasting wall of protection they had for their dad. Their actions reminded her of D.Q.

Chapter 7

Darrell got in his car and dialed Dershai. He needed to tell her he would be in town for what may be a few weeks. He didn't want to be out somewhere and run into her without her knowing he was home. That move was okay on the weekends, but he didn't want to be nervous while in public for what may be a month or more. Sometimes on the weekends he would call her and tell her he needed to see her, but she would ease his hardened pain by telling him her desires of him on the phone. He needed that right about now. Especially since he could arrange to meet her before anyone else knew he was in town. He would arrange to see her before he stopped in Richmond. If he was gonna take care of business he would start where he left off. Dershai. She was truly beginning to raise his curiosity. At first he thought it was purely a sexual attraction, and then he wanted her friendship. Now he wanted both. He had to satisfy his craving. Then he would put her off for a while until he handled the business that brought him home and spend time with Monique. If necessary he could decide later about continuing to see her.

"Good evening Shai."

"Good evening to you, sir." Shai got giddy for a moment.

She hadn't spoken to Rell in at least two months and figured the fun had ended. She really liked him but knew she couldn't push her luck. Shai didn't know much about him, but she did know he didn't like to be pushed into anything. Just in conversation about some of his past experiences he voiced a problem with pushy women. So her plan was to let him guide the relationship. Rell was a little slow in setting up a plan for them to get together, but she could ride it out. There was enough dirt in her closet to keep her horns down, for the time being. None of the relationships she had were serious, so she could always invite one of her part timers over for sexual healing.

"What's up with you, lady? I was thinking about you and decided to give you a call."

"I'm glad you did. Where are you? In Richmond, I hope."

"You always have the power to see what shouldn't be seen."

Rell wished he had waited now to call her. Once again, his nature was reaching a peak. He needed to taste her from head to toe.

"Hmm, I could only imagine. Are you in Richmond? I have a few things I want you to see."

"As a matter of a fact I am making arrangements to come home. I have some business to take care of. Death in the family and you know how that goes."

"Whew, they say it comes in three. I had death in my family too. The funeral should be early next week though. When are you coming home?"

"I don't know when the funeral is yet. I'm waiting for the call about the arrangements than I can tell you, I wanted to see you though. Maybe we could have dinner and spend a quiet evening getting acquainted."

"An evening getting acquainted should be rewarding. If I can ask, who died?"

"A relative, but I want to see you before the funeral. You said you will be busy the early part of the week, what about Saturday or Sunday?"

"Well, I guess I can get away on Saturday, the wake is Monday so that should be fine."

"Okay, Saturday it is. Let me make a few calls for reservations, and I will call you back. Thank you Ms....."

"Shai, baby just Shai. We're beyond formal names now."

"You're right, I'll call you later."

Rell hung up the phone, just as he was pulling up to his house. *"Now I need a hand job and a cold shower. Distance dating is rough on a brother."* He decided to wait until he spoke with Monique. She always helped him with the hand job, even if she didn't know it.

Chapter 8

Darrell walked in his house to the ringing of his telephone. He wanted to let it ring, thinking it was his mother again or maybe Nana. He didn't want to confirm his arrival with either of them. Mr. Moore told him take as much time as he needed. Mitch would fill in on the accounts that had pending transactions, and if there were any problems he would call him. Rell would be talking with Mitch anyway. Mitch was his roommate in college and was close enough to be his brother. They had been through plenty of hard times together. Mitch told him to call before he left and give him the funeral arrangements. Rell would have to call Mitch and give him the update on Dershai and tell him not to call anyone looking for him until Sunday evening. He knew that he would have to cut his cell phone off to avoid calls from Monique.

The phone stopped ringing and the message light began to blink. Rell went into the kitchen trying to decide what to cook for dinner. The phone rang again. Darrell glanced at his watch. The time was six o'clock.

He knew Monique would not call, unless his mother or Nana had called her.

"I hope they didn't upset that girl", Rell thought. He closed the refrigerator and paused. The phone rang twice and stopped ringing. *"What's up with that?"* Rell picked up the phone and dialed, getting his messages.

"Rell call me as soon as you get this message. I hope you're okay baby. You know this is Nana."

Rell wanted to call Nana first but his grandmother tended to be long winded at times. His part of the conversation would only be uh huhs and other sounds of agreement. She could go on a while before she would say, *"You hear me baby. What you think 'bout that?"* The conversation with her tonight would be memories. What he needed to talk to her about could wait until he got to Richmond after the funeral but definitely before he would go see the lawyer.

Rell put the phone in the cradle and opened the refrigerator. He decided to finish the meal from the night before. He was glad he could cook. It saved a lot of money during the week. Eating out could be expensive, and he splurged once a month on Monique and their weekend desires. Rell made sure he could give her what she wanted on the weekends to compensate for the distant romance. He needed to clean out the refrigerator before leaving. Rell thought about inviting Mitch and some of the guys over for a few hours to consume the beer and some of the snacks in the cabinet. He'd call Mitch and ask him to get the guys together. He could tell them about his dad and say he'd be leaving town. His circle of friends included Mitchell Carter, Keith Larson and Craig Masters from his office, and Byron Washington another college friend. They would all come to the funeral, but they would also keep an eye on his house, check his mail and call him if needed. The group had been together since Rell moved to Maryland, and if you saw one, usually you saw another.

Rell placed his food in the microwave and dialed Monique's number after he gathered his scattered thoughts. He would eat during the conversation. He wouldn't leave until early Saturday morning. The drive wasn't long and that would give him time to prepare for his evening with Shai. He would tell Monique he was reserving Saturday for his boys and, they had plans on going out. He would see her Sunday.

"Hello." Monique answered in a crackling voice. She had been sleeping.

"Hey, are you sleep? Do you want me to call you back?"

Rell would call her later if she was sleep. Monique was good for saying it was okay to talk but would fall to sleep in the middle of the conversation.

"No, I'm just laying here. I guess I did doze off. What time is it?"

"It's seven thirty. I called you after I got myself situated here."

"Hmmm, I bet. You must be eating."

They both laughed. Rell always started the conversation with food or got food while they were talking.

"So what problems are bringing you home? I wanted to think you were coming home because you want to spend time with me."

"Tempting, tempting, and I do, but it's about some family business. Money, my dad died two days ago, and I have to come home for the funeral and some legal matters. They haven't called me yet with the arrangements. I have no idea how long the legal matters will take. My mom seems to be okay now, but she may go through some things with me being out of town. She seems to be taking it all in but when reality sets in who knows. I'm worried about Nana too. My father was her youngest and the first to die. She'll have some problems dealing with that, I'm sure. My uncle will be in town, but she may need my support. She told my mom to make sure I was coming home. She just called here and left me a message."

Monique was crying silently. She lost her parents in a car accident earlier in the year during a January storm. She had been in shock for weeks. Her doctor prescribed medication to help her sleep. Darrell had been there for her through the early phases. He stayed with her for two weeks and every weekend after until she came to grips with things. Monique knew the pain she felt and could only imagine what Rell was going through. She wanted to asked questions but let Rell go on.

"My mom said Nana called to say he didn't make it through the night. He was in the hospital and died due to respiratory failure. That's what the letter from the lawyer said. I have to call the lawyer to let him know when I arrive in Richmond. He suggested we meet with him one week after the funeral. He said I could contact him to confirm a date and time. My mother got the same letter. It's for the reading of his will. The funny thing is I am the executor of his estate. Nothing will be done without my signature. Seems weird huh?"

"Wow Rell, I don't even know what to say."

"Yeah, I still have questions from the last surprise my dad sprung."

"I don't think he meant this to be a surprise."

"That's the other thing, he was in the hospital sick, and no one even called me."

"Rell, would you have gone to the hospital if they did call?"

"I don't know, but they should have said something. Here we go again with these family secrets."

"Wow, I wonder what is in the will."

"I really don't know. My father never discussed his business with me. When I graduated from college he laughed saying he needed a good accountant. That was that. I know he owns a lot of stock, was the President and CEO of his company, and owned valuable property. He employed at least fifty people at the Richmond location and I think they had a few satellite offices in a couple of states. My dad was a business man, he had money. He worked hard for it. He even owned a few resort spots. This should be interesting."

Darrell started thinking about his father's gains. There was indeed an extensive list. That had to be the reason he was chosen as the executor. D.Q. knew Rell would maintain the finances and disperse his assets properly. His brother Darryl was a contractor. He had his own company, and he hired an accountant to maintain his books and finances. D.Q. had done the same by turning his affairs over to his son. Monique began to understand Rell's need for a leave of absence. It could take a few weeks to tie up D.Q.'s loose business ends.

"Who else will be at the meeting with the lawyer?"

"That I don't know. My mom got a letter too. I would assume Nana and Uncle Darryl would have received one. I don't know about any other family members, unless he left something to Uncle Darryl's children. I don't know though, there is six of them."

"Is there six? I thought there were five. I guess I lost count after the twins."

Monique couldn't keep Rell's family members straight and shook her head at the thought of his family drama.

"The last one isn't Aunt Francine's. The mother died during birth. They're raising her now."

"Is that his hobby? I thought the oldest was out of wedlock."

"Yeah, they raised him too. But the youngest child's grandmother had her, and now she is real sick, so, they took her in."

"I told you your family could be on a daytime talk show." They both laughed.

"I got the leave I asked for so I will be at your house on Sunday afternoon sometime. I want to stop by my mom's first. If I go to Nana's from there I will call you. But I will be in your lovely presence on Sunday for sure."

"Why not leave Friday night? Then we can spend Saturday together."

"The fellas want to get together before I leave. We made plans for Saturday afternoon and night. I think something is going on at the sports bar. Anyway I won't be seeing them for a while, and they are my local support system."

"Okay, sounds great. Aren't they coming to the funeral?"

"I know Mitch is. I haven't spoken to the others yet, but I'm quite sure they will. Mitch only suggested we get together before I left, and I agreed."

"How much laundry do you have to do?"

Rell dreaded laundry. He sometimes would convince Monique that he had to bring it with him. She would wind up doing it for him. Monique was prepared for at least four loads.

"I just did my clothes yesterday. I'll do the rest Friday before I get ready to leave."

"Really, that's a new move."

"I was coming to see you as a surprise this weekend. It's funny how things fall in place. Hey, babe look, I need to call Nana before it gets too late. Can I call you back once I speak to her, unless you're going to sleep?"

"No, you go ahead. Call me when you're done."

"Thanks, love you."

"Love you too."

Rell called Mitch before calling Nana. He told him of his plans with Dershai and the guys getting together tomorrow. Even if Monique called, nothing would seem unusual about them being over his house on a Friday night.

Chapter 9

"Hey Nana, it's Rell."   Rell was hoping he didn't call her too late. He knew she would say no if he asked her was she resting, they both knew she would need her rest for the stress of the days to come.

"I'm returning your call. You're not too tired to talk are you?"

"I'm not sleep baby, I been trying to find your father's papers that this lawyer is talking about. You are coming this week aren't you? I need you to look through this stuff, so I can give it to the lawyer."

"I should be there Sunday. We have time to go through that stuff after the funeral. Have the arrangements been made?"

"Boy, it's done. Your Aunt and Uncle helped me handle it before they left their home. They will be here in the morning if you want to talk to them."

"When is the wake?"

"Monday evening. The funeral is eleven o'clock Tuesday morning. Are you going to both?"

Rell looked at the phone. He had to rehash what she said. *"Why wouldn't he go to both? Maybe she was talking about the wake."* He really didn't want to attend two wakes.

"What time is the wake?"

"Monday, there will be one from three o'clock until five o'clock and another from six o'clock until nine o'clock. I think I will attend the earlier viewing. That other one is too late for me. I told Darryl that was too late but he said other people may find that time more convenient. The early time is for them business folks D.Q. 'sociated with. I can understand them, but who wants to be standing over the dead nine at night?"

"Yeah, I hear you Nana. I will probably go in the afternoon too. I don't want to deal with all those people I don't know."

Nana thought about what he said. She wanted to be there when the truth revealed itself. She didn't know how Rell would take being a part of his father's drama. Nana had told D.Q. to straighten out his mess years ago.

Nana loved Rell. He was her favorite. Darryl had six children at last count, Darlene had two, and D.Q. had three. Nana was aware of the extramarital affairs that produced her grandchildren. She was stern about her offspring taking care of their own and the responsibilities that came with them. Darryl made sure his children knew each other, but then again, Francine was a fool for his antics. Nana would have left Darryl years ago, but she always said, *"It takes a fool".* Darlene, her oldest, had no use for men at this point in her life. Nana prayed for her constantly. Nana described her as one evil child. After her last romance left her pregnant and homeless she wrote relationships off. Once she got on her feet, there was no limit to her success. Nana took her and her two girls in. She finished college, worked and now had her own beauty salons and hair care products shops. She stayed busy and used that as an excuse to avoid relationships. She agreed with Nana though, her brothers loved the drama that romance brought. She stayed away from their wives and their side pieces.

Rell didn't even know who Darlene was. He thought D.Q. had one brother and a sister-n-law. Nana didn't feel it was her place to tell him any different. Now that D.Q. was dead, who would be there when Rell found out about the family he never knew?

Darlene already said things were beginning to stink. She told Nana that she would pick her up for the reading of the will, but she didn't know what condition she would be in afterwards. She would try to contain herself but knew there would be problems between Nikki and Tonya. Problems she intended to address since D.Q. couldn't stop her.

Nana loved Nikki too. She didn't care for "that winch" he married. She knew that Darlene understood Nikki's side of the problem, since she too had been the other woman. Darlene didn't know that her daughters' father was married until she met his wife at his job. She told D.Q. that if she got to know Nikki she would probably build an alliance with her destroying their relationship as brother and sister. So she chose not to meet Nikki or Rell. Tonya and Darlene never hit it off and once Tonya knew that Darlene and Darryl knew about Nikki, she distanced herself and her children from D.Q.'s family as much as possible. Tonya thought she was the best thing God gave breath to and his family needed to know it. Nana stayed away from her to keep from putting her in her place. She did fancy the children.

Nana always thought Tonya kept them away from the family to spite D.Q., more drama. However, she saw Rell all the time until he moved two years ago.

"Rell you think you gonna move back this way? Your Momma might need you more now that your Dad is gone."

"They weren't together Nana, remember? They haven't been together for at least a year and a half."

"Yeah, I think that's what killed your Dad too. He hadn't been right since then. Losing someone you love can kill you. He should have been with your mom all along. I don't know what he was thinking. That wife of his never wanted him, just his money."

Nana was careful not to mention the children. She thought that Rell knew about the marriage and knew nothing about the children. The lawyer told her that information was to be discussed at the meeting. They would all meet and he was to read the will that declared Rell as D.Q.'s oldest son and the executor of his estate.

Rell didn't tell Nana that no one told him his father was married. He made the assumption after his father and mother broke up. Nana just confirmed his suspicions.

"Hmmm, but he made that choice. I don't think I will ever understand his motive. Almost killed me too, I can talk about it now, but I went through a thing."

"I know baby, I went through it with you."

"And I thank you Nana, you are my heart and soul."

"And you are mine. So I will see you Sunday sweetie."

"Sure will Nana. If I need to I will call you.

"Alright Sweetie, we'll talk later."

"Hey Nana, how long was he sick?"

"Baby a long time, he didn't even know he was sick. By the time the doctors stopped giving him medicine for his pressure, stress and depression, he was bleeding internally from an ulcer. They rushed him in for surgery and seemed like he took a turn for the worst. They thought he would pull through. Three days later he developed a breathing problem. I thought it might be pneumonia, but they said no it was an upper respiratory infection. He developed complications and couldn't breathe on his own. They hooked him up to those machines and he still died. I was running in and out of the hospital so much I wanted a bed."

"Why didn't you call me Nana?"

"Baby it was so much confusion with that wife of his, drama, nothing but drama."

"I guess you're right as usual. I'll call you before I leave here."

"That's fine baby."

Nana hung up the phone. Rell was glad he found out about his sickness before getting back to Richmond. He couldn't tell whether or not his mother knew the full story, but now he didn't have to decide what was sugar coated. Nana was not one to sugar coat much. If she did, it was for someone's benefit, and would be explained later. He felt better about meeting with the lawyer. The last thing he needed was more drama.

Chapter 10

An evening with the mystery man, Shai hung the phone up smiling from ear to ear. Maybe it would start a relationship that would last longer than a month or two. That's what she averaged before finding out the men she dated thought she got serious too soon. Shai felt it was time to be in a relationship that would lead to commitment. She had graduated from college, started working as a Medical Technician and moved from her parent's home all in the same year. She was a proud black woman and didn't mind flaunting her success. She appreciated all her parent's had done for her, but she was grown and nothing proved it more than her responsibilities. She handled her handle. Unlike her brother who followed the wind no matter which way it blew. Although she was the youngest she felt responsible for his failures. When she landed her job and got her apartment, her brother was still living at home with their parent's. Shai told him to pack up and move in with her until he found his own place.

Derek was two years older than her but no one could tell. He looked for her to give him advice, guidance and support. Their mother didn't show them much support and their father worked all the time. D.Q. would tell them they could accomplish anything they wanted and if they needed him, he would be there for them. As children they found it more comforting to share their happy and sad times with each other.

Shai called Derek to see how his day went and to tell him about her mystery man. She wanted to know if he had gone on his job interview, and she prayed he got the job. Derek needed another job, something that dealt with computers and web pages. He was great with computer graphics. His interview was at a new web designing company just outside of Richmond. If he got the job they would give him a bonus for joining the company, top computer equipment and a company car. Derek needed all of it to steer his life in a new direction. Dershai never got around to her news about her date for Saturday after Derek told her his news.

"Hey big brother, how is your day going?"

"Hey girl, I got the job."

"Wow! That calls for a celebration. I knew you had it." Dershai uncrossed her fingers and let out a sigh of relief. Derek had his father's name but his mom's attitude. If he didn't get the job it would have been the end of the world.

"Did you call your mother and tell her?"

"No, she doesn't even consider web designing a job. She will though when I can pull in those clients that will help me live on her eye level."

"She might come down off the clouds after the funeral though. Did Nana or Uncle Darryl call you?"

"Yea, I got the call earlier. Monday is the wake and the funeral is on Tuesday. I have to go to orientation on

Monday. Will you wait for me before you go to the wake? I figured we could go together, we'd get there around six thirty."

"Your orientation is on Monday? Yeah, I guess I could wait. I'll tell mom, so she won't think we just refused to come."

Derek laughed. "I don't think I could do both wakes and the funeral anyway. Dad knew so many people, I don't know if two wakes is enough."

"Being the President and CEO has its advantages and disadvantages."

"Shai, did you get a letter from an attorney's office?"

"It came yesterday, I forgot to tell you. I guess it's just the formal reading of his will. I can't imagine it being any deeper than that."

"I miss Dad already. He would have been proud of me finally landing a good job. Now maybe Nana will call me D.Q."

"No, I don't think anyone can fill his shoes for her. I need to call her too, you know, to see how she is feeling."

"I hope your mother doesn't cause any problems during the funeral or the reading of the will. You know how she is about Daddy's people. They probably have been named in the will."

"My mother, you act more like her than I do." Dershai meant that from her heart. She never considered herself to be like her mother. She was more like Nana than either of her parents. She wasn't much on causing, or being a part of drama.

"If she starts her shit Derek, I'm out. Regardless to if it's at the wake, funeral or the lawyer's office."

"Okay, don't get mad at me if I stay. I wouldn't miss it for the world. Nana will get her chance to put Tonya Mince in her place."

Chapter 11

arrell hadn't called his mother back to confirm his arrangements. He wasn't sure Sunday would set well with her since Monday was the wake. He wanted her to be strong, knowing she would break the closer it got to Monday. Sunday would be a hard day for her. Mitch called the crew and they all agreed to get to Rell's house by eight o'clock that Friday evening. Rell went on the computer for hotels and fine dinning outside of the Richmond to make reservations for his date with Shai. He kept in mind not to be too close to the city. If he was to get caught it wouldn't be in Richmond. It was ten o'clock. If he was going to call his mother, he'd better call her before she went to bed.

"What's up, my Lady?"

"Hey Rell, I was waiting for your call. Did you get in touch with your grandmother or uncle?"

"I spoke to Nana. I think Uncle Darryl is on the road. She told me the arrangements had been made."

"Oh good, she called me back after I spoke with you. I figured I would wait for your call or call you in the morning."

"I will be there on Sunday. I got a leave from my job. Mr. Moore told me take all the time I needed."

"Sunday, why not leave tomorrow since you got the time off already? You are off aren't you, or are you working tomorrow?"

"No but I have a few things to take care of here. There's nothing pressing that has to be done before Sunday. Nana wants me to go through Dad's things at the house but that can wait until after the funeral."

"Well, your uncle will probably jump to the opportunity to look through his stuff. He always wanted to know your father's personal business."

"I don't know if Nana is gonna let him. She was looking for papers the lawyer needed. I don't think she is up for Uncle Darryl's nonsense."

"Then she probably will put his papers and things away before Darryl gets there."

"Did you find out who else got letters?" Rell hoped his mother could give him some insight on what was expected from this meeting.

"No, she didn't even mention the letter or the papers you're talking about. I guess it would be the immediate family."

Nikki was careful not to mention his father's wife or the children. She didn't know what Nana had said to him, and she didn't think Rell knew about D.Q.'s other family. Since the lawyer didn't mention it, she didn't know if it was necessary to bring it up now. Darryl called saying he would be in Richmond Thursday night or Friday morning. He never said if he got a letter, but she was sure he had. Darryl never talked to much about Tonya or her children, so she didn't know if they would show up at the meeting. Before the funeral, when she got a chance, she would definitely sit with Rell and tell him everything.

"Yeah, that's when the fun begins. Are you alright Mom? I know it's got to be hard on you to play shadow. I mean not to have your input in any of the arrangements."

"It's okay baby. Like everything else, your dad knew this day would come. It's just another thing he thought he could have avoided. Only this time he can't hear me screaming at him." Nikki laughed a little. She thought about him saying 'Calm down baby'.

"Yeah, so he could tell you, 'Calm down baby'."

They laughed. It was a good moment for both of them. It seemed to release some of the tension the topic had brought up. They were stressed, wondering what the other would say or would do before this all was behind them. Nikki wanted to spend some time with D.Q's mother before the arrangements were finalized without Rell hearing the conversation. She was sure Rell would stop at his grand- mother's first before coming to her house.

"What time are you getting here on Sunday? Do you know yet?"

"I'm not sure. I think I might go to Nana's first. I hope we don't have to go through too many things to get the papers the lawyer needs."

"Call her first, maybe your uncle will find it for her between now and then."

"Well I have to see her on Sunday anyway, it can wait."

"I don't think you'll have to do that before Monday. The lawyer said the appointment won't be 'til a week after the funeral."

Rell sensed his mother didn't want him to speak to his grandmother until after the funeral. *"What was she hiding now?"* He definitely was going to his grandmother's house first.

"I'll call her but I'd rather stop at her house first, then come to your house. Just in case I want to spend time with you, I don't have to worry that I didn't stop to see Nana. Then again, she might have company who knows."

"Yeah, people may be running in and out of her house on Sunday, especially the church folks."

"You're right I forgot about them." Rell thought about it again. *"I don't want to be bothered with those church people. Baby this and Sugar that."* He definitely didn't want to deal with that. He would call her tomorrow and set up a time to see her on Sunday.

Nikki hoped she had convinced him that Sunday wouldn't be the best time for sorting through D.Q.'s belongings. She needed Rell to be in a good mood then she would spoon feed him the details of the secret that was about to expose itself. Even though he wouldn't like it, Nikki knew she could talk to him better if they were alone.

"Well, you let me know so I can have your dinner hot for you."

"I'll call you when I know for sure. Right now everything is in the air. I have to pack tomorrow and take care of some business here. I'll call Nana. I'll call you tomorrow night."

"Okay baby. I'll talk to you then."

Chapter 12

Darryl and Francine arrived at Nana's just before eight o'clock Friday morning. Nana was up cooking breakfast when they came in. The aroma of sausages, eggs, and grits could be smelled when the door opened.

"Mama sure smells good in here!" Darryl shouted as he entered the kitchen. He and Francine had dropped their suitcases in the living room.

"Did y'all bring that girl with you? I don't hear her complaining about being hungry."

Alesha was always hungry when she got to Nana's house. Although she was eleven she had the appetite of two teenagers. Francine told Nana that Alesha didn't eat like that at home. Nana would tease saying 'the child was hungry 'cause nobody fed her'.

"Nana, I'm hungry."

They all laughed. Alesha had just come through the door with two more suitcases. Her brother, who was now 6'1" and nineteen, came through the door with an overnight bag.

"Well did everyone make this trip?" Nana didn't know if Darryl had all his children with him or not.

"No Mama. Just Alesha, and Michael." Francine saw the look on Nana's face. "The others are coming together on Sunday night. They're staying with Tonya. She said she would enjoy their company and since no one was staying with her, she had the room. Did Darlene call you this morning?"

"I spoke to her last night. She said she would see y'all some time today. She had some running around to do so things could be managed while she was off next week."

Francine knew that meant Darlene wasn't trying to see them. She hadn't been herself since D.Q. died. Darryl said Darlene thought someone should talk to Tonya before this meeting with the lawyer. Darryl argued the point that Tonya was D.Q.'s wife, and she probably set up the meeting with the lawyer. He told her Tonya wanted the family to know that she would be getting all D.Q. had worked for. Darlene told Darryl he was wrong, as usual, and there were some serious issues about to surface. They argued their points until they hung up the phone. That was the morning after D.Q. died. Darlene and Darryl hadn't spoken since.

"Nana, do you want me to put these suitcases in the rooms now, or after we eat?" Michael's way of letting his grandmother know he was hungry.

"You got time to put the bags in the rooms, then come and eat. That goes for you to Alesha. Help your brother move those suitcases."

"Nana, he can move those bags. I carried them in the house."

"Girl, get a move on." Darryl waited to make sure she heard his voice. "What is her problem? She's been moody all morning."

"Darryl I really believe that damn Tonya knew what he was planning. She got colder toward him soon after she found out he was sick. That's why I was running so to the hospital, me and Darlene. Tonya wouldn't go but maybe twice a week. I guess to make sure he hadn't died without her permission. But praise be, his papers was in order long for his body gave out!"

Darryl and Francine looked at each other. Alesha and Michael excused themselves from the table and told their parents they were going to catch up with their friends in the neighborhood. After a nod of approval, they both walked out of the back door. Francine started the dishes as Darryl continued the conversation.

"You mean you know what is in the will?"

"No honey, I don't know what or who is in the will. I just know that Tonya didn't have her hands in it. Thank God."

"So what other things need to be decided?"

"That's where I need y'all to help me. Tonya doesn't want Rell to be recognized in the obituary. I can understand her not wanting to mention Nikki but Rell was D.Q's first born. No matter what went on, that ain't Rell's problem or his fault."

"I can understand her not wanting to be embarrassed at the funeral though."

Francine spoke without turning from the sink. Nana and Darryl gave her a puzzled look. Nana didn't want to start with Francine about who should be embarrassed. She thought to herself, *"No, you wouldn't be embarrassed. You would invite the other woman and the children to stay with you. It takes a fool!"*

Darryl didn't know what to say. He was just as guilty as D.Q. His first born was a one night stand. He met his oldest son's mother while on vacation with D.Q. and some other relatives. The woman moved to Detroit after she discovered she was pregnant. She threatened she would tell Francine. He told Francine and soon after his son was delivered to him one Saturday afternoon by the woman's aunt. That was twenty five years ago. Then there was Alesha. She was the result of a temporary break up with Francine. He didn't hear from the woman's family until the girl was nine and her grandmother couldn't care for her anymore. He had no idea she even knew where he lived. Alesha's mother died during childbirth and the grandmother called Francine and told her it was time Darryl took care of his responsibility. Francine went and picked her up. That was two years ago. Francine's response was always, *"Well what you gonna do?"*

"Well she can't ignore the fact that Rell is his son. Mama is right. So what solution did you and her come up with Mama?"

Darryl wanted to know what his mother expected them to do.

"We didn't and I wasn't about to argue with her at Watson Funeral Home. So we will go there sometime today and talk with her."

"Does Dershai or Derek know about Rell?"

"I don't know if she told them, I know D.Q. didn't. I don't know what he was thinking."

"Does Rell know about them?" Francine asked as she dried her hands and sat at the table with the two of them. "If not, that's another problem."

"I don't think Rell knows either. Remember when he found out Nikki and D.Q. weren't married he left town. Neither Nikki nor D.Q. told him. D.Q. was still trying to get Rell and his relationship stable before he got sick. I don't think he wanted to add that fuel to the fire."

Nana was sure Rell didn't know anything about other children. He would have said something by now if he did.

"I think you're right Mama. Rell talks to me two, maybe three times a week, we've talked about D.Q. and Nikki. He never mentioned Dershai or Derek."

"Darryl, did he mention the letter from the lawyer or the funeral arrangements?"

"No he asked Francine when we would get here and that was it. I think I was out when he called."

"Yeah, he called before you got home on Wednesday."

Francine was sure he had asked about the arrangements when he spoke to Darryl. That was Wednesday, maybe she was wrong. Before she could ask Darryl had he talked to Darrell later that day, the phone rang. Darryl gave her a "don't say a word" look, and she went into the bedrooms to unpack. Nana answered the phone not noticing Darryl's look of warning.

"I don't know what you talking about Darlene. Darryl and Francine are here now. I guess we will just have to talk with Tonya about that too. Okay, I'll tell them. Uh huh, three o'clock is fine with us. I'm sure. Okay, bye honey."

"What's the matter with Darlene?"

Darryl waited for his mother to answer. She walked past him waving for him to follow her into the living room. Nana opened a folder with what looked like legal documents in it. It was one folder of the ten stacked neatly in the corner of the room.

"Tonya done called D.Q.'s office looking for his things from his desk. Darryl, he emptied his desk three weeks ago or more. He brought home all his personal papers and things 'cause the doctor told him to take a medical leave. This is them here in these folders. Now you look through this, and see what she is looking for."

Darryl looked at his mother and called for Francine to come into the room with them. There was a lot to sort through. Each contained insurance, contracts, and other legal documents. Nana didn't have a clue what she wanted. *"First it was the lawyer looking for papers and now Tonya. What was D.Q. hiding now?"*

"Darlene wants us to meet her at Tonya's at three o'clock. Tonya called D.Q.'s office and told them she would be there to pick up his things. When she got there, she didn't have much to pick up. Only the things he left out. You know stuff on his desk, nothing in it worth her snooping. The lawyer went and got most of his stuff the day after he died. I called the job and they said Mr. Simpson had been there already."

Darryl interrupted his mother. "She was looking for a copy of his will Mama. Here it is. She wanted to know who was getting what."

The large envelope was marked 'legal will' in capitalized red print. There were papers inside it, and it was sealed.

"Let me call Mr. Simpson, I'm sure D.Q. wouldn't have copies of those papers right in his office where anyone could get hold of them."

Darryl and Francine stopped looking through the folders. They waited for Nana to return into the room.

"Darryl, I thought you and Rell talked later in the evening on Wednesday. Why didn't you tell your mother?"

"Fran, Rell was still up in the air about even coming to the funeral. He wanted to know what this meeting with the lawyer was all about. His letter has named him executor of D.Q.'s estate. I don't know if Nana knows that. It doesn't bother me but it may bother her. I don't know who she feels should be the executor of the estate, Rell or Derek. I'm gonna leave it alone and so are you."

"D.Q. left a real mess. I'm glad you straightened out our problems before they caused this much drama." Francine could only imagine trying to deal with arrangements for Darryl. Nana returned to the living room shaking her head and smiling.

"That Mr. Simpson is something else. He said we can drop off the folders today, or he'll come by and pick them up. He said he'll go through them."

"But Mama what's in this envelope?" Darryl was holding it ready to open its end.

"Put it down in that pile Darryl. Mr. Simpson said he has the will. The envelope was marked that way to tease Tonya. He said we will get all the papers back the same way we give them to him but there was a contract he was missing. He thinks the contract is in that envelope."

"Well if it's just a contract, we can open it."

"We ain't gonna open it at all." Nana knew Darryl was just being noisy.

Francine took the envelope from Darryl and placed it on the stack with the rest. Nana sat back in her chair. Darryl told them he was going to check D.Q.'s closet and pick a few suits for them to choose from. Francine picked up the phone and called home letting her other children know they arrived safely. Nana dozed off in her chair.

Chapter 13

Darlene had two more stops to make before picking up her daughters and going home. She told them to be ready right after the program at the academy was done. They were working at the Christian Academy Day Camp, and it was the first week of on the job training. Marci, her oldest, had been a counselor, since she was in junior high school. As a part of her internship for college she chose to work again with the Academy. She was in her last year at the University of Virginia and hoped to be a Social Worker for the state. Although she changed majors two times before, after two colleges, Darlene was just hoping she would see this one through to graduation and a degree. Mia chose to work at the academy full time as a Program Director. She had chosen a community college and completed the business course before landing her position. They both loved working with children.

They decided since they were going to Aunt Tonya's house they wouldn't drive separately to work. They met at their mother's house that morning and Darlene drove them to the academy. It was Darlene's intention to leave the academy going straight to Tonya's house. Now, after picking up Mia and Marci, she wanted to change her clothes to be as comfortable as possible. A family meeting at Tonya's could be uncomfortable enough.

"Mia, Marci, listen, I'm going to stop at the house and change my clothes first."

Darlene wanted them to know they weren't going to Tonya's right away.

"Ma, Dershai and Derek are not going to be there. I called Dershai and she said it was going to be nothing but family drama, and she really couldn't take much of that. Derek has a job orientation Monday. He's on his way to Maryland to hook up with some of his boys for the weekend."

Marci had a close bond with Dershai and Derek. Mia tagged along when they got together enjoying the company, but she didn't hang out with them much. Marci and Dershai were usually together even with their other friends. Darlene knew when Marci mentioned Dershai and Derek wouldn't be there, that was an excuse for Marci and Mia not to go.

"Well if you like we can meet later for dinner."

Darlene was looking for an excuse not to stay at Tonya's too long.

"Mama you know after you leave Aunt Tonya's you, Nana, and Uncle Darryl will need your own meeting. How about calling us when you get there, and we'll call you back on your cell phone and break up the meeting somehow."

They all laughed. It was the same technique they used when they were on dates. They would prearrange a time for the first call. Then they would wait for the call that would interrupt their date.

"So you're bailing out on me."

Mia and Marci said, "Yeah", in unison. They all laughed again.

Darlene hadn't told them all the details about this meeting or D.Q.'s personal problems that spilled over into everyone's life. They didn't know Nikki or Rell. It probably was best that they did miss this meeting. They pulled into the driveway. Both Mia and Marci kissed their mother and said they would wait for her call. They talked in the driveway for a moment, gave each other a hug, got in their cars and left. Darlene waved and went in her house.

Chapter 14

arlene entered the house through the garage. The entrance put her in her laundry room. She stopped and put a load of clothes in the washer that she had left on the floor. She walked in the kitchen and noticed the letter from the lawyer's office.

"Damn, what were you thinking D.Q.? This ain't going to be easy on Mama or Rell." Darlene had been talking aloud to D.Q. since he died. *"This shit ain't cute."* She smiled, D.Q. would say the same thing to her when she had got herself in serious trouble, or whenever she had deliberately done something that was totally wrong. Their mother and Darryl would say you got yourself in that mess, get yourself out. D.Q. would let her vent and try to give her some solution. *"Q. I can't even think of a solution for this mess."*

The phone rang. Darlene looked at the clock that read two thirty. She answered the phone, she was sure it wouldn't be her mother.

"Hello."

"Hi Aunt Darlene," It was Dershai. "Is Marci there with you?"

"No, honey she just left. You can catch her on her cell. Is something wrong?"

Darlene had not talked to Dershai or Derek since their father had passed.

"No, I'm okay. I wanted to know if she was going to her house or coming here first. We are supposed to go to the mall."

"Well, Marci and Mia just left here. They are in their own cars though so she may be coming straight to your place. You better call her to check with her."

"Okay, thanks."

"How's Derek? Is he okay in all this confusion?"

"Yeah, he's fine. He just got a new job with Carson Web Designing. It's what he wanted. He got a position in the arts department, illustrating for different corporations. He's going to celebrate with some of his friends in Maryland. He'll be back Sunday, so he'll miss the bickering and fussing."

"That's good he's been waiting a long time for something to open in his field. I wish I was going to celebrate with him instead of being a part of this mess."

"That's why I will be at the mall. Y'all are supposed to be at my mom's house at three o'clock right?"

Darlene glanced at the clock which read two forty five.

"About that time I guess. I'm not in a hurry to get there. Who is staying with your mom?"

"Ronnie, Chantell and the twins, are staying as far as I know. They're coming in on Sunday night. Uncle Darryl and the rest are at Nana's. I don't know if anyone else is supposed to be there."

"I think most are just coming in on Monday, and if they stay over they'll spread out between all of us."

"If they know like I know they'll skip my mother's house. She's in a foul mood. I can understand grieving but she's mad at everyone. Did you get a letter too?"

"I got one. I think all the immediate family got one."

"Well she's been ranting and raving since she got her letter. She was trying to tell me and Derek about daddy having an affair and the woman trying to get money now that he's dead."

"There is another woman involved Dershai."

There was silence on the phone. Dershai was stunned.

"Dershai, didn't your mother tell you about her?"

"No, I guess she tried, we told her we didn't want to hear it. My mother has been throwing this dirt at daddy for years."

"Shai, they were together for years. Your dad and this other woman were an item for a while."

"Why didn't you tell us? We would believe you. My Mom and Dad have been arguing so long we just didn't want to take sides."

"Well it wasn't for me to tell. Your dad should have told you and Derek long before now. I know you can't talk with your mom at this moment, but you and Derek need to sit with her. I would suggest before we all meet with the lawyer. He's supposed to contact us with a definite date and time."

"I know that's right. I guess that would make me mad too. Maybe I should come to the meeting."

Darlene didn't know whether Tonya had mentioned Rell to Dershai or Derek, but she knew the meeting wouldn't be a good place for Dershai to find out she had another brother.

"No baby, you and Marci go to the mall as planned. Your mother may not want to talk to you in front of all of us. It would be better if the three of you talked alone."

"You're probably right Auntie. I'll talk to you later. You better hurry up. They'll be waiting on you."

"Yeah, or I'll be the first topic." They both laughed.

Darlene went in her bedroom to change her clothes. She glanced in her closet and noticed the jogging suit she wanted to wear wasn't there. She went into the guest room and found it on the chair. She pulled down her jeans and paused. She pulled them back up and thought aloud. *"I'll keep these on, change my blouse and put on my sneakers."* The clock read three fifteen.

Chapter 15

Nana woke up from her nap to Alesha and Michael yelling at each other in the kitchen. Darryl shouted from the bedroom adding to their noise.

"Your grandmother is napping, hush all that noise. Take it outside you two."

"I sure ain't napping now. You ain't made it no better yelling at them. What y'all want in that kitchen anyway. Didn't y'all eat lunch? I heard y'all in the kitchen earlier. What you looking for?"

"Nana I just wanted water. Michael wants the water that is cold too. Ain't but a little left and he snatched the jar from me."

"Michael, give that gal that water. You get you some water and ice from the freezer. Y'all come outta my kitchen now."

Michael mumbled he didn't want any water.

"Suit yourself lazy boy. But still come outta my kitchen."

Darryl came into the living room and sat on the couch. "Mama, do you think this meeting will be long?"

"I can't say Darryl. I guess that would depend on how stubborn Tonya wants to be."

"Or how stubborn Darlene wants to be," answered Darryl.

"No, I think Darlene would agree with us on this point. Rell is the oldest out of them kids D.Q. left, and he should be included in the obituary. I don't care how she feels. The boy is a Mince and should be recognized as such. His father recognized him as a Mince, even if his wife didn't. What time is it anyway? I slept all day."

"It's close to two thirty. Guess we all better get ready to go."

"Well you know your sister will be late. We can't talk about her if we ain't there on time."

Nana went to her room to find her loafers. She sat on her bed saying a silent prayer for peace. Darryl went to tell Francine they would be leaving in a few minutes.

"Darryl don't you think I should stay here?"

"Why? Baby you are a part of this family too."

"I don't want to influence Tonya, one way or another. She knows I accepted Michael and Alesha. She knows they both were from the outside affairs you had. I don't want her to feel I was there to persuade her."

"That's nonsense baby. Our relationship has nothing to do with her and D.Q. He was with Nikki for their entire marriage and Tonya knew it. He didn't break it off. Even at the end Nikki told him she had enough."

"I just think it would be better if you, your mom and Darlene went and handled this. It's not like I feel left out, I just don't feel it's my place to be there."

Tonya and Francine had many debates over the years about Rell being allowed to visit his father's home to meet his brother and sister. This conversation stopped once Francine knew that it wasn't just Rell that kept D.Q. in touch with Nikki. He loved Nikki. Everyone knew it except the children. D.Q. would say he couldn't choose one over the other. He loved them all and he loved Nikki as well. Tonya stayed with D.Q. for his money not his love. She wanted D.Q. to love her like he loved Nikki, but his love for her died early in the marriage. The family knew it but they never spoke much about it.

"If you feel better staying here, then stay. I'll call you if it gets too late."

Darryl stuck his head Nana's bedroom door. He whispered he was ready whenever she was. Nana turned from her closet saying she would be right there. Darryl went to the bathroom, closed the door, and he leaned on the sink looking into the mirror.

"Q, they say when you become an angel you can hear those who you care for when they pray. Man, my prayer is simple in nature but a difficult task. I want strength brother, strength to deal with these women you left me with. All of them have different reasons to be mad as hell with you, and you left them here with me. The least you could do for a brother is give me strength."

Darryl opened the bathroom door and looked up.

"Amen."

"You can say that again." Nana said as she passed him in the hall.

They walked out the house together laughing.

Chapter 16

onya looked at the clock in disgust. *"They can't even get here on time. D.Q., you and your shit. All this will be over shortly, and I will be rid of you and your lame ass family."* Thoughts ran rapid through Tonya's mind.

She had made finger sandwiches and lemonade. She was prepared for them to stay awhile, but she wasn't offering to feed them a meal. If it had been just D.Q.'s mother she might have gone all out. Tonya figured if she could satisfy Mrs. Julie Mince the rest of the family didn't matter. The problem was Mrs. Mince and her desire to have this outside "grandchild" in the funeral program. As far as Tonya was concerned there didn't have to be a program. Say a few words and get it over. They could meet with the lawyer Tuesday right after the burial, the sooner the better. She had been waiting for this day a long time. *"D.Q. had enough time with that tramp to say what he wanted and now that he's gone, I'll speak for him. They had their day while he was living. I'll have mine now that he's dead."*

Tonya's thoughts were cut off to the sound of the front doorbell ringing.

"Hey Darlene, you beat your Mama and Darryl this time."

Tonya spoke with an inviting smile one Darlene knew to be aware of. She was usually last at all the family events. She did this, so she wouldn't have to be there long. Darlene could tell Tonya was prepared for possible drama.

"Come on in girl. Do you want some lemonade?"

"Yeah, I'll take some. You make yours just the way I like it. Not too sweet. Thanks."

"Sure, I'll set everything over here at the bar. Help yourself."

"How are you handling things Tonya?"

"Well, I don't have to pretend with you. It's been rough. I don't think it's so much about his death. I mean don't get me wrong, I love your brother, but he left so many things undone, too many things."

"You're right, and probably a lot we won't even know about until later on."

"I know that's right. I don't even know where to start with his business matters. It's enough with the family issues. Darlene, I still have to tell Dershai and Derek about this other son and his mother."

"I spoke a little earlier with Dershai before I came over here. I told her that the three of you need to sit down before we all have to meet with the lawyer. I hope I didn't talk out of turn."

"No that's fine. Maybe now they will talk to me. They've been avoiding the topic for years. We haven't been a family since D.Q. left to live with your mother. Thank you, I hope she will tell Derek we need to talk."

"She said she would. He's going away this weekend though."

"Going where?"

"He didn't tell you? He's celebrating. He got a new job in web designing."

Darlene could tell by Tonya's expression, she knew nothing about Derek's new job or his trip to Maryland. It was times like these that Darlene avoided.

"Dershai knew about this job offer?"

"I don't know if she knew about the offer. She just knew he got the job and was celebrating with friends this weekend in Maryland. I hope I didn't start any trouble for him with you."

"Oh no, it's just. You know kids don't think. D.Q. has a will that leaves a large business to be run. Why would Derek think that it didn't include his input, maybe in some position within the company? Why would he take an interview now?"

"I guess 'cause D.Q. never offered him a job before he died. Tonya if D.Q. thought that Derek could maintain the demands of the business, he would have groomed him into it before now."

"You're right, just like he didn't tell them there was another son that would be included in the reading of his will. I guess we all better prepare ourselves for what is to come."

Darlene was relieved to hear the doorbell ring. She got up from the bar stool to answer the door. Tonya went to the bathroom to freshen up. The conversation had overwhelmed her and tears had begun to form.

"Hey, Mama. Hey, Darryl." Darlene greeted them with a kiss and a hug. "Come on in. Tonya went into the bathroom, she'll be right out."

"How long you been here?"

"Since about three forty five, a few minutes. There's lemonade and sandwiches over at the bar. Mama, do you want something?"

Darlene walked over to the bar area. She already knew her mother would say yes to the lemonade. Tonya made lemonade to die for. Darryl walked to the bar and fixed himself a drink. Darlene gave him a look of confusion. Darryl only drank on holidays or birthday celebrations. Darryl poured vodka in his glass and headed for the kitchen.

"What's up with that?"

"If I have to go through this little meeting with three hotheads, I might as well get mine hot too?"

"Who's got a hothead?"

Tonya entered the room smiling. Darlene could see she had touched up her eye makeup and brushed up her hair. Tonya was an attractive woman. She took care of herself with constant pampering and spent a lot of time in Darlene's beauty salons. Her complexion complimented her eyes. She had light brown eyes and hair. Darlene wondered why women like her didn't just show their natural beauty instead of always covering it up with beauty products. It was profit for her but women like Tonya didn't need constant enhancement.

"Hey, Mrs. Mince. How are you? Are you holding out with all these phone calls and such?"

"Chil' them calls don't bother me. If I want to talk, I talk. If not, I say goodbye. People know not to get too personal with me. I ain't never been one to talk a lot on no phone."

Everybody started laughing. They all have been on the phone with her when she went on and on. Her conversations about the church could take you through most of the night.

"I guess y'all think its funny 'cause, I talk to y'all. I don't talk to them like I do y'all. That's the truth. Darlene give me some lemonade please."

"Mrs. Mince, I have some sandwiches here."

"Not right now dear, the lemonade is fine. Go see what Darryl is looking for in your kitchen honey. He acts just like them two at the house, in the refrigerator, for nothing, just looking."

Darryl came back to the living room with his glass complimented with cranberry juice.

"No Mama, I knew what I needed, and I found it. Thank you."

Tonya picked up her pad and pen from the end table and sat back in her chaise chair.

"Shall we start family? I'll write the information as we decide what we want."

Chapter 17

ershai and Marci met at their usual spot in front of the Nine West Shoe store located in the Belt Mall. Dershai was looking in the window when Marci walked up behind her.

"Hey girl."

"Hey, where's Mia?"

"She had some work to catch up on. She said for us to call her later and let her know what we're doing for the evening."

"Girl, these shoes are hot. Let's go in so I can see if they have my size."

"Shai, you know you never can get your size in this store. Let's look around first and then come back."

"Okay, which way do you want to go first?"

"Let's go towards Victoria's Secret. I need some bath gels and lotion."

"Are you hungry, do you want to eat first?"

Marci paused. The lunch at the academy had definitely left her stomach a hunger notice.

"Yeah, they had some kind of meat with egg noodles for lunch. I didn't eat any. I could go for anything right about now."

Dershai looked around. Let's do Friday's, they have a pretty good menu."

"That's fine."

The two walked to Friday's laughing and talking about the family members they would probably see at the wake and funeral. Marci told Dershai about her mother trying to get out of going to Dershai's mother's house for the family meeting. When they got to Friday's, they took a booth and ordered two lemonades while deciding what to eat. They decided on two seafood platters and gave the waitress the menus.

"Marci, I have a date with the mystery man Saturday." Dershai was smiling from ear to ear.

"With who? He must be someone new."

"Remember the guy I told you I met at the mall about two years ago."

"The guy you went to dinner with once, he's the one who moved to Maryland right?"

"That's the one. He called me yesterday saying he had to come back this way to handle some business with his family. He said he may be around for a couple of months and wanted to hook up with me."

"Well he didn't forget you."

"We've been keeping in touch off and on. You know, phone, e-mail, things like that. He sent me a few "thinking of you" cards."

"Hmmm, and you are going on this date to see if he compares to your other part time lovers?"

"I do want to compare him, but I'm following his lead. I told you I wanted to try him the day I saw him in the mall. I decided to approach this date differently. I am not going to even suggest what I want. If he can hold out, I can be patient."

"Whew girl, that could be dangerous. Well, at least dangerous for him."

Marci couldn't help but laugh. She knew her cousin had a little freak in her. She loved talking with her about her sexual escapades. Marci knew this new approach would not hold Shai's desires for long.

"I know that's right. But Marci you have to meet him. He is gorgeous. He reminds me of my father. He has deep dark brown eyes and thick curly hair. He keeps it cut close, but you can tell its nothing but curls. His complexion is butter brown or maybe caramel. He's about 6'3" or maybe 6'4" and I would say he's got to be a Leo, but I'm not sure."

Marci stopped her in the middle of her description.

"You didn't ask him his sign?"

"I don't even know his birth date."

Dershai always asked men what their signs were. She wasn't into the zodiac heavily, but she sometimes made comparisons to men by their zodiac sign.

"What makes you think he's a Leo?"

"He takes his time. He analyzes a lot before he makes a move. He loves the chase. I guess that's what is turning me on. Marci this feels so different."

"Shai, even if he is the "one" didn't you say he'd only be here for a couple of months?"

"For now, Marci, for now."

"So, after you knock him down, you won't get bored with the relationship? You know how your relationships go."

"Marci, what would give you that impression."

"Hooker, I know you! If he lived in Richmond you would know more than just his name. By now he would be another number in your book listed by his size."

They both laughed. Their food arrived, hot and smelling good. They blessed the food and continued their conversation.

"Marci, I think this date could take things to a different level. He said it was an evening to get acquainted."

"Well, I guess you will know more than his birthday after tomorrow."

"I'm gonna try to get to know as much as I can. Especially what makes him tick. I like his conversation and the fact that we can talk about anything. I know more about him than that damn Tyree."

Tyree was her last fling. They had been dating for six months when she found out he had baby mama drama. He was scared to let the mother of his child know he was involved with someone else. Dershai would call him when she wanted to see him. The lack of backbone told Dershai he wasn't the man for her, but he wasn't bad in the bedroom.

"So what is this man's name?"

"Oh, it's Darrell."

"Darrell, Darrell what?"

"Marci, I don't even know. When we talked the other day he tried calling me by my last name. I told him we didn't need to be formal after all this time. He doesn't know my last name either. That's funny."

"Well you make sure you find out. He may be a stalker or something."

"Girl you watch too much television. We've been talking for two years Marci, stalkers don't stalk that long. Not long distance anyway."

"Depends on how horny they are." They laughed.

"What time are you going to see him tomorrow?"

"He should be calling me today sometime I guess. He just said he wanted to spend Saturday afternoon and evening with me."

"Are you guys going out?

"You got me again girl. But to be honest I hope we start in. In each other's arms and a bed. That man gets me riled up just talking about him."

"Okay, do we need to change the subject?"

"No, I'm just saying. This may be serious for me. When have you known me to know a guy this long and not test the waters? I'm telling you Marci; I'm going to take this one nice and slow."

"You're right, that just don't happen with you."

Marci was the one who waited before sharing the sack with a guy. She needed her evaluation of them to be clear. She would tell Dershai they had to connect with her inner being. Dershai would laugh replying she had an inner spot they could connect with, and if they couldn't reach her spot that was enough of an evaluation for her.

"Well my sweet cousin, I will be getting my thing off with someone who I truly want to have a relationship with. If he should decide he wants me, it's on."

"Dershai, take it one step at a time. At least find out his name."

They laughed and talked through the balance of their lunch and desert. The two walked through the mall shopping, talking and enjoying each other's company. After two hours, they decided to go to Mia's and fill her in on Dershai's date.

Chapter 18

"Well I guess we can start with the prayer card. That's simple. Tonya did you pick out a prayer for the back of the card?"

Nana knew this would give Tonya an ill feeling. She didn't go to church much and probably hadn't thought about the prayer card at all.

"No Mrs. Mince, maybe you can select something appropriate. I thought the funeral home did that."

"Mama please don't pick the one that everyone has on their cards."

Darlene collected most of her prayer cards and kept them in an album for keepsakes. She wanted D.Q.'s card to be special.

"What verse is that Darlene?"

Darryl didn't know the bible well enough to recite verses. He knew most of them from hearing them over and over. Nana was determined to let Tonya pick the verse.

"Tonya can pick the verse when she reads her bible. They have other verses in Psalms that you can use Tonya. Go through it and pick one that suits you."

Tonya recognized this as the first round. *Mrs. Mince, one, Tonya, zero.*

"You can tell Mr. Watson what you want on the card when you take him the program information." Nana knew this would stir Tonya's emotions.

"Oh I thought you or Darryl would take the information to Mr. Watson when you took D.Q.'s clothes." Tonya answered ridding herself of what she considered a trivial chore.

"You don't want to see what we pick out?" Darlene waited for her response to the question before adding her comment to Darryl's question.

"Well, after all Darryl, he stayed with your mother for the last two years. Is it really my place to choose his clothes for his funeral?"

The bell for round two rang. Darlene walked toward the bar to get another glass of lemonade. She wanted to have distance between herself and Tonya.

"He is your husband and if you are wondering what your place was in the arrangements why are we here discussing the program with you?"

"Darlene, I don't want to be embarrassed by telling a congregation the news of his bastard child."

Tonya spoke out before she thought. She turned immediately to Nana.

"Mrs. Mince, excuse my mouth but this has been a long time coming. I don't think D.Q.'s funeral is the place to air his dirty laundry."

"Well child you said one thing right. It's D.Q.'s dirty laundry. Now I'm not gonna get into a dispute with you about how much you contributed to this dirt. If it's your reputation you're worried about, people know that you and D.Q. didn't have the perfect marriage."

Tonya rose to her feet walking to the bar to get a glass of water. She looked at Darlene who was nodding in agreement to the statement Nana made.

"Darlene, you can't possibly agree with your mother. Why should everyone know that he had an affair and a child while we were married?"

Tonya put her glass down on the bar.

"So the three of you think you can come in my home and force me to agree with this bullshit? There doesn't have to be a program as far as I'm concerned. But if there is, that Bitch and her bastard son will not be included!"

"Tonya you can cuss all you want. We ain't going nowhere and there will be a program. You are right. You don't have to be a part of this. I have a long time relationship with Mr. Watson. My word will make all the arrangements final. Now we can do this in a civilized manner, with everyone's input or me, Darlene and Darryl can leave and write it the way we want."

Round two was over Mrs. Mince, two. Tonya, zero. Tonya returned to her chair, pen and pad. She knew her back was against the wall. Why couldn't they see things her way? The funeral would be over in a couple of days. If they wanted to tell it all over town after Tuesday, she could care less. Not at the funeral in front of all D.Q.'s business associates and her co-workers. Tonya kept her home life separate from her business. Some of her co-workers didn't even know that she was married. Did they even consider Dershai and Derek?

"What about Dershai and Derek? They don't even know, are they supposed to find out this way too?"

Tonya broke; the tears began to run down her cheeks. Darryl went to get her tissues from the bathroom.

Darlene started back to her seat on the couch. Nana gestured to Darlene she wanted another glass of lemonade.

"Listen Tonya, and hear me when I say this. D.Q. is gone. He left a mess and we all in it, like it or not. Dershai and Derek are your children. You owe it to them to tell them before they get to the church and read it in the program.

"Darlene said Derek is not in town. He won't be back until Sunday sometime." Tonya was still crying between her words.

"Dershai knows about Nikki. I told you we talked this afternoon before I came here. She didn't say what time Derek was coming home on Sunday. If I know him it will be late. Maybe you can talk with Dershai first."

Darlene didn't really think that would work. Dershai and Derek didn't talk much to their mother in person without the other being present. They kept each other from going off on her. Tonya hadn't won any mother of the year awards.

"She won't talk to me without Derek being around. They told me that would never happen again."

"What kind of mess?" Nana couldn't believe her ears. *"What child can't talk to their mother? Drama."*

"Mrs. Mince it's been like that for years. They talked to their father. They worshiped the ground he walked on. When they got old enough to understand what an affair was, I started to explain. I wanted them to know about this woman and the child, she and D.Q. had together. Nikki never called or sent messages here and neither did her son. It looked like I was bad mouthing D.Q. They didn't see what was going on. D.Q. kept it from home. He was away too most of the time. Dershai and Derek thought it was always business that kept him away. They didn't know the difference and neither did I."

"So nobody told them about their brother?" Darryl handed her the box of tissues. "Where is Derek?"

"He's in Maryland, celebrating his new job." Darlene answered knowing Tonya didn't know. She handed her mother her glass of lemonade.

"He left knowing his mother might need him?" Nana was really confused about their relationship.

"It's okay Mrs. Mince. I'm fine. I'll get through this if we could just not include them on this program. I want to talk with Dershai and Derek before everyone else knows."

Round three ended. Mrs. Mince, two. Tonya, one.

"Well if Dershai knows about Nikki that's a start. I'm sure she has questions now. She will speak to Derek before the weekend is out. Why not tell her to ask Derek to come home early on Sunday so you can talk with both of them?"

Darryl thought that made logical sense. He went to the bar and looked at the sandwiches choosing one with tuna salad.

"Anyone else want a sandwich while I'm up?"

"Please Darryl, I'll take one." Darlene was getting hungry. She thought about the phone call to Marci and smiled.

"Darlene, you okay. What's got you tickled?" Nana and Tonya both were looking at her strange.

"No, I'm okay. Darryl, pass me a napkin too."

"Darryl, that's a good idea. I can ask Dershai to call Derek and ask him to come home early on Sunday. Then I can talk to them at the same time."

"Alright, now that we know they will be told about Nikki and Rell, what about the program? There should be a way to work this out." Nana had heard enough and wanted to get to the program.

Round four began. Tonya was getting sick in the stomach and her head was beginning to hurt. She didn't want to be bothered with D.Q.'s family or a program. If his mother had a solution then she was willing to give in. It wasn't a fair match anyway. The Minces came with a plan. The reading of the will would be her triumph. So Tonya prepared to surrender.

"Do you have an idea Mrs. Mince? What about you Darlene?"

"Well let's just go through the program and how we want it set up. We need to provide them with a picture."

Darlene figured the obituary would be the most difficult, so she took everyone's mind off the problem and moved to something easier.

"All but the obituary, the soloist and the picture will be set up by the funeral home. Tonya make sure you order enough cards and programs. There may be a lot of folks."

Nana hated when the family didn't have enough programs or prayer cards to give out.

"Mama, do we have to give out programs at the wake?"

"No, I don't think so. Darlene, Tonya how y'all feel about that. I don't think we need a program until the service on Tuesday."

"That's fine with me. We'll have the prayer cards at the wake and the funeral though."

"That makes sense, Tonya. You'll remember to give Mr. Watson a verse now."

Tonya thought to herself, *"Mr. Watson can pick the verse for all I care."*

"Tonya do you have a nice picture of D.Q.?" Darryl went for his wallet. D.Q. had given him his picture about one year earlier. "I've got a recent one if you don't."

"Let me see Darryl. I think that's the one he gave all of us."

Darlene went in her pocketbook to look for her picture to compare the two. Tonya went into the library to get the recent photo book. Dershai kept the book up with current pictures of everyone.

"Maybe, I think he gave one to Dershai and Derek too. If he did Dershai's should be in this book. There are others in here too. Mrs. Mince you look through here and see if you see one you like. D.Q. always took good pictures so it doesn't matter to me."

Tonya was right. D.Q. was photogenic. Darryl stood behind the couch to get a view over Nana's shoulder. Darlene sat on her left and Tonya sat on her right. As they turned the pages they laughed and talked about the pictures and the memories that came to mind. Darlene grabbed the tissue box when she saw her mother had tears in her eyes. They all took a tissue and wiped their own tears. They selected a picture from the book and agreed it showed D.Q. just as they remembered him. They decided to let the church's gospel choir sing. Nana told them that D.Q. loved to hear them when he went to church with her.

"D.Q. went to church with you Mama?" Darryl was surprised.

"Sure did, and enjoyed it too. He would have been there for about five years now. He joined the church about four years ago. He was on the usher board."

Tonya cried more now. She didn't even know he had joined a church. There was so much about him that was secret. It was like he lived a dual life. Darlene felt Tonya's pain.

"Tonya it's okay. Things will work out."

"Darlene, I didn't even know he had joined the church. What else don't I know about this man who was my husband?"

"It will all come out in time."

Darlene was right about not wanting to take sides in this drama her brother had caused. She could see clearly both sides of the problem. She couldn't understand D.Q., *"Why would he treat Tonya this way?"* She let the thought wander off. She **probably** never would find out. Darryl could see Tonya was hurting.

"You just don't know when. That's why you have to talk with Dershai and Derek. It's gonna affect them too."

Darryl knew that was the reason he told his children and Francine. His secrets were too heavy for him to carry. Nana bowed her head as if in prayer.

"Well Tonya, let's conquer this problem now. The program." Nana sounded as though she had new energy.

Round four had turned out to be a draw. She didn't have to surrender. They played fair that round. Now it sounded as though Mrs. Mince had reloaded. *Round five began.*

"Since I don't want to see Dershai and Derek get more upset than need be I think there is a way to settle this with less stress."

Tonya was getting mad now; her thoughts showed. *"What does she mean she doesn't want them upset? What about me? D.Q. I am sick of you and your family's shit!"* Tonya held her tongue but Darlene caught the change in her expression.

"Tonya, you alright? You want some more water?"

"Yes please. Mrs. Mince what could possibly settle this. Either they are mentioned or not."

"Let's go through the obituary first. There are so many things that D.Q. was into, let's begin to list them. I don't think the smaller things have to be listed. Like those community activities he did. If we just list he participated in the organizations, I think that will be fine."

Darlene agreed. "That will take up most of the room for the program."

Darlene brought Tonya her water and sat next to her. They all began naming organizations D.Q. belonged to as Tonya began to write them.

"Okay we've got his education, his job and the organizations. Is there anything else other than who he left to mourn?"

Darryl was getting hungry. It was six thirty and Tonya's sandwiches weren't holding.

"Okay Darryl we got the hint." Nana, Darlene and Darryl looked at Tonya. She lifted her head from her pad.

"Oh, are you waiting for me?"

"Tell us when you're ready to write."

Nana already knew how she wanted the obituary to read. She knew there would be little input from Darlene and Darryl. She hoped Tonya would follow their lead.

"Oh, go ahead, I'm ready."

Nana started narrating D.Q.'s life. Tissues were passed out again as certain parts of the obituary touched their memories. Just when she was about to name who he left to mourn Tonya spoke.

"Would it be improper to just say he had three children? I mean he has a lengthy obituary. If we just named you Mrs. Mince, Darryl, Darlene and myself; three children, a host of nieces and nephews, so forth and so on would that be okay? This is a lot for an obituary and people wouldn't notice much if no names were listed."

Nana didn't answer right away. She thought of Rell, Dershai and Derek. Mr. Simpson would straighten out this mess, as soon as he read the will. That day couldn't come soon enough. For now all they needed to do was get through the wake and funeral.

"That's fine Tonya, it will be just fine. You and your children aren't the only ones who will be affected by this mess. D.Q. done left all of us buried in his dirt. I don't want none of those children hurt by this. So if that suits you, it suits me fine."

Darlene and Darryl were in agreement. If their mother accepted Tonya's suggestion, they didn't need to dispute it. It was going to be her way anyway. *Round five ended in a draw.*

"Good, Mrs. Mince. I can type this up and come to your house on Sunday and drop it off."

Nana thought about Rell coming in on Sunday.

"Bring it to the house tomorrow that way you can look at the suit and see if it's the one you like. Darryl can take this and the suit to Mr. Watson in the afternoon so the body can be ready Monday for the viewing."

Darlene had begun taking the glasses in the kitchen.

"Darlene don't worry 'bout that stuff girl, I'll clean up. I'm going to call Dershai. You said she went to the mall with Marci?"

"They might be done by now. Call her anyway, they probably are still together."

"Do Marci and Mia know about Nikki and this outside child."

"Tonya stop, with the outside child, bastard thing. His name is Darrell, it's pronounced Da Rell. We call him Rell. He was named after me. He is part of the family, and I'm quite sure the lawyer is going to tell us that at the reading. He is D.Q.'s first born. I know it hurts to say so but D.Q. included him and his mother in his life."

Darryl was getting tired of her ragging on the situation like his brother was still actively cheating on her. Tonya rolled her eyes at Darryl and Darlene spoke before he could say another word.

"Well it is what it is. Rell is an executive at Sheldon Finance Company in Maryland. He will be in town I guess until the business at hand is taken care of and return to Maryland. I am quite sure he got a letter just like we did. We don't have to like the situation or the problems it will bring, but we do have to deal with it. So, I say we deal with it like adults with an open mind. I have never met Nikki or Rell, but she has never caused any confusion or drama for us. What was between her and D.Q. she kept between them? I like her just because she didn't bring no baby mama drama. Rell found out about you Tonya, what was it Darryl, two years ago?"

Darlene had no idea that Rell didn't know about Tonya when he left home. Everyone including Nana assumed he knew about D.Q.'s wife and not the children.

"It's been about two years. Darlene is right, they have never stepped into your world. D.Q. stepped into Nikki's and a child was born to them. They respected your marriage, even though D.Q. didn't. Who knows what he told Nikki for her to stay with him that long."

"Well it will all be settled soon." Nana got up from the couch and headed toward the door. "C'mon Darlene, you and Darryl take me to get something to eat. Tonya, I'll see you tomorrow. Don't forget to get that passage for the prayer cards."

"Thank you, I won't forget. See you guys tomorrow."

Tonya closed her door and stood for a moment saying, *"D.Q. when this is over, I hope never to speak your name again."*

Chapter 19

It was seven thirty. Rell had called Nana twice and his Aunt Francine said she hadn't returned home yet. She didn't say where she was, but she did say she was taking care of the program for the funeral. After calling the second time he decided to leave the message with his aunt for Nana to call him when she returned. He wouldn't call his mother until he spoke to Nana. Maybe he didn't have to go see her on Sunday. His aunt and uncle were there to see about her, so she should be alright. He would go by her house early on Monday. If she still needed him to look through the papers he would do that on Wednesday or Thursday. Rell was certain she had found them because she didn't call back complaining about his uncle snooping through his father's belongings.

Rell had ordered sandwich platters and hot wings to go with the beer, wine, and Hennessy. He had begun to play mixed CDs as he waited for his company to arrive. He planned to leave Maryland in the morning. He had made reservations outside of Richmond at the Ramada Inn off of Interstate 95. Rell had been there before and loved the suites for preferred guest. He would spend

Saturday night there and ride into Richmond Sunday in the early afternoon. He didn't want to put a definite time for his arrival in case he decided to spend the morning with Dershai.

Rell still had to call her with the final arrangements. He wanted to tell her to drive to the hotel but that wasn't his style. Rell wanted to pick her up, but since he didn't know where she lived in Richmond, that might not be a good idea. He was determined to spend the afternoon with her without being noticed by anyone who knew him. Rell dialed Dershai's cell.

"Hello. What's up lady?"

"Hey Rell. How are you?"

"I'm good. What do you drink?"

"Bailey's and Crème."

"Okay, I want to make sure I have what you like here."

"Thank you."

Dershai knew that meant they would be alone at some point and time. He would definitely be giving her what she liked.

"Hey, there's a Ramada Inn where I will be staying, outside of Richmond. You can drive your car there, and we can leave, spend the afternoon doing anything you like, go to dinner, maybe dancing and return, ending the evening with a romantic night cap."

Rell wanted her to drive her car back to Richmond the next day, so he wouldn't have to drop her off. Until he knew for sure she didn't live near Monique, her family, or her friends, she would be driving to meet him. This was perfect though because he would tell her that he wanted her to meet him half way. He knew restaurants and clubs near the hotel because he had clients who he entertained when they came to town.

"That sounds fine. What time do you want to meet?"

"Is two o'clock too early?"

"No that's fine. I don't have much to do in the morning."

"If you need more time let me know. I will probably be checking in the hotel at eleven in the morning. Call me if you need more time."

"Okay, should I bring anything with me?"

"Anything like what?"

Rell knew she meant clothing, but he played dumb.

"You said dinner and dancing. That might require a lady to change and get ready for the evening."

He smiled. If that had been Monique, she would have just come without an outfit, and while they were out she'd ask for a new one for the evening. She played him like that often. The game was cute in the beginning of their relationship, but lately it had played out. The thought of comparing Monique's actions with Dershai's surprised Rell. He had never compared Monique with any of the women he had dinner or went to the movies within the past. He couldn't understand his feelings. What was specila about Dershai? Rell put the thought aside continuing their conversation.

"You're right. You can bring what you want to wear. We will be dining and dancing at a club that requires me to wear a jacket so you can choose your outfit accordingly."

"And after?"

"You can bring what you want for before and after. It's up to you."

The door bell rang before she could answer.

"Shai listen, that should be Mitch or one of the fellas they're coming over tonight for drinks. Hold on."

She waited, thinking about how her Saturday would play out. She didn't even mind the drive to meet him. She would ask what that was about later though. Shai didn't want to spoil the date with thoughts, he was playing hide and seek with his girlfriend.

"Hey baby, it was Mitch. Do you know where the Ramada Inn is?"

"Yes, I have been in that area."

"Well if you need me to direct you tomorrow don't hesitate to call."

"Rell, why didn't you offer to pick me up?"

Rell knew, listening to her question, she was sharper than Monique. Monique never questioned his actions. *"Okay, Shai will be a tempting challenge."* He liked that. Monique had become predictable.

"Where in Richmond do you live?"

"I live in the condominiums near the University. Are you familiar with the area?"

Rell thought about it. She lived on the opposite side of town than Monique. She was actually closer to Interstate 95 then he thought. That was good for him. Monique didn't travel much on that side of town. He would stick to his story though.

"I'm driving into town for a funeral and business, remember? I don't want to be tempted to stop at a family member's house and get caught up without seeing you. That's why I booked a suite outside of town."

"I just wanted to know. I'm not one for drama. If that's what it is, it will reveal itself."

"C'mon babe, we've been talking on and off for two years. I never asked you about your personal life 'cause, I knew at the time I couldn't be a part of it full time."

"And now?" Shai was hoping he would say things may have changed.

"Well let's just say things may have changed. I don't believe I will be moving back to Richmond, but I may have to come closer than Maryland. And I'm not one for drama either."

"What about your job and your position?"

"That may have to change too. Shai, I want to see you because lately I think about you a lot. Let's just leave it there for tonight. I promise to answer your questions tomorrow. That's if you are still interested."

"I'm sure I will be interested."

"Hey, let me call you in the morning. I would say later tonight, but I would be lying. These guys will probably have a contest on who will get drunk first. I usually lose at that game."

Shai laughed. "Have a good time, I'll talk with you tomorrow."

"Thanks baby, good night."

Chapter 20

Mitch walked in on the end of Rell's conversation with Shai. He wanted to know more about Rell's interest in Shai and what happened to the "solid" relationship he had with Monique and took the opportunity to ask questions.

"So what's up my brother? Is tomorrow set?"

"Pretty much, I packed already and that was the hard part. I may need you or Byron to bring some of my other things after the funeral. That would depend on how long I may have to stay."

"Or how long you may want to stay; what's up with Monique? You haven't mentioned visiting her, just your hook up with Dershai."

"Man, I think she's tripping again. I don't want to give her the impression that we will be living together. I don't think I'm ready for that. I don't know how long it will take me to finalize this mess with my father, but I don't think I'm gonna start staying with Monique for her to get any ideas. I'll stay with my mother until she undoubtedly gets on my nerves. My Aunt and Uncle won't be in town for more than a week or two, and I'll stay with Nana after they leave."

"It would be hard for you to meet Dershai if you stayed at Monique's."

"Mitch, man at first I thought of her as a nice weekend lay. Now, I don't know man. I may want to try to get to know her better. She's sharp or maybe she's more experienced than Monique. I think that's the attraction. Maybe I'm just bored with this driving back and forth for a weekend that ends with Monique begging me to change my mind. If it wasn't for my dad's funeral, I think I might have met Dershai and nixed Monique this week."

"I thought you spoke to Monique the other night and planned on visiting her this weekend anyway?"

"Yeah I said that but after talking to Dershai, man my feelings leaned toward spending time with her. That's how it usually starts. I talk with Monique and think about Dershai. Lately, Monique has been begging me to let her come and live here. When I tell her she'll regret leaving her job, she then talks this compromise shit. I don't need the hassle right now."

"Rell, man she shouldn't hassle you now knowing what you might have to deal with. You know, the lawyer, your mother and who knows what else."

"I think telling her what was up just may spark her to push harder. I thought about it last night man, I'm not staying with her on a regular, nothing to even hint that it may be my intentions. Just an occasional overnight at the most. I don't want her to get used to me next to her every night. That shit is addictive."

They both laughed. The door bell rang it was Keith and Craig. Rell answered the door and saw Byron pulling in the driveway.

Chapter 21

After hanging up her phone, Dershai, started to call Marci, but she decided to go through her closet. She started coordinating the easiest outfit first. An afternoon doing what she wanted to do, Dershai could not remember the last time a man told her that. They never told her that. They always had set plans and most of the plans were the man's if he arranged the date. Rell was different. It was as though she knew him or his personality. She always felt comfortable when talking with him.

"Okay Shai, what do you wear when you want to keep a man's attention? Nothing!" Shai laughed to herself. *"A skirt, dress, pants, whew. I don't know what to wear."*

The phone rang. Shai fell across her bed to reach the phone on the nightstand on the other side of the bed.

"Hello." Shai rolled on her back looking up into the ceiling.

"Dershai, hi, it's Mommy."

"Oh, hey, Ma what's up?"

"Why didn't you call me earlier?"

"I was at the mall with Marci. Besides you had business to handle with Nana, Uncle Darryl and Aunt

Darlene." Dershai wondered what argument this would start. She could hear it in her mother's tone.

"Hmm, where's your brother?"

"Call him on his cell, he'll answer."

"Where is he?"

"I'm not quite sure, somewhere in Maryland visiting friends."

"See Dershai, that's the shit I'm talking about. You and your brother get together and do shit to annoy me."

"I'm here in Richmond. What are you talking about?"

"What is he doing in Maryland and your father's funeral is Monday?"

"Mom he'll be back on Sunday night. It wasn't like he was needed to do anything. You took care of the arrangements with Nana yesterday and y'all did the program today. What was Derek supposed to do?"

"Step up and be the man in the family. It's time he stepped up."

Dershai knew her mother had to have had a few drinks in her. Derek never stepped up to do anything for himself let alone for anyone else. His biggest accomplishment was the job he just got.

"Ma, he's celebrating getting a new job. He is probably in the same condition you are. Drunk!"

"What new job? And I am not drunk!"

"We'll know tomorrow when you don't remember this conversation. Anyway he got a job at Carson's Web Designing. His orientation is Monday. We will be at the six o'clock wake."

"You're not coming to the early wake? You're your father's children. What will it look like when people don't see you there?"

"It will look like we couldn't take coming to see our father laid out all day and then follow it with a funeral. Even if he didn't have the orientation Monday, I don't know that I would want to come to both wakes. That's a lot Ma. Maybe you need to consider not staying long at both of them."

"I will be attending both. I am your father's wife and no one else will get that recognition for the next couple of days."

Shai thought to herself. *"Lady, you are drunk."* Her mother babbled on for a few minutes about her father's business partners expecting to see her at the early wake and the family not wanting her to be around at the late wake. She intended to turn heads at both.

"Shai, I need to talk to you and Derek on Sunday. We need to sit and talk. Me, you and Derek. I need to tell you about your father and that winch he had before he died."

Shai cut her off before she continued her statement.

"Ma, I'll call Derek. If he is coming home, I'll call you with a time. I can't talk about this now. Bye."

Shai hung up the phone thinking. *"Damn that woman irks me."*

Shai called Marci. She needed wardrobe guidance. She couldn't pick an outfit even for the afternoon.

"Marci, I need the fashion police."

"Shai? What's up now?"

"Rell called and said the date for the afternoon was whatever I wanted to do. Then we would be dining and dancing at some club that requires the men to wear jackets, and afterwards we would have a romantic discussion in the suites at the Ramada Inn."

"Some day, go ahead Miss Thang.   So what's the problem you have plenty of clothes."

"That's just it, what do I wear?"

"What do you wear when you want to hold a man's attention?"

They both chimed in together.

"Nothing!" They both laughed hysterically.

Chapter 22

Nikki hung up the phone and went in the kitchen to do the dishes left from dinner. She spent most of her day giving the arrangements for D.Q.'s funeral to her family and friends. They gave her their condolences telling her they would see her at the wake on Monday. Her cousin, Simone, called to say she would fly in from New York Sunday night and stay with her awhile. Nikki and Simone were very close. Simone was Nikki's Aunt Peach's daughter, who was her mother's only surviving sibling. Nikki's parents were deceased and she was an only child. Nikki's family was small but they stayed in touch. Most of them lived in New York or Philadelphia.

After doing the dishes, she decided to call Rell. He didn't call to say what time he was coming in on Sunday. Now that Simone was coming, she would need to do some shopping tomorrow for snacks and things she knew Simone enjoyed. She forgot to ask Simone if she was traveling by herself or if her son would be with her. It didn't matter, Nikki would buy enough for everyone. She dialed Rell's phone and sat in her favorite chair in the living room. Nikki loved murder mysteries and she began to scan the channels for what would keep her attention for the evening. After finding one of her regular shows, she dialed Rell's number.

"Hello." Rell answered loudly.

The sound of laughter and music followed in the background.

"Rell, this is Mama. Did I interrupt a party?"

"No Ma, that's Mitch, Craig and them. We're emptying my fridge of the beer and stuff I don't want to leave behind. I couldn't think of a better way to clean the refrigerator out."

Nikki shook her head at the thought.

"Well, it sounds like you're having fun cleaning. I was calling to see if you called your grandmother. Are you going there first on Sunday?"

"I didn't reach her. She was out with Uncle Darryl taking care of the funeral programs."

"Oh, well Simone is coming in Sunday, and I was gonna cook for everyone. I didn't know what time you were thinking about coming. Are you going to stop and pick up Monique?"

Rell hadn't called Monique. "I probably will."

"If you like I can call her and tell her to meet you here."

"No, I will pick her up on the way from Nana's."

"Call me when you get to Nana's. That will be better. I might have to pick Simone up at the airport."

"Alright, I will call you Sunday. If you need to reach me leave a message on my cell, I might not answer it, but I'll check my messages."

"Why won't you be able to answer it?"

"We're going to some event at the sports bar tomorrow afternoon it will be an all night thing."

"Two nights in a row, you're living dangerously huh?"

"Kinda, but I don't know when we'll hang out like this again. It will be strictly business for a while."

"Have a good time. I'll talk to you Sunday."

"Thanks. Night Ma."

"Good Night Rell."

Nikki thought about Rell having to take care of business. She still didn't know what the lawyer wanted with her. She could understand Rell. Maybe D.Q. left him some money or property, but what did he have in store for her. Nikki had been on the computer to keep up with D.Q.'s business and some of his properties. He owned enough to give everyone a bulge in their pocket. Nana would know what the lawyer wanted. She would call Nana and find out.

Chapter 23

Darryl took his family to visit other relatives in Richmond for the evening, that left Nana enough time to go in D.Q.'s room and put his papers under lock and key in the safe in his wall to wall closet. Nana was sure Darryl had spotted the safe. If they didn't get to the lawyer's soon after the funeral he would ask her what was in it. She had no intentions of Darryl opening that safe. D.Q. had given her directions to follow in case of his death when he moved back home with her. D.Q. told her about Mr. Simpson and explained he would take care of the rest. Well, now that D.Q. was gone, Mr. Simpson stepped right in like he knew it was his turn to help her through the turmoil.

Nana had always been a strong woman. She was married at a young age to a man that her family didn't care for. D.Q. had a lot of his father's qualities and all of his good looks. That's what won Nana over. They were married for forty five years before he passed away. Nana couldn't imagine living again and not marrying Maurice Mince. She truly loved that man. Darryl worked hard like his father. He never wanted to work for anyone else.

He graduated from high school and went to a trade school for masonry. When he moved, he opened his own business and D.Q.'s business was up and coming. Darryl had the same ambitions as D.Q., but they definitely had their differences. This caused them to compete for their father's approval. D.Q. oftensaid he would use his brains rather than his hands.

Years passed and they both became very successful. Yes, Mr. Mince would be proud. Nana closed the closet and thought about Rell filling his father's shoes.

"Lord, I sure hope Rell got the backbone Maurice had. Keep him steady Father, 'cause there's plenty to knock him off balance. Give him the strength to manage what needs to be managed and throw away what he will not need."

The phone rang interrupting Nana's prayer.

"Now who could this be this time of night?" It was close to ten o'clock.

"Mama Mince? It's Nikki?"

"Hey, Nikki, are you okay?"

"Yes, I'm fine Mama Mince. How are you doing this evening? Rell told me you were out taking care of some of the arrangements. I wanted to call you earlier, but I thought you might still be out."

"I'm holding on baby. I got back here about eight o'clock. Darryl and Francine went visiting with some relatives in the Heights. I didn't want to be bothered."

"I see, I guess you'll see enough relatives for the next couple of days."

"You right about that. Some I don't want to see. You know a funeral sure has a way of bringing out what you don't want to be bothered with, including people."

Nikki laughed. "You're so right. Did you get everything done?"

"I think we did. Darryl is going to pick out one of D.Q.'s suits for him to wear. They were already cleaned. D.Q. had just picked them up from the cleaners before he went into the hospital this last time. We got a photo for the program. Tonya is supposed to pick a prayer for the back of the prayer card, and we wrote the obituary."

"Mama Mince, I am so sorry I couldn't have been a help to you. You know under the circumstances, I guess you could say my hands are tied."

"Baby it won't be long. I'm just mad it took D.Q.'s death for him to be free of….."

Nikki cut her off. She knew Nana didn't care for Tonya, but she never allowed her to talk bad of Tonya or speak about the relationship she had with D.Q.. Although D.Q. was dead, Nikki still wouldn't allow it.

"Mama Mince, I need to know what to expect at this meeting with this lawyer, Mr. Simpson."

"What do you mean? You must be in D.Q.'s will if you got a letter."

Nana was told by Mr. Simpson who got letters. He explained they all were mentioned in the will and would need to be at the meeting once Rell would be asked to set the time and date. He told her D.Q. wanted Rell to set the time and date because he wanted him to be there. D.Q. felt if Rell was told when to come, he wouldn't show up. Nana didn't know much else.

"I was hoping you could tell me what the meeting will be about, and what it has to do with me. D.Q. was still married when he died right?"

"Unfortunately, but he could leave what was his to anyone. They had a legal separation, and she got a good portion in money and property. He filed for a divorce, but it wasn't final. He died 'fore he could get it finished. I believe Tonya got what she was entitled to at that other proceeding they had. Who knows what she will start up now though. She doesn't have to be his beneficiary. I guess we will all have to wait and see."

Nikki was stunned. Thirty plus years and just when D.Q. files for the divorce, he dies. Nikki started crying softly.

"Nikki, child are you okay?"

"Yes, Mama Mince, it's just D.Q. always waited until I got fed up to make a move. Mama, no matter how I pushed him to get a divorce, he wouldn't do it and now...."

Nikki was crying a little louder.

"Nikki, we both tried to get D.Q. to leave Tonya. He stayed with her for those kids. You did know about them didn't you?"

"I found out the same day Rell found out we weren't married. I never told Rell about them though. It was hard enough for him to know we weren't husband and wife."

"This funeral sure gonna turn some graves. Even those who ain't related gonna turn over on this one."

Just the thought of what Nana said made Nikki laugh.

"I know that's right. They're probably getting front row seats in heaven and D.Q. being the business man is selling tickets."

They both laughed. Nikki felt a little better knowing her relationship with Nana had not changed. She loved Nana and she loved the fact that Nana loved and embraced them although D.Q. had a wife and family.

"Well child it's getting late. I'm going to bed. It's calling me by my first name. Will I see you Sunday?"

"No, Mama Mince, I think Rell is coming to see you Sunday. My cousin Simone is coming in from New York for the wake and funeral so I will be here with her. Thank you for the invitation though."

"How is Simone? Give her my regards. Rell sure talks about her. Have you ever met Tonya?"

"No, I never met her or their children."

"Well you won't be able to say that for long. You get your rest baby. You'll need it to restrain yourself."

"Aw, Mama Mince, I'll be fine. Have a good night's rest."

"You too baby."

Nikki hung up the phone and thought about it. *There has never been a formal introduction. Oh well, Nana's right; Tonya won't be able to say that after the funeral.*

Chapter 24

onique came into her apartment hoping Rell had called. She stayed out later than she expected. A coworker from her office got a promotion and a few of the girls went out for drinks after work. Monique liked the restaurant and took a brochure to show Rell, Monique thought maybe she and Rell could go there while he was in town.

Monique was in a good mood knowing Rell would be in town for what could be a couple of months. Maybe if his father left him the business Rell could move back home. Rell could move in with her, or they could find a place together. Monique would definitely forget her rule about space. Rell made good money in his position at Sheldon's Finance, but if he inherited what his father had, the thoughts ran through Monique's mind. *"Damn"!* She would be set when they got married. Rell hadn't made any hints toward marriage, but they had been together two years. Long distance or not that had to mean something. If she played her cards right, she would be sharing that inheritance.

Monique had been setting the stage for marriage for a while. Rell seemed to always be preoccupied with family matters or work. Monique liked his signs of devotion to the job and family, but it seemed that their relationship was at a stand still. There were times she felt like she was his weekend date, a safe sex relationship, and not much more. He would buy her gifts to appease her, or he'd surprise her with a four day visit. Rell would say he loved her, but she wanted more. Nikki liked her and so did Nana, they didn't give her any sign that she was just someone he was dating.

Well, at the end of this ordeal she wanted him to be in love. Monique had plans to help him. There was no other woman in his life when he was depressed and alone, Rell always called her. Monique wanted to be certain there would be no other woman he would share that inheritance with, and she would definitely clear her list of friends she had been seeing when she and Rell were on the outs. She checked for messages, no one had called. Rell must have been busy.

"That's odd he usually calls just to say hello. I'll call him in the morning before he gets with Mitch."

Chapter 25

Rell woke up to the sound of Mitch and Craig talking and laughing in the hall near his room. He looked at the clock, it was nine-thirty. As he sat up his head and stomach felt like they had been in a fight. He made his way into his bathroom and looked in the medicine cabinet for something to help him win the fight that was about to knock him down.

"Shit." The medicine he needed was in one of the other two bathrooms in the house.

"Mitch, man, bring me something from the medicine cabinet for my head and stomach."

"Say what?" Craig yelled back from the hall. "Mitch went out to his car. What do you need?"

"Damn." Rell couldn't yell again.

It would send serious pain to his head. He decided to try to make it to the other bathroom. Craig met him in the hall.

"You look like shit, bro."

"Thanks, this is what you and your boys did."

"You know what you can handle. Looks like you went over the limit. Good thing you were at home."

"We all must have gone over the limit. I see you're all still here." Craig laughed, Rell could only muster a smile.

"Byron left about an hour ago. He was fine though."

"He didn't drink much, he never does." Rell usually drank like Byron, neither of them could handle as much as Craig and Mitch.

"Rell, man, you want some coffee. There's some in the kitchen, Mitch made it a few minutes ago."

"Yeah that sounds good but first I need something for my head."

"You make your way into the kitchen, and I'll search the bathrooms for you. What am I looking for?"

"There's headache medicine in one of them. It doesn't matter what."

Rell probably could have found it quicker but his head was killing him. Mitch came through the front door and noticed Rell making his way to the kitchen. He laughed. He walked ahead of Rell in the kitchen and poured his hung over friend a cup of coffee.

"I guess good morning wouldn't be the thing to say."

"Man, that's the last time I drink that much. I guess I'm getting old. I can't hang like that anymore."

Mitch laughed. "Remember when we used to get drunk in college and wind up with some chick we wouldn't talk to sober."

Rell just shook his head. "That's when I first vowed not to drink like that again. Now I know why I'm being punished. We didn't call those girls last night, did we?"

They both laughed. Craig came in the room with medicine for both Rell's stomach and his head. He got a glass, filled it with water and gave it to Rell.

"Thanks, man. I can't be feeling like this today. I need to drive, entertain and get my shit off with the hottest chick I've seen in two years. I need a quick recovery."

Craig patted him on his back saying, "Well bro, I wish I could help you, but I got some things to take care of this morning. Mitch, call me with our time of travel on Monday."

Craig began to make his way toward the front door. Mitch walked him to the door looking on the front steps for the morning paper.

"I'll call you after I speak with Mr. Moore Monday morning. I probably will be leaving from the office to pick you and Byron up. I guess we can get a room once we get to Richmond."

"I'll make reservations today. We can get a suite at one of the hotels in town. Just call me though, I'll be at Laurie's house, call me on my cell."

"Alright man, later."

"Later, Rell hope you feel better man. Call me later."

"Yeah, Craig. Later man."

Mitch returned tossing the morning paper on the table and poured himself a cup of coffee before sitting at the table joining Rell.

"So my brother, what time are you pulling out?"

"I told Shai to meet me at the Ramada at about two o'clock. I wanted to leave in enough time to check in and rest a minute. I may have to rest before I leave from here."

"Where are you staying when you get to Richmond?"

"I think I'll wind up at Nana's. I thought I told you that."

"I heard you but if you're gonna be seeing Dershai, it ain't happening at Nana's."

Rell hadn't thought about that. If he and Shai hit it off, he definitely would want to see her again. He needed to keep his room out of town for that purpose alone.

"I guess I'll stay at the Ramada. You're right. I probably need to play it safe with this family business too. I don't know what my father's will might uncover. I'll check their monthly rates."

"How long do you think you'll have to stay?"

"I don't have a clue Mitch; my father has a lot of assets. If I'm to be the executor, I will need to learn things about him and his business I didn't know."

"That could be time consuming. I'm not going to ask the what if's, you could never answer them all. If you should find yourself in charge of his business keep a brother in mind."

"You got that. You, Craig and Byron. Working at Sheldon has its advantages, but working where you can build your own is better. You guys know that's what we want, and if I can get us there, I will."

"So what's up with you and Monique? Suppose this Dershai is what she appears to be. How long you gonna roll with two?"

"Man, I don't know. I love Monique but she's been irritating with this living together thing. If this turns out to be a large inheritance she will be clinging all over me. That's her personality. She already thinks there's someone I'm dealing with here, in Maryland. This was even before I called Shai. I've been out on a few dates but nothing serious. I only talked to Dershai off and on. I just decided to meet with her because I want to test her waters."

"Did you tell her about your dad?"

"I told her it was a relative's funeral. I did that on purpose man. I don't want two women trying to get me to settle down. If Monique keeps pushing, I'm out. I'll keep Dershai in the dark about the business until I know for sure she's not about the money or the status."

"I never knew Monique was about money."

"Mitch, I think she got to know about my father's business by talking with Nana and my mother. I don't know how much she knows, but his business is on the web and she could check it out there."

"Yeah, she could run a check on you too. Wow. Monique doesn't look like the gold digging type."

"What do gold diggers look like? I need to know." Rell poured another cup of coffee for them. "I'm sure I'll become the next best catch in Richmond."

"Well if you need a body guard, I can fill that spot too."

"You really want to leave Sheldon Finance, huh."

"Rell, I want to see the light, and know it's shinning for me. I'm doing well, just like you man. Now I want self satisfaction. We don't make a decision that Mr. Moore and the others don't sit down and take apart. I would like to know that the decision I make stays my decision and benefits the company."

"I guess I understand. My dad used to complain that all the decisions fell in his lap. Mitch, he would sit hours with paperwork in his office at home and come out smiling. I guess because he didn't have to ask anyone's opinion. The beauty of it all was he made sound business decisions. I don't know how he messed up his personal life."

"Gotta be dumb in something. Not that I'm saying your dad was dumb or, well you understand."

"I do. A wife, a woman, and a child left to deal with his will. Drama."

"Look man, I'm gonna get outta here and let you get ready for that ride. Call me if you forget or need something before Monday."

"You have your key right?" Rell had given Mitch and Byron a key when he bought the house.

"If I don't Byron has his."

"Alright, I'm going to shower, shave and get myself together. I'll call you tomorrow, hopefully to say she is thorough."

"Man, call Monique before you leave so she won't be calling me complaining."

Rell picked up the phone. "I'll call her now, later man."

Mitch went out the door and waved bye to Rell. Monique's phone rang three times. Rell hung up and dialed her cell phone.

"Hello Rell."

"Damn, why you sounding like that."

"Why didn't you call me yesterday? You said I couldn't get you today after you get with your boys."

"I got caught up with a few loose ends and packing. I'm packing for more than the weekend. I went shopping for a few things too."

"Did you get me anything?" Rell could feel Monique smiling at the possibility.

"No I didn't. We'll go shopping for you when I get there."

"Hmm, so what time will you be coming over Sunday? Did you decide what you're going to do?"

"I have to talk with Nana, so I'll pick you up on the way to my mother's. I don't know what time though. I'll call you from Nana's when I'm leaving. Didn't we talk about this?"

"I guess we did."

"Monique, why are you taking me through this again if we talked about it?"

"Rell don't get mad at me. If you paid more attention to our conversations you would remember. Listen I don't want to argue. You have enough on your mind with the funeral and the meeting with the lawyer. We both know how you act when you're pushed."

"So why do you push and then say you know how I will act. Listen I have a headache, and I want to have a good time for the rest of the day. I'll talk with you tomorrow."

"What's up with that? If you have a headache, cancel your little outing with the boys. I'm not stopping you from having a good time."

"Monique, please. Stop with the bull. I'll call you tomorrow."

"Bull? Rell I don't know what's wrong with you, but you can't blame me. Maybe you dialed the wrong number. I wasn't with you last night. Enjoy your day."

The phone went dead. Monique hung up.

Rell looked at the phone saying, "That's that bullshit!"

Rell hung up the phone and headed for the shower. He still had a headache, but he didn't have time to let it slow him down.

Chapter 26

*T*onya's day started with her searching the library for the bible. She didn't know where it was, and it annoyed her that she allowed D.Q. to take the one they kept in the bedroom. She took her shower and got dressed early thinking. She would treat herself to breakfast at the diner. After breakfast, she would meet with her lawyer and discuss her next move. Once that was done she would drop off the typed information for the program and prayer card to D.Q.'s mother.

Tonya knew D.Q. was filing for a divorce. Although her lawyer fought to get her share of D.Q.'s properties and assets when he filed for the separation, Tonya wanted more. D.Q.'s business grew daily. He made real estate deals at least twice a month. Before she got to his lawyer, she wanted to know what she may have to fight for. There was no doubt in her mind that D.Q. left money to Nikki; *"Maybe her and that son they had together."*

Tonya knew the business had legal ties with other partners but who would D.Q. leave his part to? Derek was no business man but Darrell was. She looked up

Sheldon Finance Company on the internet. They had information on all their Executive Officers. Darrell Quincy Mince stood out among the rest. He was D.Q.'s child. Tonya knew that from the picture. His features were identical to D.Q.'s when he was younger.

Darrell had an impressive write up. He definitely made a name for himself. He wouldn't be easily fooled. His mother wouldn't be the problem, he would.

Tonya had called her lawyer and his secretary gave her an appointment for this morning at ten o'clock. Once she found a passage in the bible she could leave. She looked at the clock and decided Mr. Watson could put the prayer on the card.

The ride to the lawyer's office wasn't long but Tonya needed to get the business for the day started. Tonya got to the offices of Calhoun and Monroe and took a seat in the waiting area hoping not to be there long.

"Mrs. Mince, Mr. Monroe will see you now." The receptionist smiled opening the door for Tonya to enter.

"Thank you".

Tonya walked into Mr. Monroe's office and noticed he was not in the room. Puzzled, she took a seat and waited for him to arrive.

"Good Morning, Mrs. Mince. How are you?" Mr. Monroe entered from a door in the corner of the office. "I'm sorry you had to wait. I just got in and this morning seems to be filled with drop in appointments."

"I wanted to speak to you on the phone but your secretary said it would be better to have an appointment."

"Yes, I sometimes forget to return all my calls in a timely fashion. What can I do for you?"

"It's my husband Mr. Monroe. He died and will be buried Tuesday of this week. I want to know what I am entitled to."

"I'm not sure I understand Mrs. Mince. We settled your entitlement during the proceedings of your legal separation. You agreed to what you were afforded. I'm not certain there is much more for you to claim."

"Mr. Monroe, I was still married to him. If he is leaving anything in his will I have the right to claim it, don't I?"

"Mrs. Mince, I'm not sure. If he declared a beneficiary other than you, it is their inheritance. I would have to check into what he has left. This may be a fight that would have to go to court. It's not as simple as it may seem."

"I don't understand. I was still married to him. We didn't get a divorce."

"Mrs. Mince, I understand what you are saying. You were legally separated. Didn't Mr. Mince file for a divorce? I seem to remember the two of you had a court date coming up."

Mr. Monroe reached for the folder on his desk marked Tonya Mince which his secretary placed there for him prior to Tonya entering the office. Tonya knew the information before he read it.

"Yes, but he died before it was final. We had a court date for late next month."

"Mrs. Mince I'm in looking through your file; I don't see where you requested any other compensation. So I am to assume if he were living you wouldn't be seeking any other monies or property from him."

"I'm not sure, well yes, that's true."

"Why Mrs. Mince? If you thought he owed you more, why would you not pursue the matter if he were living?"

"Mr. Monroe, what difference does it make? I am his wife and what he leaves behind after death is mine. Is it not?"

"I don't think you are his beneficiary Mrs. Mince. You can only claim what is acquired during marriage. Your separation was final. Your divorce was filed and pending. It would have to be decided in court by a judge. What is it you're fighting for?"

"The will is to be read within the next couple of weeks. I want what's entitled to my children and me."

"Your children are grown Mrs. Mince. They would have to make a claim for themselves, if they needed to."

"Are you going to be able to help me or not Mr. Monroe?"

"Mrs. Mince, you said the reading of the will is in a couple of weeks. Why don't you wait and see if there is a legal leg to stand on first? This may not be a fight you can win. You got a settlement in your separation hearing. I can't say you are entitled to much more. Mrs. Mince you signed a legal document that stated you were satisfied with the settlement and would not seek further compensation from your husband."

"And....?"

"And that included what he would leave behind after his death."

"We'll see about that. Mr. Monroe I don't intend on anyone else getting what my husband left behind. That includes his tramp and that bastard son of theirs!"

Before Mr. Monroe could respond, Tonya got up and walked out of the office slamming the door behind her.

Chapter 27

arlene wanted to see the suit that Darryl selected for D.Q. She wanted to get to her mother's house before Darryl went to the funeral home. She didn't want to be the one that had to inspect the body when it was ready for viewing. She used her key to her mother's front door and walked in.

Alesha was in the living room reading what appeared to be a home décor magazine. Nana told Darlene she subscribed to them because Nikki loved new ideas. Darlene didn't even get into it with her mother. *"Why would she buy magazines for someone else and get them delivered here?"* Drama. Alesha looked up from her magazine and smiled.

"Hey, Aunt Darlene!" Alesha got up and gave her a big hug.

"Hi baby. How have you been? You sure grew."

Darlene took a step back to look at her from head to toe. Michael came in the room and grabbed Darlene from behind.

"Boy, if you don't let me go. How tall are you now? Give me a hug."

"I'm six one, Auntie. I think I'm still growing though." Michael hugged Darlene and kissed her on her cheek.

"Where's your mom, dad and Nana?"

"They're sitting on the deck in the back."

Nana had a screened deck built on the back of her house. She loved the outdoors but hated the heat and the bugs. The deck served as her getaway. It was decorated beautifully thanks to Nikki. No one else knew who had done such a marvelous job of arranging the furniture, Nana's flowers and other items that made the deck so cozy. The two large ceiling fans that hung overhead weren't needed today because Mother Nature hadn't teased them with what the summer months' weather would bring. Darryl and Francine were sitting at the bar talking and laughing between them. Nana was nodding in her rocking chair that everyone died to sit in.

"Hey all, how is everyone today?"

"Hey there Darlene." Francine spoke first.

She was surprised to see her. When Darryl and Nana told her that Darlene went straight home from Tonya's she thought Darlene was still a bit angry with Darryl.

"Francine, y'all got two big children in there. No more babies huh."

"That's for sure." Darryl got up and hugged his sister. "You want me to get you something to drink?"

"No, well yes. What y'all drinking?"

"Just iced tea girl. We thought we would wait until later when we would need a drink," replied Darryl, laughing at his own joke.

Nana opened her eyes and smiled.

"I thought I heard your voice. How you baby?"

"I'm fine Mama. I thought I would stop by and see what Darryl picked for D.Q. to wear into heaven's gates."

"Well I would hope they don't have a dress code."

Nana always added humor to comments about people going to heaven. "If they do it's a lot of folks that will be turned away," Darryl added. They all laughed.

"Did Tonya get here yet? It's close to three o'clock."

Darlene laughed to herself. She knew she should keep the comment she was about to make to herself, but she said it anyway.

"I sure hope she ain't still reading Psalms looking for a verse."

They all began to laugh.

"Now y'all know Ms. Thang is gonna leave that information blank for Mr. Watson to put a prayer on the card." Darlene spoke while trying to contain her laughter.

Nana waved her hand in the air. She reached for her glass of iced tea and took a drink.

"Mama, don't let Mr. Watson put that same old verse on D.Q.'s card."

"What verse, Darlene?" Darryl still didn't know the verse they were talking about.

"Darlene, if Tonya doesn't give Mr. Watson a verse for the prayer card then I'll call him and give him another verse for the card."

"Thanks, I just want something different for D.Q."

"Why don't you pick the verse then Darlene?"

Francine knew how to pluck a nerve. Darlene looked at Nana. Nana just snickered. Darryl turned his head the other way. Francine looked at them and continued drinking her iced tea.

"Francine, the job was given to Tonya. It was more like a test. We all knew she wouldn't take the time to pick a prayer from the bible." Darlene explained.

Darlene didn't think it had to be explained, but she understood and liked Francine even though she was naïve when it came to some things.

"Let the truth be told, Darlene don't know another verse either. That's why she wants me to give Mr. Watson the prayer."

Laughter filled the air again. Nana loved teasing Darlene but she knew Darlene read her Bible and knew the book of Psalms well. Darlene told her mother often that Psalms was her favorite book in the Bible.

"So did Tonya call?" Darlene wanted to know how long it would be before Tonya arrived.

"No she didn't call here. Did she call you Darryl?"

Nana figured she might call Darryl and avoid talking to her.

"No, she knows I'm here, why would she call me?"

"Well she didn't call then." Nana didn't seem to be bothered by it.

"What time are you taking the clothes to the funeral home?

"Whenever Tonya gets here. I ain't in a hurry. I don't want to take them anyway. We should send Tonya on that mission alone."

Darryl knew that his mother was not letting that happen. She was just venting. Before they could say anything else Tonya stepped on the deck. They could tell by her looks she had been drinking.

"Good afternoon family. Sorry I'm late but I had business to take care of this morning, and it took longer than I expected."

"Sit down girl, before you fall down. Where did you have lunch?" Nana knew immediately Tonya had more than one drink.

"I didn't have lunch, why?"

Darlene shook her head. Drama, Tonya knew better than to drink and come to Nana's house. D.Q. had told them that most of their problems stemmed from her drinking. Tonya always denied her over the limit drinking, saying she didn't drink any more than anyone else.

"I got the information ready for you Mrs. Mince, right here in this envelope. Y'all can look it over if you want to before giving it to Mr. Watson. I did a spell check on the computer so everything should be correct. Oh, I didn't really know what verse to select. I guess Mr. Watson can pick one. I really think you should Mrs. Mince. You can do it being his mother and all."

Darryl reached for the Vodka bottle and offered to pour a drink for Darlene, who readily accepted. Francine started laughing knowing his gestures were meant to be a joke. Nana was getting angrier by the minute.

"Tonya, it took you all day to come here with this paper, and then you have the nerve to tell me what I should and can do?"

"Mrs. Mince, I am having a terrible day. I thought I would have gotten good news earlier, but it is just adding to my existing problems."

"We all have problems, drinking ain't never solved problems. You go on, leave that envelope right there. I will look at it the minute I get a chance. Mr. Watson will get it sometime this evening. Say your goodbyes Tonya 'cause your visit is over."

"I didn't see the suit Darryl picked for D.Q."

"You wouldn't remember it if you did see it. You'll see it Monday. I can and should take care of that too. Good day Ms. Thang, Darryl you drive Tonya on home. Darlene you follow them and bring Darryl back here."

Nana walked back in the house leaving Darryl and Darlene looking at each other.

"I can drive myself, I got here didn't I?" Tonya's speech was beginning to slur.

"Mama wants to make sure you get home alright. I'll drive you, c'mon Tonya. Mama ain't gonna say it twice." Darryl didn't wait for Tonya to move. He led her to the door where she made her entrance. Darryl and Darlene walked with Tonya around the house and put her in the car. Darlene walked past Darryl heading for her car.

"Darryl, do you think she will be drinking through this whole thing?"

"Darlene, if she went and got drunk, she must have received some bad news. Believe me, she would love to have the upper hand in all of this. If she is willing for Mama to help her, she's looking for an alliance for what is to come. Tonya is still Tonya but Mama knows her game."

Chapter 28

Dershai woke up still angry that her mother called blaming her for Derek not being in town. Well, she would be more upset when she called and found out that Dershai was out of town too. She could reach Shai on her cell if it was important. She hoped her outing would last until Sunday night. She called Marci and Mia telling them she would be leaving by noon. They talked for a while letting Dershai know her mother was wrong but it was the alcohol talking and she should enjoy herself before the problems of next week began.

Shai agreed. She packed clothes for what seemed to be a week. She figured if she left them in her car at least they would be with her if she needed them. She dialed Rell's number to let him know she was leaving Richmond.

"Rell, it's Shai."

"Hey, sweetie. How's your morning going?"

"I guess I'm doing fine. I'm not running late. That's usually a sign of things going well."

"You're right. Are you leaving now?"

"Yeah, where are you?"

"I'm ten minutes away from the hotel. I got a late start. Call me when you are parking. I'll meet you in the lobby."

"Okay, I'll talk to you then."

Shai hung up smiling. *"This is the beginning of what may be the best weekend ever."*

Her thoughts drifted to her memories of Rell in jeans and his designer shirt. "Damn, I can't wait."

Shai picked up her garment and overnight bag. She locked her condo door and started toward the parking lot. She thought about her mother but decided against calling her. Marci knew where she was if anyone needed to reach her before Monday. Derek would call her on her cell, so she was good to go. She got in her 2006 black Toyota Avalon and put in a mixed R& B CD. She knew her way to the hotel, so she prepared herself for the drive.

Chapter 29

ershai pulled into the parking lot of the Ramada Inn at two fifteen. She could have been there sooner, but she didn't want to give the impression that she was flying down the highway. It was a shorter ride than she expected. She still hadn't thought of a place to pass the time until dinner, she wanted to arrive closer to the time for dinner. After talking to Rell, the anticipation of them being together for the evening had her hormones ticking. Marci was right. This could be a dangerous situation for him. It had been a while since Shai had been satisfied with a lover. She prayed that Rell wouldn't disappoint her.

Shai thought about taking charge by asking for his room number to surprise him. She talked herself into keeping her promise of allowing him to lead. She hoped he was as horny as she was. Shai dialed Rell's cell number and waited for him to answer. There was no answer. She got out of her car and looked into the lobby area. There were no guests in the area just the hotel employees. Shai decided to dial the number again. Her thought was maybe he couldn't get reception in his room.

"Damn, I don't know his full name."

If she knew his name, she could have the front desk call his room. Shai was standing at her car looking at the hotel. She thought about what Marci said and laughed. She would make sure she found out his last name. She was about to get in her car and call again, when Rell came walking out of the door. Shai dropped her phone on the ground by her car. Rell was dressed casually, his jeans fit him perfectly. He had an opened powder blue button down shirt with a white muscle shirt under it, a matching fitted baseball cap and casual shoes. His accessories included two diamond cut necklaces, and a gold Rolex. Shai hadn't noticed before but his ear was pierced with a small diamond stud. His shades had a powder blue tint.

Rell made his way over to her car smiling as he picked up her phone. He didn't wait for her to speak before he kissed her lips.

"Hey baby. I saw your number on my cell and just came down. The phone breaks up in the hall and on the elevator."

Shai had an internal rush and still couldn't speak. Rell was more attractive than she remembered. When they went to dinner before he left Richmond, he seemed more refined. He was leaving a business meeting and met her for dinner afterwards. Although he was sexy in the suit, somehow he turned her on more dressed this way. Shai had worn a white jean suit with a silk multicolored blouse. Her belt was silk also to match her blouse. Her shoes were blue with a matching handbag. She had let her hair hang down curled under. She decided she would fix it different for their dinner date.

"Are you okay? Do you want to go into the lounge before we get going?"

Shai wanted to tell him no. She wanted to go to his room. She put her phone in her bag smiling as she nodded yes.

"I didn't keep you waiting too long, did I? Is that why you haven't said anything?"

"I thought you forgot you told me to meet you in the parking lot."

"I just was down here. I saw the sun was still out and decided to get my glasses."

"Are they prescription? The sun won't be out long."

"No, they're not but I do wear them most of the time. Even without the sun being out. The tint is not that dark."

They reached the lounge and Rell pointed to two seats at the bar.

"Or would you rather sit at a table?"

"The bar is fine. I didn't pick anywhere for us to go. I didn't really know what you would like to do."

"Okay that's easy. I just want to spend a day with you so it really doesn't matter where, or what we do. We both like window shopping but the malls may be too crowded. We don't have a lot of time before we need to leave for dinner, and it is now two forty five."

The bartender cut Shai's comment off by asking what they would like to drink. Shai ordered a Bailey's and Crème, Rell ordered Cranberry Juice.

"Cranberry Juice? What's up with that?"

"Well the guys… well I drank more than I wanted to last night. My stomach is still riding the waves. I want to drink tonight so, I'll drink this for now."

"Oh, I thought you were setting me up."

Rell laughed. Shai just didn't know she was already set up and trapped. Her jeans were fitting her body showing him exactly what he wanted to see. Her thighs invited him to what would become his new addiction. He wanted to tell her they had to go to his suite before leaving. Rell couldn't remember the last date he had been on that he wanted to have sex first. Even with Monique they would wine, dine and tease each other first. Shai had teased his masculinity for two years.

"How much time do we have?"

"Baby, we have all the time we need."

Shai smiled. The bartender brought their drinks. Rell nodded thank you.

"You know what I meant, time before we have to get ready for dinner. Don't start something you can't finish."

"And I have all the time I need. But you're right. This is a date of getting to know each other better. So, let's not start something that will take all night to finish." Rell liked the chase.

Shai liked Rell. She had thoughts running over thoughts. *"This is going to be an all night thing. He planned it that way. Shit! I sure hope he is thorough. I don't need this man to have any sexual phobias."* Shai looked him over again. He was FINE. She thought to herself about the possibilities saying, *"They always say when they're fine like him they have some kind of hang up."*

"You're right we need to get to know each other better. The weekend festivals started at Byrd Park, would you like to go there and walk around?" Shai asked about the festivals because she had been to festivals in Byrd Park before and enjoyed the atmosphere.

"Sounds like a plan. We can ride in my car. It's parked in the back. Do you want to walk with me or should I pull it around?"

"I don't mind walking with you." Shai smiled and finished her drink. Rell left the money on the bar as they got up to walk to his car.

"Do you want to move your car or is it okay with you where it is?

Shai thought before she answered. *"I'm not hiding anything. I wonder if he is, and if he is, too bad."*

"No, it's good. If I need to, I'll move it later."

"I parked my car in the back because I have the suite for a month so far. I had quite a bit of clothing to carry. This spot is closer to the entrance where the suite is."

"A month? Do you think it will take that long to settle your business?"

"I don't know, but I don't like moving around. I'd rather be in a spot where I wouldn't have to move if things get shaky."

"Shaky with who, or maybe I should say with what?"

"I really don't know it's just a precaution. I don't like to be in the midst of drama. So the suite keeps the playing field even."

Shai didn't quite understand and Rell preferred it that way. He would explain later if necessary. For now she was a date. If they hit it off, he would let her get close to the real Darrell.

"Who are the players on this field?"

Rell knew where she was going. She wanted to know if she is being played, whether or not he was a player. Shai was sharp.

"I have a lady that I see off and on in Richmond. I don't know how much longer the relationship is going to last. I was dealing with her when I met you at the mall. I am not one to lead women on so I'm keeping it real. I like you. I like you a lot. We've been talking for almost two years, and I have wanted to be with you more and more. But I didn't want to start another distant relationship. So Ms. Shai, I took a chance to call you, see what you were about, and possibly take it further."

Rell heard himself talking but he couldn't explain why he was saying it. It was more than he wanted to disclose. If things went well, this would have been his comments on Sunday morning. Shai's comments had changed his thoughts about expressing his feelings. Rell didn't want to go through a whole night of Shai wondering if he had a relationship with someone else and where she fit in. If that thought lingered she might not relax and be herself.

"Okay, Mr. Darrell. I like your honesty. Let's take our time about this since you are involved with someone and see if we both feel the same when the getting acquainted date is over."

Shai loved a challenge. She understood Rell was looking for an out. He didn't want to break up with his girl, but if he had a good reason he would. Shai couldn't think of a better reason than herself.

Rell hit the unlock button on his key ring. A beep sounded not far away and lights blinked on a 2007 Midnight Blue Mercedes. The interior was cream, the detail and chrome were gold. Shai was stunned again. This man had beautiful taste. He didn't mind spending money. This told her another thing about him. He didn't have any children.

"Your car is beautiful."

"Thanks, I like the Avalon you have. I always wanted a Mercedes, so I got one once I moved to Maryland. I've been driving one ever since. I drive my truck most of the time, but I didn't think you wanted to climb in a truck this evening going to dinner."

Shai laughed, "Yeah, I'm clumsy. I might have wound up under the truck."

They both laughed. Rell opened her door and walked around to his side. He drove out of the parking lot while turning the stations on the radio.

"What type of music do you like?"

"I like all kinds. I prefer R&B and jazz."

Shai felt her body easing into a comfort mode. It no longer felt like the first serious date. She looked for signs of his girlfriend in the car. There were none. He had a writing pad in the passenger side door pocket. Rell reached across Shai's lap and opened the glove compartment. He took out a pack of gum.

"Would you like a piece? The cranberry juice left a after taste in my mouth."

"No thank you. Do you know your way to the park from here?"

"I think so. I've only been there once or twice but it was from the opposite direction. When we get close you can give me directions."

"No problem."

They drove for about twenty minutes making small talk along the way. Shai did ask a few questions that she knew Marci would ask her. She never asked his last name. They walked through the park holding hands. The jazz group was one neither of them had heard and they both enjoyed their performance. Rell kept an eye on the time and told her it was close to the time for them to leave. Shai felt like they had been a couple for the past two years.

"So how do you feel? Are you hungry?"

Shai wanted to answer his question honestly. If they had truly been a couple for two years she would have told him the hotel bed was serving the best meal. Nevertheless, she was determined to keep her promise to let him lead. Shai answered still allowing Rell to remain in control of the date.

"I could go for something to eat. How about you?"

"My stomach is feeling better now, so I guess I could eat a little. I hope you enjoy the spot I chose."

"I'm sure I will. I will need to get my clothes from my car."

"I'll park my car next to yours."

They pulled into the parking lot and Rell parked as he said, next to Shai's car.

"Rell you didn't tell me where we're going."

"A Riverboat Dining Cruise, in Norfolk.'

Shai had heard about the dining cruises in Norfolk. She smiled thinking to herself. *"This man is really trying to impress me."* Shai got out and walked to her car to get her garment and overnight bag. Rell grabbed her overnight bag as they walked into the hotel together. Rell allowed Shai to get on the elevator first and followed her, pushing the button for the penthouse.

They entered his suite and Shai noticed immediately small touches Rell had added. There was an aroma of scented candles in the air. Shai didn't know the fragrance, but it added an essence of comfort. Rell told her where she could change and shower if she liked. He said he would be doing the same in the room on the opposite end of the hall.

Shai resisted the temptation to call Marci once she was in the room. She would never be ready on time if she called Marci with a blow by blow update. Shai would wait until she got home tomorrow. She decided to wear a gold after five dress. The bottom was shear and fell softly on her body. It was airy enough to blow in a breeze. She selected gold accessories, taupe shoes with a matching handbag. Shai changed her hairstyle three times finally letting it fall on her shoulders with freshly done curls. Her touch of makeup enhanced her natural beauty. Shai was ready for the evening.

Rell had begun to change his clothes thinking of how the conversation at dinner would go. He selected a black double breasted suit. The jacket was a little longer than a standard suit jacket. He coordinated it with a cream shirt and a black and cream tie. His breast pocket held a matching handkerchief. Rell finished his outfit with black shoes. Rell was ready for the evening.

When Shai walked out of the room, she noticed Rell was at the wet bar fixing a drink. She saw he had her drink waiting for her. Rell heard her walk in the room, turned and smiled.

"Very nice. You are beautiful."

"Thank you. You look good too."

"I made you a Bailey's and Crème. I hope it's okay. I'm afraid I'm not much at bartending."

"I'm sure it's fine." Shai picked up the glass and took a sip and nodded yes. "It's good. Thanks."

"The ride is about an hour, so if you're ready, we'll finish our drinks and be on our way."

Shai placed her glass on the bar. She looked around the suite at the décor. Shai had been in suites like this with her parents. On vacations and some weekend business trips, they would take her and Derek along. They would stay in suites with the hotel employees at their beck and call. Her mother would insist that they see what money could afford them. Rell was staying here a month, he had to have money. She smiled. Finally, she was with a man that could afford her taste and didn't mind spending money. In the past, whenever she suggested to the men she dated, outings that cost more than the average date, it had to be planned in advance. It was the basis for most of the arguments she had. It was the basis for most of her breakups. The men she dated felt that if she wanted them to spend that type of money she was hinting toward marriage. The other problem was them knowing she was the daughter of Derek Mince. Rell made her feel at ease. He didn't need her status or money.

They finished their drinks and Shai went to the bathroom to check herself for final touches. She came back into the room and saw that Rell was standing at the balcony window. He didn't turn around right away and Shai walked right behind him. Rell turned and smiled. He looked into her eyes and kissed her. The kiss was all they needed to trigger feelings they held for each other. He kissed her on her cheek and whispered.

"Let's go before we get to the finishing touch of a lovely date."

Shai was there already. She had mentally stripped him and was taking off her clothes. She giggled.

"Lead the way."

Rell held her hand as they went out the door.

Chapter 30

Nana waited for Darryl and Darlene to return. She got her bible and picked a verse from the book of Psalms for the prayer card. She put all the paperwork for Mr. Watson in a folder. D.Q.'s suit and his other clothing were put in a garment bag. Francine was in the closet looking for a pair of his shoes that would match.

"Mama, does he really need shoes. They won't show his feet in the coffin."

Francine handed her a pair of shoes.

"Baby, Mr. Watson said a complete outfit. I think that would include shoes. If not Darryl can bring them back with him."

"What are you going to do with D.Q.'s suits and things? There's a lot of quality clothing here."

"Whatever Darryl can't wear or doesn't want, I will see if Rell can use it. I don't think they wore the same size clothes but his shoe size is close. Derek might be able to fit the suits."

"Darryl said we would be able to help you with packing up some of D.Q's things. He has one of his foremen handling the business while we're gone."

"Is Michael still working with him?"

"Mama Michael loves it. Darryl is thinking about giving him his own crew. When he goes back though, he will be in the office handling new accounts until we return."

"We won't be doing anything with D.Q.'s belongings until Rell goes through them. D.Q. wanted Rell to look over a few of his personal papers. We have to respect his wishes."

Francine didn't know why D.Q. wouldn't want Derek to be a part of that as well. "When will Derek and Dershai meet Rell?"

"I guess at the funeral. I don't think they'll get a chance to meet before then. I don't want to be in the middle of that. They all will come running to me when they find out. I'll be the one helping them through the emotional damage."

"Mama, do you think D.Q. wanted it to happen this way? Do you think he was going to introduce his children to each other after he got the divorce?"

"I don't know. I don't know what D.Q. was thinking. He sure left a mess though. D.Q. only left instructions. Mr. Simpson has most of them. I guess we'll find out at this meeting."

"Is Rell staying with you?"

"No, I think he will be staying with Monique or his mother. I don't know though, Rell is like his father and Darlene. He avoids drama. He may stay in a hotel."

"I guess that would keep him from being bothered."

"Francine, see if those other black shoes are in that closet. These shoes don't look right with the suit."

"Mama, does it really matter."

"Yes it matters to me."

Darryl and Darlene came into the room laughing.

"Did you get Tonya home okay?" Nana asked.

"Yeah, we took her in. She wanted to apologize about upsetting you. I don't think she realized we knew she had been drinking. She kept asking why you were upset with her." Darlene answered taking the shoes from Francine.

Francine closed the closet door telling Darryl the suit and papers were in the living room.

"I got business to handle. I don't have time for Tonya and her mess. What bad news could she have gotten that made her get drunk like that in the middle of the day? D.Q. said she drank a lot. I didn't get into their business. She'll reveal herself as the days go on."

They all walked into the living room. Darryl was ready to take the clothes to Mr. Watson.

"Mama, is this all that's going to the funeral home? I'll tell Mr. Watson to call us if there is something else he needs."

"Darryl wait, I need to get D.Q.'s handkerchief."

Nana went back into D.Q.'s room and got a matching tie and handkerchief. She remembered his cuff links and grabbed the box off the dresser.

"Darryl, look in this box and pick out a pair of cuff links for that shirt. I'm not sure which ones would be better."

Darlene took the box from her mother and opened it.

"Darryl here's a pair. They have the initials D.Q. on them."

Francine and Darryl looked at Nana.

"Derek or Rell might want those cufflinks Darlene. Leave them in the box so they can choose them if they want."

Darryl spoke responding to the look on Nana's face.

"No Darlene it's okay. D.Q. had more than one pair with his initials. If you look in that box you should find the others."

Nana put the cuff links and the handkerchief in Darryl's hands.

"And Tonya is wondering why I'm upset."

Darryl picked up the garment bag.

"Fran, come on ride with me over to the funeral home."

"Mama, do you need anything else?"

"No. Darlene, are you going with them?"

"They can handle that I'm sure. I'll stay with you until they come back."

Darryl and Francine walked out the door. Darlene saw Nana was tired. The stress and aggravation were beginning to get to her.

"Wait Francine, Mr. Simpson asked us to drop these papers off to him. Darlene, hand Francine that envelope on top of those folders in the corner there. Just put them in his drop box outside his office. I don't think he's still in his office. I told him we would drop it off. I spoke too soon. I thought Tonya would have gotten here earlier."

"Okay Mama, we'll be back in a while."

"Mama, what do you think Tonya is up to?"

"Darlene ain't no telling what Tonya is up to. I guess she is trying to find out what D.Q. left. I don't know why though. She got hers when he left her. She got a pretty penny and property too. If D.Q. were still living she wouldn't be acting this way. When has she ever greeted us as 'family'?"

"You're right. I hadn't paid much attention to that, but she did say family. Do you think she talked to D.Q.'s business partners?"

"She probably tried, but D.Q. had already schooled them about Tonya's mess. Remember they were around during the beginning of the separation. They tried to talk to D.Q. out of leaving her, but he said he would pay her before he would stay with her."

"Mama, why didn't D.Q. leave her earlier? Why did he stay? I know that Dershai and Derek were the excuse when they were younger, but they have been grown for years now."

"I know Darlene but I can't answer that. All I know is that D.Q. and Nikki broke up shortly after Rell moved, and D.Q. said that was it. He lost what seemed to be his being when Nikki wouldn't take him back. He knew Rell was mad and he hoped to put it all together. I believe losing them both killed him slowly."

"He should have left Tonya when the love for her left." Darlene felt pain for D.Q. She knew what lost love felt like.

"Child, that would have been when their children where in grammar school. He has loved Nikki since before they were born. He married the wrong woman. D.Q. just stayed because he thought it was the right thing to do."

"D.Q. still wasn't doing right. Nikki held on all her life to a love that never became complete. Now where does that leave Rell?" Darlene was trying to make sense out of her brother's motives.

"Rell is strong but he reminds me of you a lot. He is not one for drama and lies. He will avoid it at all cost. It's like he gets mad with the world and stays to himself to grasp the full meaning. He was better after he moved to Maryland. At first he would visit me with questions, mostly why. I couldn't answer and would tell him he needed to talk to his parents. The questions stopped. I think he began to accept things as his parents' mistake. Nikki was bad off for a while after Rell left. So I couldn't talk with her about the situation to even help Rell."

"Mama, you mean Rell didn't talk to her at all?"

"Not at all. He only spoke to me and Darryl. Darlene he is so easy to love. He's a sincere, honest young man. He ain't lazy like Derek either. He looks like your brother when he was young. You seen his picture haven't you?"

"I don't think so."

Nana didn't keep her pictures out. They were all in books. Rell and Nikki had a separate book to keep people from asking about them. She went in her den and got the photo album for Darlene to see Rell's picture.

"Mama, he is handsome. He sure is D.Q. all over again. Looking at him now, I see Derek favors Tonya more. Dershai has D.Q.'s smile and color, Darrell is definitely a Mince."

"Child, don't I know. This has been my burden for over thirty years. D.Q.'s secret. I told him to straighten this mess out. All he would say is Mama, one step at a time."

"D.Q. would always say that. It might have worked as a business plan but life is a little different."

Darlene flipped through the album looking at the other photos.

151

"Nikki is a nice looking woman. I guess now I wish I knew them both. I was afraid of my feelings and disregarded theirs. Especially since D.Q. led them on for years. I wonder what he kept saying that would make Nikki stay in that type of relationship."

"Darlene, he didn't have to say anything. Nikki loved D.Q. She didn't love his money or status. She loved D.Q. with all his secrets, lies and alibis."

"And Tonya didn't love him?"

"Tonya wanted what she saw coming over the horizon, his success and his money. She told him for a long time that she couldn't have children. Before Rell was born, he fought with the idea of telling his wife about his affair with Nikki. He finally told her when Nikki got pregnant. She told him he was a liar. He asked for a divorce. Tonya wouldn't even consider it. Well, Derek and Rell are just about two years apart."

"So what's going to happen now?"

"Well I'm following the instructions he gave me while he was in the hospital. Each day he would have me repeat what he wanted done; the rest Mr. Simpson will handle. I don't know anything about that set of instructions."

"What did D.Q. want you to do? Why didn't he ask me or Darryl to carry out some of these tasks?"

"A lot of it has to do with Nikki and Rell. You made it clear you didn't want to be involved with them. The rest has to do with Rell going through his personal belongings. He wanted Rell to sort through his things before anyone else."

"Mama D.Q. has other children. Why is he excluding them?"

"Why did D.Q. do half of the things he did? Dershai wouldn't be able to handle it, and she would leave it undone for someone else to help her. I don't think he wanted that to be Tonya. Derek never cared much about details and business. Some of his personal items are linked to the business. I can't say I am right though. We will just have to see what Rell uncovers."

"The next couple of weeks could be rough."

"Darlene it will only be rough for those not prepared to handle it."

Chapter 31

The music on the boat had changed the mood calling all couples to the floor for a dance under the stars. Rell didn't allow Shai to take her seat. He pulled her close to him and kissed her forehead and cheek. As the music played their bodies moved together to the beat getting closer with each step. Shai closed her eyes feeling at ease in his arms. She fought off the temptation of kissing him while they moved slowly to the record that followed. After the DJ played the third slow cut, the boat roared as it made its turn signaling they would be headed back to the dock.

Rell checked his watch knowing that they would dock around eleven. They wouldn't return to the hotel until twelve, and he would ask Shai if she would like a night cap. He didn't want her to think he assumed she would stay. The weight of her overnight bag told him she came prepared to stay.

"Do you want another drink?"

"Yes, what are you drinking?"

Rell looked at his glass. "Vodka and cranberry juice; heavy on the cranberry juice."

They both laughed.

"I don't think I could take another serious night of drinking. I can't drink much anyway. I can handle beer but liquor seems to beat me down after too many."

"I guess you need to know your limit."

"Believe me, I do."

Rell walked away from the table heading for the bar to replenish their drinks. Shai had enjoyed her evening; Rell could tell by her reactions to his gestures and questions. At different times during the evening, she would reach for his hand at the table fondling his fingers as she spoke. She didn't talk a lot but their conversation was steady and interesting. Rell was certain about this becoming a new relationship.

Shai watched as Rell walked away. He enjoyed her company. Shai could tell by his attentiveness. Most men put on their best for the first date and maybe a few calls afterward. Rell seemed to be the same all the time. His telling her about his girlfriend scored big in her book. They had a deep discussion about goals. Rell told her he wanted more than being an Executive Officer because he deserved more. She liked that. She told him about her career as a Medical Technician and her desire to get into medical research. Rell told her she would always have something of interest to talk about with a career like that. They both laughed. His rhythm on the dance floor told her he had a lot to offer. If he was as big as the impression in his pants, she was certain about this becoming a new relationship. They docked about two hours later. Rell asked her if she was hungry on the drive back to the hotel.

"We can stop and get something if you like. I have fruit, chips, dip and drinks in the suite. I didn't know your taste in food, so I didn't make arrangements to have any food there when we got back."

"I'm not that hungry. What you have is fine."

"I don't want to get ahead of myself Shai, but it's rather late. Please feel free to stay the night."

"Why did you say you were getting ahead of yourself?"

"I didn't want it to sound like I was trying to get you to spend the day with me to lead you to my bed."

Shai thought about it. She wanted to say *"Why not?"*

If she were leading, they wouldn't be talking about the bed they would have been in the bed. Now she wasn't sure if he would pursue the issue. It was just her luck, a fine man who was too polite. Once back in the parking lot Rell pulled up next to her car.

"Do you want to move your car to the back now?"

"It's fine." Shai didn't even look at her car.

Rell smiled. "Do you need anything out of it?"

Shai caught on to the joke. "No, Rell I don't."

"Good." Rell drove to his parking spot in the back of the hotel.

Chapter 32

They entered the suite talking about the food they had for dinner. Rell told Shai he was happy she enjoyed the evening, and that he had a great afternoon at the festival. He went to the refrigerator and pulled out a platter of fruit. He put it on the bar along with chips, pretzels and other snacks.

"Babe, I need to get out of this suit. If you want to get comfortable feel free. That includes your shoes."

Shai noticed that Rell had already taken off his shoes and was headed toward the room he changed in earlier. Shai couldn't wait to talk to Marci. This was incredible. Usually, her date would have rubbed her the wrong way, at least twice.

She would overlook it for a good roll in the bed and at times that would be their third strike. Shai brought shear lounge wear with her. She was wondering if it might be too much for tonight. It would be putting it right in his face. She didn't want to appear too anxious. She would wear it in the morning for round two. Yes, something to make him invite her back. She had a black silk pajama set. It was a three piece; a teddy, pants and a thong. She got dressed and walked into the living room. The lighting was dim setting a romantic tone. Again she smelled the scent of the candles. Rell had moved the fruit platter to the table next to the couch. An all night oldie's station was tuned in on the radio.

"I like that station. I listen to it often when I'm relaxing or about to go to bed."

Rell smiled and replied. "I'm glad we have a lot in common. It makes it easier to talk. How long have you lived in Richmond?"

"All my life, it's funny. As much as I have traveled, I love Virginia."

"Hmm, I can relate to that. I am growing fond of Maryland though. I think it's the change. I still get lost there so I'm always stumbling on different spots of entertainment or dining. Most of my job relies on business meetings at restaurants or tickets to shows or sporting events."

"You sound like my dad. That's how his business was, always keeping him on the road, entertaining clients."

"What kind of business is he in?"

This would be the first time Shai talked about her father since his death. She felt comfortable telling Rell about him, now she had to hold on to her emotions as she told him he was dead.

"He's no longer with us. He passed away."

"Oh, I'm sorry to hear that." Rell didn't want to mention his father at all. He wasn't ready to talk about it openly.

Rell stood up walking to the bar. He wanted to change the subject.

"I don't want you to think I'm trying to get you drunk. I'm going to have a beer. Can I get something for you?"

"Do you have any wine?"

"Yes, do you want ice? It's chilled already."

"A cube of ice is good."

Rell had on silk pants and a white tank shirt. His muscles were well sculpted. He definitely had the look of a model. Shai didn't want to talk any more she'd rather get cozy. She wanted to get acquainted physically. Rell sat next to her on the chaise chair handing her the glass of wine.

"Thanks."

"No thank you Shai for such a lovely day and evening. I enjoyed your company."

"Well you helped make the day and evening complete. I guess we share in the enjoyment."

Shai put her glass down and slid back into the chair so her feet extended to its end. Rell put his hands on her feet massaging them gently. His hands found the way up her leg to her thigh. Shai touched his hand and pulled him toward her. He paused kissing her thigh through her pajama pant. His kisses continued to her breast. He could feel her nipples begin to rise as he kissed them gently. Rell's lips found her neck and ear where he used the tip of his tongue to arouse her more. Shai closed her eyes as she prepared herself for the kiss. Their lips met and their tongues touched giving both of them pleasure that reached the points between their legs. Shai massaged his chest and worked her hands down his stomach to the brim of his pants. His penis met her hand, and she used her fingers to stroke the tip.

Rell began to work his way back to where he started. He gently pulled at her pajama pants and Shai helped him with the removal. Rell stood up and unsnapped the top of his pants. They fell to the floor. His penis stood erect. Shai gave a smile of satisfaction. Rell was as beautiful below as he was above. Shai said a silent *"Thank You."* She knew she would reach a climax at least three times. She could feel herself getting wet with anticipation.

Shai raised her legs for Rell to remove the thong. He leaned over her pulling the thong toward his mouth and removed it slowly with his teeth. He spread her legs wrapping them around his neck. He began licking and kissing her inner thigh. This foreplay had him hard and her moist. Gently, he kissed her clitoris and began licking it for their arousal. Shai's clitoris stood erect for him. Shai began to moan softly. She had oral sex before, but he took care to take his time and this turned her on more. Rell sucked her clitoris like he had her breast. He put his finger at the edge of her vagina and massaged it in and out until her juices began to flow. The sounds of her juices began to turn him on. He moved up to put his penis in and Shai sat up to return the favor. She began to tongue the tip of his manhood while she held his sack in her hand. As she massaged him Rell leaned back and put his finger in her vagina moving it slowly in and out. Shai took him all in. As her mouth would return to the head, she would touch the tip with her tongue. As the taste changed, she wanted all he could give her.

Rell was about to explode, and it was then he thought about a condom. She hadn't said anything, so she must be prepared. He thought to himself. *"Shit I can't stop right now."*

Shai laid back. She couldn't remember if she took her pill. She tried to think what day she had taken her pill last. Since she wasn't active sexually often she had fallen off taking them daily. She thought about it. *"Shit I can't stop him now."*

Rell penetrated Shai, they both moaned, he didn't rush. Since he set the most sensual pace Shai had experienced she knew she could go all night. Rell was going deeper than any man had gone. He pulled himself out and began kissing her navel. Once again, Rell returned to his original spot. He licked her hardened clitoris until Shai was trembling with arousal. He penetrated her again.

Shai wanted to scream. He didn't cum; he was hard as a rock. She couldn't imagine a man being erect that long. Rell moaned and pulled out again. He licked her juices and sucked her nipples before his penis found the comfort of her vagina again. Shai couldn't hold it any longer. She felt herself exploding and trembling. Rell picked up the pace, but he was gentle. It was as though he didn't want her to feel how large he was. She felt every inch of it and enjoyed it all. He pulled out again and smiled at her as he went down one more time. He knew she was satisfied.

Rell felt himself filling up. He had reached his goal. He put his penis in her warm cove again, and he began to set a new pace. Shai was in another world. She had never felt that good before. Shai was ready to ride Rell all night. He began moaning. "Oh, baby. Yes, this is aww....."

Rell exploded. Shai felt the warmth of his cum and she began to tingle again. Shai joined his moaning with a chorus of her own. "Oh, oh, oh, awww....."

Rell was still hard. He slowed the pace down. Shai could feel him filling up. Before she could make a move to show him what she was working with he exploded again. "Oh, oh, oh shittt......." Shai kept moving to his rhythm. She could feel his penis pumping cum into her body.

She thought to herself. *"Damn this is good."*

Rell pulled his penis out and laid next to Shai. He wasn't even breathing hard. He kissed her breast and put his finger in her, playing with her clitoris again. Shai was horny as hell. Her clitoris said so and so did his penis. Shai decided she would ride him at least once, so she could say she did him. She rolled him on his back. Rell smiled and his penis came to attention. She mounted him. Shai moaned the whole time she rode him. Rell let her have her way. He had mastered the art of control, and he wanted her to have enough of him to want to come visit him for more. Shai moved up and down until she could feel the warmth of the movement. Rell played with her nipples, he sat up sucking her breast. Shai repositioned herself so that they both could enjoy oral sex. Shai was about to burst. She could feel his penis throbbing waiting for his third explosion. He turned her over on her stomach. Rell penetrated her from behind. He set the pace again. Nice and easy, he doggy styled her until they came together. Tears of pleasure ran down Shai's face. Rell picked up the pace and again his rod filled with cum. He exploded immediately. Rell moaned in harmony with Shai. They laid on their backs totally satisfied.

"Baby are you okay?"

"Yes, and you?

Rell touched her thigh saying, "I couldn't be better."

He thought again about the condom. "Shai?"

"Yes."

"I know the question is late, but you are on birth control right?"

Shai almost forgot about that. "Yeah."

Rell pulled her in his arms and kissed her. He asked Shai to join him in the hot tub in the bedroom where he got dressed. Shai smiled and followed him into the large room equipped with a step in hot tub. The room was beautiful and Shai now realized where the aroma she smelled earlier was coming from. Rell had lit candles around the perimeter of the tub. Rell went into the bathroom and got two big towels. He walked over to Shai and kissed her passionately. He led her to the tub.

They sat in the tub talking about intimate pleasures and past sexual disasters. Shai listened intently when she found out Rell's reason for setting a nice and easy pace while making love.

"I'm not bragging but I was told once I was too large. I was a little upset because I was ready for a night of pleasure. The young lady stated this right before I was ready to penetrate her. I went into the bathroom and it took a while for me to get myself together. I was hard even after the cold shower."

"So you have always had this problem?"

"Not with every female, but there are those that feel a man can't be gentle. I've had to stop right after they saw my size."

"I noticed that about you. You are a gentle lover. I never experienced that before. Most men increase the pace forgetting a female's feelings. The slower pace turned me on. It was different."

"If I see that I'm attracted enough to have sex with someone, the ultimate pleasure is for us to be emotionally and physically fulfilled. I think sex is a beautiful thing. I want the moment to be remembered each time as the best ever."

Shai couldn't believe her ears. She felt most men didn't care how the female felt as long as they got theirs. This man was different. She would definitely be seeing him on a regular.

They relaxed in the tub for about twenty minutes. Rell went and got the fruit and their clothes from the living room. He returned to Shai, who had gotten in the bed.

Rell smiled. "I think we both had the same idea."

"What's that?"

"The day is complete. Let's rest together for the night."

"Exactly my thought."

They slept in each other's arms for the night.

Chapter 33

Tonya had tried talking to Darlene and Darryl about the issue of D.Q. leaving his money or property to Nikki and Rell. They had no answers to her questions. It was as though they didn't want to talk about it, or they had been threatened by Mrs. Mince not to talk about it. She still didn't have any clue what D.Q. left behind. Tonya told them to apologize to Mrs. Mince for her even though she didn't understand why their mother was upset with her. Tonya held on to the statement that she wasn't drunk.

After leaving the lawyer's office Tonya had to sit in her car for what seemed to be fifteen minutes to get herself together. Mr. Monroe didn't understand her problem. She didn't care that she had agreed to the settlement after her separation from D.Q. She didn't want Nikki to benefit at all from his death. Tonya didn't know Nikki had a home, car, and vacation time share all of which D.Q. had purchased. Tonya didn't know that Rell was put through college and wanted for nothing because D.Q. took care of them as he had Dershai, Derek and her. Tonya thought Nikki was a weekend thing, a part-time lover. There was a lot Tonya didn't know. Between her thoughts, Tonya needed a drink. One drink led to another, and before she began to feel better she had drowned her problems with a few doubles. Tonya left her stress at the bar.

Tonya had to speak with Mrs. Mince and clear the air before the reading of D.Q.'s will. She needed her to be on her side. Tonya decided she would eat her dinner and then call Mrs. Mince to get a feeling of where she stood with her.

Tonya hadn't heard from Dershai or Derek. She called them both and left a message. Tonya thought to herself. *"Where is Dershai? I don't believe they haven't called to at least check on me."* Tonya needed them on her side in this mess too. They all could be on top. Although D.Q. was a Mince, he was her husband and their father.

Tonya picked up the phone and dialed Mrs. Mince.

The phone rang three times before Alesha answered.

"Alesha, is your grandmother home?"

"Yes, who's calling?"

Tonya was about to snap as she thought. *"This child doesn't need to know who I am so Mrs. Mince could refuse the call."*

"It's your Aunt Tonya baby".

"Oh."

Tonya heard her put the phone down. She could hear voices in the background. It sounded as though there were a lot of people at the house. Mrs. Mince picked up the phone.

"Hello"

"Mrs. Mince, this is Tonya. I want to apologize for upsetting you this afternoon. We all are under a bit of stress. I know you are stressing a lot more than we are. I

166

should have taken that into consideration before coming to your home straight from the bar. I went there thinking a couple of drinks would help me cope with the stress I'm having."

"Tonya, I'm really busy trying to get paperwork together for the funeral home."

"The funeral home needs more paperwork? I thought we took care of all of that." Tonya couldn't believe the funeral home needed more.

"Well Mr. Watson just called, and he needed another part of his insurance papers." Nana had lied to get her off the phone and Tonya knew it.

"Mrs. Mince I don't know what I should really be doing. I guess since D.Q. wasn't living there when he died, I don't know if the family accepts me as his wife. First there is the funeral and including this other woman and her child. Then there's this secret meeting with the lawyer. No one has told me anything about the letters or who got them. I don't know why the lawyer never called me about the reading of his will. It's a lot. I guess what I'm saying is, I need your insight and help."

"I'm sorry too Tonya. I don't deal with people who go overboard drinking. I will not accept that in my house from anyone. You are D.Q.'s wife by name only. He filed for a legal separation and divorce. That tells me he was done with you and your marriage. The other woman, Nikki, and the child, Rell, were apart of D.Q.'s life. Rell was D.Q.'s child too, his first child. D.Q. took care of you and the children the two of you had. He didn't treat them any different than he did Rell. You knew about Nikki and you decided to stay in the marriage. I can't tell you what D.Q. discussed with the lawyer, or what business he wanted him to handle at the time of his death. I have instructions also. I believe the lawyer will respect his wishes just like I will. You will have to deal with this situation the best you can, just like the rest of us."

Tonya couldn't win. She didn't know Nana knew how long Tonya knew of Nikki and the affair. D.Q. was closer to his mother than she thought. It was obvious that Nana had accepted Nikki and the child. It didn't sound like Nana was going to interfere with D.Q.'s request for them to be a part of the reading of the will. Tonya had to rethink her strategy.

"Mrs. Mince, I don't want to take up your time. I understand and I'll try to deal with this better. I guess we all will have to just respect his wishes."

"That's all we can do. I'll talk with you later."

"Okay good night."

The phone went silent. Mrs. Mince was still upset with her, but it wasn't about her drinking. Tonya thought about it, *"I have to win her over. I have to play the part of the loving wife who didn't want a separation or a divorce. Someone will have an understanding for my feelings."*

Tonya went into her bedroom knowing she would sleep late into the morning.

Chapter 34

Darryl and Francine spent the balance of the evening with Nana watching her favorite television shows. When Tonya called it gave them an excuse to go in the bedroom. There they could talk in private.

"Darryl, have you talked with your mother about the business?"

"No. I didn't think it was the right time.

"Are you thinking about waiting until the funeral is over?

"Francine, I don't want Mama to think all I'm concerned with is D.Q.'s money. D.Q. probably told her about me asking him for the loan. I don't want to tell her about the debt my company is in until I find out what D.Q. may have left us. We got a letter to be at the reading of the will, so we'll wait."

"Your mother said Rell needed to go through D.Q.'s belongings before anyone touches them. I can't believe D.Q. left all that responsibility to Rell."

"If I could see some of his papers, I may find out his assets. I'll see if Rell really wants to deal with searching through all those papers, or if he needs me to assist him."

"What if D.Q. didn't leave you enough to get the company on board?"

"Francine we'll see. I'll talk to Mama after the reading."

Chapter 35

Nana got up early Sunday morning, just as she planned. She wanted to go to the morning service to avoid the crowd that attended the eleven o'clock service. She knew they would be stopping by her house after service, and she wanted to get back in time to finish cooking her dinner. Nana knew with the church people stopping by, they would want to nibble on something while they visited.

Nana told Francine and Darryl if they didn't have any intentions on attending either Sunday service, they could start the macaroni and cheese and her collard greens. She had prepared both to be ready to cook when she got home. Nana would fry chicken, make rice and gravy and serve her homemade biscuits. There would be plenty for everyone, but she had to get to the early service, so she would be home in enough time to see that the cooking was handled.

Nana knew Nikki wouldn't be at church this morning even though D.Q. wouldn't be there. Nikki went to the early service to avoid running into D.Q. at the later service. Nana and Nikki would go to church together often when Nikki and D.Q. were together. Nikki liked the earlier service. Nana had too much church business to attend to for the earlier service. She could get so much more done during the week if she personally met with the members that attended the eleven o'clock worship.

Reverend Wallace Wilcox was the minister. He loved seeing Nana come into his office. He was a widower and he didn't mind telling Nana that didn't mean he was dead. She would smile and continue to talk the business at hand. After she told Reverend Wilcox that D.Q. wanted to become a member, he came by the house a few times to talk to D.Q. about organizations in the church that needed male participants. Nana knew this was his excuse to see her away from the church.

Nana told Reverend Wilcox that she would be attending the early service, and she wouldn't be handling church business that morning. He assured her that whatever business needed her attention could wait until she handled it. Nana thought Reverend Wilcox was a man that aged well. He was a good looking man with a bald head and a beautiful smile. He was always well dressed and overly polite, but she couldn't see how she could date a Reverend. The thought would come and go.

The church was filled with members for both services, although most of the members at the eleven o'clock service were new. The regulars attended the eleven o'clock service if their group was singing or ushering at the service.

Nana didn't wait for Darryl or Francine to respond to her alerting them she was leaving for church. She started up her Cadillac that she hadn't driven in months. It wasn't that she couldn't drive, but she preferred not too. However, this morning she decided she would need the time to herself.

Nana hadn't taken time to grieve. She kept herself busy and prayed, but she didn't grieve. She hoped to start the process today. Nana understood that the reality of losing someone only came after one grieved for their death.

"Good morning, Mrs. Mince."

Nana was greeted by two girls in the parking lot of First Chapel Baptist Church. She returned their greeting and proceeded into the church headed for the Deacon's office.

"Morning Mama Mince, how are you this morning?"

"Good Morning Deacon Smalls, is the Reverend in yet?"

"Yes, Ma'am, he's in his office."

"Thank you, Deacon Smalls. You have a great day now."

"I will Ma'am, you too."

Nana walked down the hall to Reverend Wilcox's office and knocked on the door.

"Come in."

Reverend Wilcox was sitting at his desk jotting down passages from his Bible.

"Well Good Morning Sister Mince. How are you?"

"Good Morning Reverend. I'm fine. How about you?"

"I'm good thank God. What can I do for you this morning?"

"Reverend I need to talk to you prior to the funeral services tomorrow. Do you think you can stop by this evening, so we may talk a bit?"

"I don't see why not. Is everything okay?"

"I don't see any problems, but I want to avoid them if I can, and I may need your help and guidance."

"Well thank you for the confidence, I will come to your home say about, seven this evening?"

"Reverend, seven will be just fine. Thank you, I know you're a busy man."

"Sister Mince, I would clear my calendar for you. You know that, anytime."

Reverend Wilcox came around his desk to walk with Nana down the hall. People greeted the two as they walked by.

"Thanks again Reverend. I really do appreciate your time."

"Don't think twice about it. I will definitely be there. You enjoy the word this morning Sister Mince."

Nana went to get her seat in the congregation thinking to herself. *That man would make any woman happy. Why he wants that woman to be me.....Well I'll leave it right there. I just can't see myself courting no Reverend.*

Nana sat in the middle of the church. She enjoyed her view of the altar from that seat. She was mindful never to wear hats that would interfere with people behind her. There were those in the church that would compliment her weekly on her hats that coordinated so well with her outfits. Then there were the others. Those that talked about her, D.Q. and Nikki, they couldn't figure out what the relationship was. They knew something was missing. When Rell was younger she would bring him to the church with her and tell them he was her grandson. She never introduced Nikki as a relative. She let their rumor circle grow. Nana knew they would be stopping by her house just to pick up on who was Rell's mother but more importantly, who was his father. Most of them knew Darlene only had two children. They never could tell with Darryl, and D.Q.. Their lives were also a secret.

The ladies of the church tried to catch D.Q. when he was just visiting. D.Q. was "well off" that's how they would describe him. Many women had their eyes on Mrs. Minces' son. They didn't care that he was married. They just wanted a chance. Once he joined the church most of them thought he had his eye on someone and the whispers increased. Nana giggled to herself. *"If they only knew I could be the first lady of the church. Lord would that keep them talking."*

The service ended and the congregation filed out the front door. Nana spoke with many that said they didn't know she was at the early service and how good it was to see her. She passed Reverend Wilcox and nodded her head. He took her hand and squeezed it gently and smiled. Nana noticed that the gossip circle immediately began to whisper. *"Drama."* Too many women anywhere meant drama to Nana.

Nana drove home and got out of her church clothes feeling relieved. She would talk with Reverend Wilcox about Rell and the situation it presented. Maybe he would ease her stress. Nana wanted Rell to be accepted. She loved Nikki too, but she could understand the family's reluctance in accepting her. Rell was blood.

Francine and Darryl were still in the bedroom. There was no sign that they attempted to put the food in the oven. Nana looked at the clock and knew she had to get a move on if she wanted the food to be done before people started dropping in.

Darryl entered the kitchen and opened the refrigerator getting the juice.

"Good Morning, Mama. How are you feeling this morning?"

"I'm fine Darryl. How are you? Is Francine up yet?"

"She's in the shower. We're going to take Alesha and Michael to visit Alesha's relatives while we're in town. We'll pick them up later tonight."

"I guess they'll have a good day visiting people they haven't seen in a while. Why didn't they go yesterday? They would have had a longer visit."

"It's like pulling teeth to get them to agree on days and times, so today it is." Darryl seemed agitated about the arrangements.

"Well at least they want to see them. Michael is going with Alesha to visit her folks? That's nice."

"Alesha has a cousin that talks with Michael on the internet when we are at home. They like to talk sports, that hip-hop mess, and girls. They've talked a lot so he's looking forward to visiting him.

"Well what about Alesha?"

"She'll be glad to see her relatives. It will be a good day for her too."

"So what are you and Francine doing today?"

"We'll be here with you, I guess. Do you need me to help you with some of D.Q.'s things? I mean have you begun packing his things? Or are you waiting until after the funeral?"

"D.Q. wants Rell to go through some of his things before anyone gets to them. So that will be up to your nephew. He should be here today; you can ask him what he plans to do. I would think he would wait until after the meeting with the lawyer. But I was told to just tell him the task is his."

Darryl knew what Francine was referring to now. He would speak with Rell and see what his plans were. Darryl didn't want to talk to Nana now. He would wait until the reading was over before he would discuss his business problems.

"Mama, what time is Rell coming?"

"I don't know baby. He said some time today. He may call before he comes."

"Do you think Tonya or Darlene will come over today?"

"That Tonya ain't coming here. She called last night, whining. I hope she don't come here with that today. Darlene is spending the day with Mia and Marci. They had plans to go to Norfolk for the day. She'll probably call though."

"Well if you need me, I should be back by one or two this afternoon. Francine and I have some stops to make after we drop off the kids."

"Ain't the rest of your crew staying with Tonya?"

"They're coming in tomorrow though. I think they changed their mind about spending two days with Tonya. They'll be here early Monday morning."

"Well I can't say I blame them. Nikki said they could have stayed with her too."

"If Tonya gets crazy, they may take Nikki up on the offer."

"Well I don't need a whole lot of people here today anyway. The Reverend will be here at seven. I have a few things to discuss with him and the less people here the better."

"Mama, if you want to be alone with Reverend Wilcox, Francine and I can go over to Nikki's and visit. I told her we would come by while we were here. I can imagine she's got her moments too."

"It's business Darryl, not a date. You and Francine can stay right here while the Reverend and I talk. I think Nikki said Simone would be staying with her for a few days."

"I don't know Mama; you just gave me a good reason to visit Nikki. Nikki, her cousins, Simone and there's another one, they're all good looking women. But that's another subject."

"A subject you don't need to study."

They both laughed.

"Let everybody know breakfast is ready, so they can get out of my way. I got food to prepare for dinner and y'all late sleepers holding me up."

"Mama, I'm glad you are alright."

"Darryl, I better be. Life goes on, with or without you."

Chapter 36

Nikki was up earlier than she had planned. Since D.Q.'s death, she tossed and turned constantly until the morning light came through her bedroom window. She would lay in bed thinking about their time together. Nikki loved D.Q., although they had separated. She had kept the hope that he would divorce Tonya, and they would be together as husband and wife. Nana's conversations had helped her hold it together, but she knew she was hurting deeply. Soon she would break. Nikki couldn't lie in the bed any longer. It was six o'clock and she didn't have any early morning chores to do before preparing Sunday dinner. Simone called the night before and told her she would be bringing enough clothes to stay with her as long as she needed. Nikki still couldn't understand how she got the time off from her job to stay as long as she wanted. Simone worked for a cable company in the collections department. Nikki knew there was something else going on with her, but she didn't know what. Simone would be arriving around two o'clock. Nikki hoped she would have time to speak to her about the expected drama and Simone's situation before Rell got to the house.

Nikki went to check the guest rooms and baths for adequate bath supplies and linen. Rell didn't say he was staying, but she always kept his area the way he left it. She decided to read her Bible for an hour instead of going to Sunday service. Nana would probably go to the early morning service, and she could meet her there, but she wanted quiet time away from the congregation and their condolences. Nikki didn't know whether or not they knew she dealt with D.Q. They went to church a few times together, but she preferred to go to the early morning service to avoid the gossip. Especially since most of the church members knew he was married. Nikki would tell D.Q. "They can think what they want, but I won't give them proof." D.Q.'s reply would always be the same. "They're going to talk about us anyway. Even when you come with my mother, they talk. I don't understand. We could be close friends." D.Q. would laugh after making the comment, hug Nikki and give her a teasing kiss. Nikki smiled as she thought about D.Q. not caring what people said about them. He didn't think anybody could ruin his reputation more than he had already done. A lot of people knew he didn't care for his wife as a husband should. They also knew he had an outside interest. They never said names. Nikki had walked past many women in the church discussing Mrs. Minces' son. Their favorite line was, "I wonder who pulled him from his wife? The reply would often be, "Probably one of those secretaries at his company." They didn't have a clue.

Nikki made a cup of coffee and sat in the living room with her bible. Reading would be good for her today.

She needed peace to keep her emotions intact. Nikki didn't know what it was but now that D.Q. was gone, she wanted to tell everyone that he was her man, and they were in love. Rell was right. It was hard being in the background, the shadows and having no say in his arrangements. Rell didn't know how long she had been in the shadows. It did hurt. Tears began to run down her face. Nikki was filled with anger, jealousy and fear. Nikki should have talked to D.Q. more in the past two years. Then she would have known what he was doing about their situation. Nikki felt Tonya had no right to make decisions for him. *"She didn't love D.Q. She loved D.Q.'s status and money. Why should she sit as his wife, receiving condolences like she was his devoted companion? What would this meeting with the lawyer reveal? What would Rell think and do? Drama."*

Nikki couldn't read without the thoughts repeating. She closed her eyes trying to relax. She needed someone to understand her feelings. It was time to let it be known that Nikki Robbins spent thirty years loving Derek Quincy Mince. Nikki thought to herself, *"D.Q., it's time they knew."*

Chapter 37

*T*onya rushed through the house trying to get ready for Sunday service. It was ten fifteen, and if she didn't hurry she would be late. She decided to get to First Chapel Baptist Church, and meet Nana. Church wasn't usually on Tonya's agenda. She knew if Nana spotted her in the church it would give her an opportunity to speak with her in person. Then she would apologize again. Tonya needed Nana on her side before the reading of the will. Tonya found her car keys and hurried out the door. The church was about thirty minutes from her house.

Tonya drove at a moderate speed thinking her plan out as though it was scripted. *"If Mrs. Mince is in the hall, I will speak to her there. She won't ignore me with all those church folks around. She'll hear me out."* Tonya hadn't been to First Chapel it seemed since she and D.Q. got married. Tonya always told D.Q. that she wasn't comfortable at his family's church. The church her family attended was closer to their home. Tonya used that as an excuse not to attend services with D.Q. She would often try to persuade D.Q. to come to church with her. D.Q. would go every now and then but neither of them became a member. Tonya was still out done that D.Q. joined First Chapel and had been a member for five years. *"It sure didn't change his habits,"* thought Tonya. *"He still stayed with that scank, Christian or not."*

Tonya arrived at the church as planned. It was early enough to find Nana, talk with her, and leave. She wasn't interested in the service. As she entered the church she spoke with members whose faces were familiar, but she couldn't match them with a name. She smiled as she accepted their condolences and offers to be of assistance. Tonya couldn't understand why she hadn't seen Nana yet. She walked by all the offices and rooms speaking to members who may have seen her. Nana was so involved in the church she could have been anywhere. Tonya spotted Deacon Smalls.

"Good morning Deacon Smalls."

"Good morning Sister Mince. How are you this morning?"

"I'm fine, have you seen Mrs. Mince this morning?"

"Yes I did. She was at the a.m. service."

"The a.m. service!"

"Is there something wrong, Sister Mince?"

"I can't believe this! There's plenty wrong Deacon, but you can't fix it."

Tonya headed straight for the parking lot exit leaving Deacon Smalls without saying goodbye. She got back into her car and slammed the door. *"D.Q. I am sick of your family and their bull. Your Mama will learn that she is going to have to deal with me regardless. She's avoiding me now, but it won't last long,"* She picked up her cell and dialed Darlene.

"Good morning Darlene? How are you?"

"Oh, hey Tonya. I'm fine. How about you?"

"I was good until I attempted to go to church." Tonya set the bait for sympathy.

"What happened, you didn't make it there?"

"Oh, so where are you now?"

"In the parking lot. I just had to call someone."

"It's okay. Are you feeling better?"

"I'm okay I guess. I'll go home and lay down. That's all I have been doing though, lying around."

"It's a part of grief." Darlene was beginning to feel Tonya was baiting her in.

"Darlene, I don't want you to think I'm a bad person."

"Why would I think that, Tonya?"

"I don't know. I guess from yesterday. You know, me drinking and coming to your mother's home. I just don't know what else to do. Dershai and Derek aren't answering their phones. My family called with condolences and excuses for not coming to the house. It's just all getting to me."

"Dershai and Derek should be calling you later today, I would imagine. Is your family coming to the funeral?"

"Yeah they are. None of them offered to come and be with me for a moment or two."

"Well Tonya if you like I can come this afternoon and sit with you for a while. Maybe we can watch a movie or two together."

Darlene wanted to know what Tonya was looking to find out. She never went to Tonya's just to sit. Tonya thought about her answer.

"Okay, I'll cook dinner and you get the movies."

"Sure, maybe the girls are getting together. I'll call Marci and see. If they are they can coax Dershai to come to the house while we're there."

Tonya wasn't ready to tell Dershai or Derek the situation. She wasn't sure she would tell them. Tonya decided since they thought they didn't need her, let them find out they had a brother on their own.

"Darlene, I would prefer if it were just us. I'm still uncomfortable with telling Dershai and Derek. That's the problem. How do I tell them and do I tell it all?"

"Hmm, okay then I'll come by, and we can talk it out."

"Thanks, I'll talk with you later."

"Okay, Tonya get a little rest. See you later."

Chapter 38

Darlene's conversation with Tonya made her aware that she hadn't told Marci or Mia about Rell. Just as she decided that she didn't want to be a part of D.Q.'s secret, she didn't want her daughters involved. Darlene knew Marci and Mia were close to Dershai. She didn't want to risk them talking about Rell and telling Dershai. Darlene didn't know if she had made the right decision. If all the family knew about Rell the problems wouldn't exist. Funerals were complicated enough without the extra drama.

It was a little after noon and Darlene wanted to tell Marci and Mia, she was going to Tonya's and they could go to Norfolk next week. Now the situation about Rell was on her mind. As a mother, she owed them an explanation before it hit them in the face. The funeral program would clearly state three children. She didn't want her children to look at her with questions during the service. It was her intentions to tell her daughters prior to the funeral. She would call them. Darlene knew she would have to tell them not to mention it to Dershai or Derek. Darlene was determined that she would not be a part of her brothers' drama. Now, here she was trying to figure out a way to explain his family secrets.

Darlene dialed Marci's cell number. As the phone rang, she hoped Mia was with her, and they could come by early.

"Hey Ma! What's up?"

"Well you sound good this morning. How are you doing?"

"I'm fine. I'm on my way to pick up Mia."

"I called to tell you I need to go to Tonya's."

"You won't be going with us to Norfolk? What's wrong? You don't sound like yourself."

"I needed to talk to you and your sister, but I promised Tonya I would come by her house. Give me a call later and we'll talk then."

"Ma, we can come by before you go to Tonya's. Mia is ready. I'm on my way to her apartment."

"Are you on a time schedule?"

"No and now that we're not going to Norfolk, we'll call Dershai maybe we'll go to the movies or something. I don't know what time Dershai will be ready though. We can wait for her call at your house if you want us to."

The mention of them meeting with Dershai made Darlene uneasy. She would have to let this ride out and explain to them why she didn't tell them. This was a mess.

"Marci, don't worry about it. It can wait. You, Mia and Dershai have a good time. Tell Mia to call me, so I can hear her voice."

"Are you going to Nana's today?"

"I will probably go to Nana's after I talk with Tonya."

"Well if you need us, call."

"I will baby. Have a good day."

Darlene didn't feel good at all about not telling Marci and Mia what was going on. She decided to call Nana for advice. She went to her kitchen and prepared her lunch before dialing the phone. Darlene took a few bites of her turkey sandwich and decided the call couldn't wait.

"Mama, how are you today?"

"Hey Darlene. I'm fine baby. How 'bout you?"

"Mama, this mess with D.Q. has me in a fix."

"What mess sugar? You're not talking about the meeting with the lawyer are you?"

"No Mama. I can deal with that and the funeral."

"Well what is it then?"

"How do I tell Marci and Mia about Rell without them questioning me or telling Dershai? I wanted to tell them before the services. Tonya hasn't told Dershai or Derek. If I don't tell, the questions will begin with why didn't I tell them? If I tell, they will definitely tell Dershai and Derek. That might be before Tonya has had a chance to speak to them."

"That ain't your problem baby. Your children look to you for support, advice, protection and love. If you don't tell them, you can explain why. You are trying to protect the relationship between Dershai, Derek and their only surviving parent, Tonya. Regardless of how bad a mother Tonya may be, she is all they have. If you tell and your daughters think they are helping Dershai and Derek, they will tell. If they find out from anyone other than Tonya, they will lose respect for her and what's left in the relationship they have with her. I can't tell you what to do, but that's the way I see it."

"Mama, that's what I've been thinking all morning. It's either my relationship with my daughters or hers with Dershai and Derek."

"Darlene your relationship with the girls is solid. You have been there for them all of their lives. Tonya has no foundation with her children. The relationship she had with her children left when she and D.Q. separated. Their respect for her is hanging by a thread. If she doesn't talk to them before this funeral, she will lose them. They will need to depend on someone else in the family. I reckon that will be us, you or I. Darlene those kids need our love and support. You give Tonya a chance to regain her place with those children. Your children will understand when it's all said and done. Trust me."

"I guess you're right Mama. I just don't want to have them feeling that I kept a secret from them. That destroys trust in a relationship."

"Darlene it ain't your secret to tell. Let the chips fall where they may. Dershai and Derek loved D.Q. It's gonna hurt them when the reality sinks in, the parent they loved is gone. There are a lot of secrets to be revealed, but it's not our place to tell them. It's Tonya's, now that D.Q. is gone."

"I sure hope Dershai and Derek will be alright when it's all said and done."

"They'll be fine. It's Tonya, who will suffer the lost; first a marriage, then a husband, and now possibly her children."

"Mama, how did it get like this?"

"Tonya accepted D.Q. as he was; his faults and his success. D.Q. told Tonya early in their marriage he loved Nikki. He told her when she got pregnant with Rell. Tonya chose to stay. Did you know she told D.Q. she wasn't able to have children? Some lie about a female problem. When she found out Nikki was pregnant she set her mind to becoming pregnant herself. Derek's birth didn't phase D.Q. much. He loved him and it always showed, but when Dershai was born D.Q. was wrapped up with her being a girl. It was sometime after her birth, that D.Q. remembered what Tonya told him. They argued constantly about him spending time with Nikki and Rell. D.Q. told Tonya he wouldn't leave Nikki regardless. Tonya used the threat of divorce and keeping Derek and Dershai away from him to keep D.Q. in their marriage. His business grew and he got scared he could lose it all. Tonya planned both pregnancies. She knew sex was a weakness for him. Darlene to tell you the truth, for a while I questioned whether or not they were D.Q.'s children. Anyway Tonya and D.Q. were both guilty about keeping this a secret from those children. They're adults now and I'm determined to let her deal with it."

"Wow, Mama, I had no idea, that's a mess."

"Yeah baby, Drama."

"Well thank you. I just didn't know what to do. My conscious can rest easy now. I'll talk with Marci and Mia after it's said and done."

"If you need me to sit with you when you talk to them just let me know. I want all my grandchildren to have a clear understanding. Maybe after the meeting with the lawyer I'll call a family meeting, so we can move on after all of this is over."

"That's a good idea Mama. I think that will help all of us to understand better."

"Well, are you coming by later?"

"I'm going to talk with Tonya. I'll see about coming by after that if you want me to."

"It's up to you sugar. Reverend Wilcox is coming by at seven. I need to inform him of what is going on just in case it gets crazy at the church."

"Mama, do you think things will get that bad at the church?"

"I've seen it happen. No telling when reality will set in. Nikki ain't no weak woman and if Tonya tries her…..well…"

"Well, call me later."

"Okay, baby. I'll talk with you later."

Darlene hung up the phone and sat back to think awhile. *"This mess is deeper than I thought."*

Chapter 39

Kershai opened her eyes and smiled. She recognized the smell of coffee, and the fragrance of a man's cologne in the air. She got up and walked into the living room with her robe tied around her waist. Rell was sitting on the edge of the couch in his jeans and an unbuttoned sports shirt. This was not what she imagined as an early morning wake up, but she would have to go along with it, since he was dressed.

"Good morning, lady."

"Morning Sir. I see you started early this morning."

"It's not as early as you think. It's almost twelve thirty"

"You're joking! I don't know the last time I slept this late."

"You must have been comfortable. I let you sleep. I hate being disturbed when I'm tired."

"Oh, so you thought I was tired?"

"No, your snoring said you were tired." Rell laughed and pulled her to him as he stood up. He kissed her gently on her nose and forehead.

"Are you hungry? I made you a pot of coffee. We can go to eat out if you like."

"You are too much Rell. First a lovely night, a restful sleep, and this dream is continuing into the morning. I don't know what to say. You are definitely a gentleman's gentleman."

"My mother would appreciate that. She took time in grooming me to be a ladies man."

"Did she now?"

"Well you know, she told me things that women appreciate. Those things that make women beg for more."

"So you want me to beg?"

"Not quite. I want you to want me, like I want you."

"How's that?"

"Well without getting too deep. Let's just say I like you a lot. Let's take it a step at a time so we won't fall over each other. I don't want to trip and fall into love. I want to walk into it knowing what's going on."

"Well said. I can take that walk with you without tripping. So are you hungry?"

"Not really. I ate at nine o'clock. You were on round two with your snoring."

"I'm sorry. Did I make you get up?"

"No, I don't sleep late often. I have to warn you though. There may be some mornings where I will be waking you when I wake up."

Rell smiled and Dershai knew exactly what he meant. All she could think of was what she had missed being tired. Dershai could have taken another round of his sweet loving.

"So, when will we be together again, or am I pushing things?"

"No babe not at all. I don't mind you pushing. I want to say tonight, tomorrow and the next day, but that's not real. I have to get with my family for the next couple of days. Let's promise to stay in touch by phone. If either of us is free we can meet here in the evening. I definitely want to see you before this week is out and on the weekend. Think of what you may want to do. I'll make it happen."

Rell caught himself again. He didn't know what was going on with Monique. He did know they couldn't continue the way they had been. Rell wanted to tell Monique what he had been thinking for a while. They would have a better relationship as friends.

"That sounds fine. I don't have the room number here. Does your reception work fine in the room?"

Dershai wanted to know if he would be bringing his girlfriend to the suite. If he didn't give up the number then there was a possibility that she would pick up the phone.

"The reception is bad in the hall and the elevator. It's fine in the room. But take a match book or a sheet of paper from the writing pad with the number on it. My room number is Penthouse Suite Four. You should try my cell first. I will only be here at night and in the mornings."

"Okay. Give me a little while to get dressed. I'll get the number in the bed room."

Dershai walked into the other room smiling as she left the room. Rell knew it was an invitation. He hesitated but followed her. He caught her removing her thong before entering the steamed bathroom.

"Can we postpone your shower for a moment?"

Dershai turned facing Rell in the nude. Her shapely body brought a pleasing smile to his face. Dershai's breasts were firm and her nipples said they wanted more of Rell's attention.

"I hoped you would join me."

"I will."

Rell moved closer to Shai taking off his shirt, pants and boxers. They stood together kissing and massaging each other's bodies slowly. Rell picked Shai up kissing her neck and took her to the bed. Shai opened her legs for Rell to place his fingers where they teasingly touched during the massage. Rell slowly moved his fingers around exploring her vagina, searching for the release of her juices. Shai began kissing Rell's chest and decided she would lead him through their escapade. Rell read her movements and rolled on his back letting Shai kiss him lower and lower. His penis began to fill as she kissed it gently for her own arousal. Now that she knew he made love slowly she could play the game too. Shai began massaging his sack while licking the head of his penis. Rell began to sigh and moan softly.

Shai mounted him and slowly moved up and down. She could feel him swelling inside of her as she thought to herself. *"Damn, this is better than last night."* Shai couldn't believe she had found a man to satisfy her. She felt herself beginning to tingle. *"Shit, no condom. Am I stupid or what? This can't be happening again."*

Rell rolled her over on her side. He began to speed up the pace. Shai knew what that meant. He was hot and he was taking the lead again. She was feeling too good to do anything but moan.

"Aw, Rell, oooooh."

"It's alright baby. I feel it too."

"Aw, damn......aw."

Rell pulled out. He wanted to enjoy her as he had the night before. He pulled her to the edge of the bed and dropped his knees on the floor. He placed her legs over his shoulder. He moved in close and began to lick her softly until her clitoris told him she was about to explode. Shai began to tremble. His penis was at its full size. He put his tongue into her vagina, as though he was setting up a target. He pulled it in and out. Shai was moaning for him to mount her. Rell moaned in enjoyment as he stood lifting her hips off the bed. He penetrated her holding her in his arms off the bed. Shai had never been in this position. It was as though she was lifted off the bed for him to carry her with her legs wrapped around him. Rell moved in and out of her while she rested on his hips. Gently, he laid her down in a mounted position. He slowed his pace and Shai knew he was ready to cum.

"Aw Shai......baby, baby."

Rell's pace quickened. He began to sweat. Rell knew this was a different feeling. He began to tremble. He exploded. Shai felt his penis fill and unload again. She kissed him passionately.

"Whew! Shai?"

They rolled over on their backs staring at the ceiling. They both had reached their goal. They had enjoyed each other again.

"Yes."

"You did say you were on birth control right."

"Yea, Rell. What's wrong?"

"Its gonna be hard putting on a condom with you after last night and today."

"I know that's right!"

They both laughed.

"Listen, seriously I don't want you to think I'm paranoid, but I am concerned."

"Do you use a condom with your girl?"

Shai thought about it after she said it. *"I shouldn't have asked him that. I don't want to know about their sex. I really hope this ends their relationship."*

"Yeah, she makes sure of that."

Rell didn't think much of it until now. *"Why did Monique do that?"* They had been together for five years. He couldn't remember one time that they had unprotected sex.

Shai smiled at his answer. She knew that would give him something to think about. If a woman didn't trust her man that would make him think twice. They showered together, kissing passionately, as the water rinsed the soap off of their bodies. He dried her entire body, and she did the same for him. They massaged and oiled each other's bodies as they prepared to dress for the day.

"Shai, have you decided what you wanted to eat?"

"I'm supposed to meet my cousins and go out. I think I'll pass and just have some juice."

Rell poured her a glass of juice and brought it to her. Shai was gathering her things, putting them in her bag.

"You don't have to rush. Richmond is not that far from here. It will only take you about twenty minutes to get home."

"I know you have things you need to do."

Rell thought to himself, *"Cut my cell phone on for one. I know everyone has been trying to catch me."*

"Well, it's about two o'clock. I have to go to my grandmother's and my mother's before I make any other stops. So let's say I call you later about eleven, just to say good night."

"That will be fine sweetie. May I call you earlier if I want to?"

Shai was testing his availability. She wanted to know where she stood.

"Sure, call anytime you want. That's not a problem. Did you think it would be?"

"Yeah, you have a girlfriend. I wouldn't want you receiving calls from other women in my presence."

"If our relationship was stable it wouldn't be happening. I told you, I don't know how long it will be lasting. It's gone the distance but I don't know if it still has what a relationship needs to continue. I'm not happy with it and I don't think she is either. That's another issue I need to handle while I'm home."

"So you're going to be with her while you're in town."

"I probably will be. She is close to many of my relatives. She'll be around during the funeral and all. She and my mother have a good relationship. Shai we've been together five years."

"Oh, I see."

"Baby listen, I told you about her so you wouldn't think I was playing you for a one night stand. I still want you to feel comfortable with me. I have some issues to take care of, but I know I want you to be a part of my life. I am not married to her. Distant romances don't work without both parties working at it. It worked for a while, then she seemed to think she could persuade me to move back home."

"So, you're not interested in living in Richmond."

"Shai, I can't even answer that. The business I have to handle may change all of that. But I really want to stay in Maryland that keeps me away from the drama that Richmond has caused me. Baby, I want you to understand fully. I promise I will explain it all after I find out exactly what I am faced with."

Shai picked up her bag, and they walked to the living room. Rell stopped her as she walked toward the door.

"You want to know where you stand in all of this. I understand. We work well together. We have talked over two years. We have become good associates, no, I should say good friends. I want you to be with me, but I need to clear up issues that don't include you. Mainly, I need to step out of this part time relationship I am in."

"Rell, our relationship will be part time too. You'll soon tire of me like you have of her. I have feelings for you. I've been hoping our relationship would move forward for the past year or more. I put my feelings aside because I knew how you felt about women who pushed you into situations. I want to love you. I want you to love me. How do I know that the distance won't kill what we started?"

"Shai, listen, stay here. Come back after you hang out with your cousins. Call me. I'll pick you up. We need to talk so that you will feel comfortable with this. I feel that if you go like this you may not want to come back. I want a strong woman like you in my life, someone who can stand beside me. My life is getting ready to change drastically. Only a strong woman will be able to handle this type of relationship."

"What are you looking for Rell?"

"What do you mean?"

"Are you looking for someone to lean on or what? Why would your type of relationship be hard to handle?"

"Shai, I want someone who would be able to understand me. My position, my job and how I live. I don't want someone always looking for me to provide them with everything. You are successful because you went after it. You worked hard for it. I would support you just because of that. That's what I'm looking for. I have been successful because my father instilled it in me. To be successful you've got to devote time to yourself. Well now I am successful. Everything I have, I worked for. It wasn't given to me. My girl treated me with respect when I didn't have much and was struggling to get it. Now, she expects me to give her because she's my girl. I love to splurge. I love to treat her nice and shower her with gifts, but I won't be used. Shai she sees my value as a financial asset not as a man. I need someone who values my manhood. For two years, I've been talking to you about relationships, affairs, and who knows what else. You don't appear to be a woman who needs a man's wealth to make her feel like a woman. That's why I asked you for a get acquainted date. Shai I am financially stable and then some. I don't want a woman who can't see past my wallet."

Shai said another silent, *"Thank you"*. She knew her prayers were answered. Rell had his own. She didn't know what her father left her, but she knew it would be a pretty penny and maybe property as well. She agreed with Rell. She didn't need a man who thought their relationship was a way to share her money.

"I understand Rell. You're right. I'm not that type of woman. I am pretty stable and I have trouble with men because of the same reason. I'll call you later. You don't know how much time you may need with your family or your girlfriend. We'll play it by ear."

Rell wanted her to say she would be back. He didn't want to go anywhere. He could see the two of them enjoying the evening watching a movie and teasing each other until they fell asleep.

"Wait, let me grab my keys. I'll walk you out. I need to leave now too."

Rell returned and Shai put her bag down to kiss him again. They separated and smiled. Rell picked up her bag, and they left the suite heading for the parking lot. Rell cut on his cell phone as they approached her car. Shai smiled.

"What? I didn't want to be disturbed."

"I see. Just don't cut it off today until you hear from me."

Rell laughed.

"Shai, you're too much girl. Kiss me and call me later."

Shai did as he said and promised she would call him later.

Rell got in his car and waited for her to pull off.

Chapter 40

arrell checked his messages. Monique had called four times and text messaged him twice. The last message said wherever he was he could stay. He smiled to himself. He wished he could have stayed where he was. There was no message from his mother, that troubled him. Rell was concerned about her getting through the funeral and the meeting with this lawyer. He started his car and headed toward his grandmother's hoping his visit could be short and sweet. Rell turned the radio to his favorite jazz station. His phone rang.

"Hello."

"Hello Rell. Did you get my messages?"

"Yeah, your last one said something about, I could stay where I was."

"Why didn't you call me?"

"Money, I just turned my phone back on. My day didn't start out that great. After a night out with Mitch and the guys, I spent the morning going from the bed to the bathroom."

"Craig called. He thought you were with me."

Rell thought about what he wanted to say before he said it. *"Why would Craig call her? He would have called Mitch first."* Rell knew something wasn't right.

"Rell did you hear me. Your boy called me looking for you. The one you were supposed to be with."

"What did he say and what time was this?"

"That was this morning at about eleven thirty."

"Money, I didn't say I would be with them this morning."

"Well you weren't home. It only takes a couple of hours to get here."

"Monique, we have to talk. Lately, you've changed and I don't know if I'm feeling this new you."

"So what does that mean?"

"It means we need to talk."

"Whatever!"

Monique hung up the phone. Rell looked at the phone and shook his head. *"She's writing her own exit ticket. I don't have time for this shit."*

The phone rang again.

"Rell do you love me?"

"Monique, I can't deal with this bull right now. We will talk when I get there."

"You have someone else don't you."

"What are you talking about?"

"Rell let's face it, you don't want to move home with your mother. You don't want to live with me. Lately, you don't even want to visit."

"Monique for the last time, I'm driving. I can't talk to you the way I want to on the road. I am going to Nana's house and I will be to your house after that. Okay?"

"Rell there is no need for you to come to my house to break up with me. I knew when you found out you had money I would be dumped."

"Monique, you have lost it. That's all that concerns you. Why are you worried about my money? Monique I had money without my father's inheritance. I made my own money. I don't like to be pushed into anything. That's why I won't move or stay in Richmond. I like making my own decisions. Since you don't want to wait and talk, hold on."

Monique listened, but only heard the radio playing. She didn't know what Rell was doing. She knew she had pushed the wrong button. She just wanted to know what had his attention. They had been together five years, and he had shown no signs of cheating but she wanted more. Rell was going to be rich. She needed to know she would be Mrs. Darrell Mince.

"Monique."

"Rell what are you doing?"

"I parked the car. If you don't want to see me today that's fine. I have a lot to do anyway. But understand this, I don't need a half ass relationship. You're only happy when I'm spending money on you. You're only satisfied when I give you gifts. I don't see honest love Monique. I don't think you love me the way you did two years ago. Maybe my leaving didn't fit your agenda; maybe my leaving put a strain on our love for each other. For two years, I have played pocket pool, ran cold showers and watched porno flicks to stay faithful to you. You don't even see it. You just know that I didn't send you this, or I didn't say that. As long as I am up under your ass when I leave my door, you feel safe. I don't need the pressure, the half ass relationship or your pretended concern. I have business to deal with that may change my standard of living and I don't want to think that you want me just because I'm D.Q. Minces' son."

Monique was on the other end crying. Rell had not been that mad with her since the beginning of their relationship when he found out she had been cheating on him. She didn't say a word.

"I'm not trying to hurt your feelings Monique, but my feelings count too. I don't want to be looked at as a good catch because my father left me money. Things have changed."

Monique knew Rell was changing. He told her he had moved into a new condo and bought a new car. She hadn't seen either. When she asked about his job he would only tell her it was going well. Rell never told her his promotion came with a hefty raise and commission. Rell was a top Executive Officer. Rell had worked hard for the title. He would only share it with someone who appreciated him.

"Rell I looked your company up on the internet. I saw your rating as one of the top officers in your company. Then I looked up your father's company and what you would be stepping into. I got scared. I got scared for us. That's a lot to deal with in a little time. We've been through a lot but we never seem to get past third base. When will I know this is it? When will I know that our love matters enough for us to plan a future?"

"Monique there is no future for us if all you want is what my wallet can offer. You knew what kind of business I was in and you knew what my father was worth. That didn't change. I always had the potential of being a top officer. I just never had the time to commit myself to my work. Now I do. Now I can. Now that I could inherit my father's company I have to commit myself. I don't want you wondering if I'm fucking the secretary while I work late. You don't trust me. But your trust has nothing to do with our relationship. You don't want someone else to get my money. They won't baby, believe me. But if you don't love me for me, you won't either."

"Rell you sound like you think you're the shit now. Fuck you! Fuck you and your father's money! You didn't get committed to that fucking job until I told you what you could get if you worked at it. I stayed with you through the bull before you were to inherit a dime. I was willing to go through this shit with the funeral, wake and lawyer. But now that you know you will be Mr. Big you don't need me to lean on. Don't stop by Rell. Keep stepping! Oh, and you will give your money to some bitch 'cause you never had to deal with one. You wouldn't know she got you until you fucked her and your books didn't balance. I have feelings Rell and they are real. When you realize it, you call me."

The phone went dead. Rell felt somewhat relieved. He needed to call Craig though and ask what was on his mind calling Monique. He also wanted to know how he got her number. Rell got back on the road and dialed Craig's number.

"What's up fella?"

"What's up Rell? Yo, man what's up with your girl Monique. She called me earlier trying to pick information about last night?"

"What did you tell her?"

"I told her we were together until early this morning. I told her when I left you were in the bathroom with a hangover."

"Thanks man. Listen I'll call you later."

"No problem. You good?"

"Yeah, I'm good. I think that's over man. She's been bugging for the last couple of months. I don't know what's up with her."

"Alright, I'll see you tomorrow."

"Yeah, later."

Rell didn't think Craig had called her. Monique had definitely stepped out of the box. She probably got Craig's number from the company directory online. Yeah, she's history. Rell turned the radio up and thought about Shai. He called Nana to tell her he was on his way.

Chapter 41

Dershai called Marci as soon as she pulled out of the parking lot. She was still floating on a cloud when she heard her voice.

"Hey girl, what's up?"

"Me Marci, me. I am floating girl. I think I found someone I can truly enjoy, intellectually and sexually."

Dershai began to giggle with excitement.

"I can't even begin to tell you on the phone. Where are we meeting?"

"I'm on my way to Mia's now. Do you want us to meet you there or your place?"

"Mia's is closer to where I am. I'll come there. I'm on my way."

"See you when you get there."

The conversation ended. Shai tried calling Derek but he didn't answer. She left a message saying she would be with Marci and Mia. *That damn Derek better come home, so he can get ready for his orientation tomorrow.*

Shai made herself call her mother.

"Hello."

"Hey Ma, how are you today?"

"I'll make it, I guess."

"What's wrong?"

"Do you really want to know? I didn't think you had time to inquire about my feelings."

"Ma, are you okay or are you picking an argument? I'm really in a good mood, please don't spoil it for me."

"How could you be in a good mood and your father just died?"

"Ma, he would want us to continue. I know you're not in the best mood, but if you're not ill then you're okay. Grief comes and goes for me. Right now I feel okay."

"I guess your brother is okay too. He hasn't called once. Does he even know what the arrangements are?"

"Yeah, we'll be at the later wake. His orientation won't be over until five or five-thirty."

"So you're not attending the wake?"

"We will be at the later wake. I can't say that I would want to sit through both wakes."

"Dershai, he was your father! It's not like you're there as an outsider. You are his children and both of you should show enough respect to be there."

"Ma, you're bugging. Be there for who; the executives from his business; the people from the church; his friends; your friends; his relatives; who?"

"Dershai don't play dumb. D.Q. was your father and you should be there to pay respect to him."

"We will be at the LATER WAKE!"

Dershai could feel she was getting nowhere as usual with her mother. If her mother didn't get her way she couldn't see any other way. Shai knew the conversation was ending but she wasn't prepared for her mother's response.

"Dershai, if you and your brother can't be with me through this whole thing from beginning to end, well, don't show up at all!"

Her mother slammed the receiver in her ear.

"Damn, what the fuck!" Shai was furious. "Who does she think she is? I'll be glad when this shit is over. I have a few words for her ass."

Shai dialed Derek's number again expecting to leave a new message. She wanted to warn him about their mother's attitude.

"What's up Sis?"

"What's up with you, lil' brother?"

"I'm on our block now. Gonna check in. Are you near the apartment?"

"No, I'm going to meet Marci and Mia at Mia's place."

"Oh, okay. So are you alright, you sound rattled?"

"Your mother and her shit. She said if we can't be with her from the first wake and through everything else don't show up at all."

"Well Shai she can't stop us. We're the children."

"She used that as the reason why we should be there throughout the entire thing. Derek I don't think I can go to two wakes and the funeral. It's too much for me. I was glad you said wait for you and go to the second wake."

"Listen, don't worry. Nana will be the only one who will be concerned. I'll call her and tell her we will be at the later wake. She'll deal with our mother."

"What about the way it will look to everyone else."

"Did anybody break down our door to see how we took the news of his death? How many calls did you get?"

"Shai, mommy wanted to be the wife to the end. Let her play the role."

"What do you mean wanted to be the wife?"

"Daddy left her, remember? Two years ago. If she had let go, I don't think he would have died as soon as he did. He probably had an ulcer as well as respiratory problems. It was her selfishness that killed him. Let her feel it a while."

Shai hadn't heard Derek talk like that before. She wondered when these thoughts developed. She understood what he said, but it sounded strange coming from Derek.

"Derek, do you mean that?"

"She needs to face reality. She held on to our father because she didn't want him to be happy somewhere else. It had nothing to do with us. It was her selfish heart. I won't uphold her now that he's dead, like she truly loved him. Shai you and I know she didn't."

"Wow, I didn't know you felt that way. Okay, I guess now I understand why you don't talk to her that often. I don't know what to say."

"It's okay sis. Have a great time with our cousins. Give them a kiss for me. I'll call Nana. It will be fine. You'll see."

"I love you Derek."

"You too, later."

Shai pulled into Mia's apartment's parking lot. She found a place to park opposite Marci's car. She walked to the apartment and rang the bell. Just the thought of reliving her night with Rell, perked her up. Marci opened the door asking questions. They had a lot to talk about.

Chapter 42

erek was feeling better about himself now that he was in a position to invest in a web designing business of his own. His new job came with an offer of partnership. All he needed was the funding. His hanging out with the boys in Maryland was really a meeting with other web designers who wanted to invest in the building of this new company. He banked on his inheritance to help pay his share. The offer had come up when his father was admitted into the hospital. Derek talked to the potential partners explaining to them his father was sick, and he couldn't possibly speak to him about a money investment at the time. Since his father's death, he arranged to meet with them over the weekend to request they give him time to be with his family and get business matters straight. The deal was on hold. The partners were well aware that he was the son of D.Q. Mince and the money would be no object, of course the deal could wait.

Derek called Nana. He had to make sure he stayed close to her during the distribution of his father's funds. Even if his father left the money for him in her hands, he could get her to understand him wanting his own business.   D.Q. knew that Derek didn't have business smarts. He couldn't be trusted with large sums of money. He left Nana the money for Derek during his college years after he found out he had a gambling problem. Nana had covered for him on many occasions. D.Q. sensed Derek was using his grandmother saying, she understood him when no one else did. That was years ago. Derek knew Nana would give him the money he needed. She told him many times he needed his own foundation.

"Hey Nana, this is Derek."

"Boy, where have you been?"

"I had to go out of town. I got a new job. Did Dershai tell you?"

"No, your Aunt Darlene did. Where are you now?"

"I'm at home. I have to get ready for tomorrow. I have to attend an orientation. That's why I called you."

"Why you called me? What's going on now?"

"Nana, Dershai and I only want to attend the later wake. My orientation won't be over until about five thirty. My mother says if we can't be with her from the beginning don't show up at all."

"Your mother is just talking boy. That's fine. You get that job under your belt. Ain't nothing like being stable in a job. So you and Dershai are coming together at six o'clock or sometime there after?"

"Yes, Ma'am. Is that okay?"

"That's fine. I will be home by then though. I can't take two wakes, so I'll go to the early one. Your mama can sit there if she wants to. She likes the attention."

"So, are you okay Nana?"

"I'm fine. Your Uncle and Aunt are here with me. People have been stopping by. I'm expecting the Reverend this evening. I'll be fine."

"Okay Nana. We wanted you to know why we wouldn't be at the early wake. I'm sure my mother won't tell you."

"You're probably right. I sure don't understand that woman. Anyhow, don't worry yourself about it baby. It will be just fine."

Derek told her to say hello to everyone for him and said goodbye. He went to his room to get his clothes ready for the next day. It would only be a matter of time. He had plans to finally be recognized as a Mince.

Chapter 43

Nana hung up the phone shaking her head. She said a silent prayer as she went into the living room. Rell was sitting in her favorite chair talking with Michael and Alesha. When he looked up, he smiled. Nana saw D.Q. all over him. Her eyes filled with tears. Rell stood up and hugged her. She sobbed softly and asked him if he wanted to eat. Rell followed her into the kitchen.

"No, Nana, thanks. I'm eating dinner with my mother. Nana, just so you know, I think it's over between me and Monique. I thought I should tell you before she called you."

"Baby you know I don't get involved in your personal mess like that."

"I know but I needed to tell you. I guess I wanted to know if I was right about my decision."

"Your decision? It was your decision to end the relationship?"

"I think it was. It happened so fast. I got the feeling that she was trying to sway me into a commitment. I'm not sure that I'm ready for that yet. She reminded me of the wife who was okay at home as long as the man kept her in furs and money. I don't want that type of life."

"What are you talking about?"

"Nana, I live miles away. I pay for her to come to see me and then splurge while she's there. It's become a habit; she looks forward to it. There has never been a weekend, where she would come to stay, without an outing to the mall or an expensive dinner. It's not that I can't afford it. I wanted to make sure that it's not about the money. I guess I wanted to know that the relationship meant more to her than just what I bought her. So I mentioned it."

"Well, what did she say?"

"She said she looked up my worth and dad's business on the computer, and she needed to know what our future looked like. She implied that she was my motivator and for that I owed her. It sounded as though she wanted a guarantee that we would get married."

"She's been with you all this time, and it just came to this?"

"It started a couple of months after I left here two years ago. It has been getting worse. It's like she wants to spend what she thinks I have on her, so I won't spend it somewhere else. I don't want it to be over, but I can't deal with that type of relationship. That's not love."

"Well you shouldn't have started something you didn't want to finish. You have been splurging with that girl since y'all got together. I'm not saying she's right by expecting that all the time. That ain't how life is. Even the rich eat at home sometimes. You have to go with your heart, how you feel. Don't stay in the relationship if you're not happy."

"No, I don't think I can, especially after watching my mom and dad. They played with each other's emotions for a lifetime."

They both sat silent for a moment. Nana wouldn't say a word. She knew Rell didn't know about his sister or brother. She wasn't about to explain that mess. Rell hugged his grand-mother again and thanked her for listening.

"Nana, did you get the papers you needed for Mr. Simpson."

"Sure did. Your father had them in the pile from the office. I guess you were right. We can wait until after the funeral to go through the rest of those papers."

"Where are Uncle Darryl and Aunt Francine? I was waiting for them to come in before I left for my mothers."

"I don't know. You should have asked Michael or Alesha. They come and go here so fast I can't keep up. They will be back soon though. Dinner is here for them."

"I know that's right. Anyway, I'm going to play this video game with Michael for a bit. I promised him a butt whopping."

"I promised him one too, but it wasn't no game."

Rell laughed. "What didn't he do now?"

"His usual, not picking up his clothes off the floor. I told him company may come through at any time. He's going to wait 'til they come, and I black out before he understands, I don't ask for nothing to be done twice."

"Nana, you sit down and wait for your company. I'll talk with Michael about picking up before we start our game."

Rell left his grandmother with tears filling her eyes again. She didn't see Rell heading toward the bedroom, she saw D.Q.

Chapter 44

$\mathcal{T}$onya opened the door when she heard Darlene's car door close. She left it cracked and went into her kitchen to check the chicken she was preparing. "Come on in girl. I'm frying this chicken and it needed to be turned."

"Okay. I brought some wine. I didn't know if you had any."

"Thanks Darlene. I don't know what's in the bar. For the last few days my supply has been going quickly."

"I thought Ronnie and the crew was coming in today."

"Darryl and Francine said they probably would get here tomorrow morning; something about Chantell getting to the house later tonight. I guess they thought she wouldn't be coming in from school until late. Maybe her flight was arriving late. I don't know, girl."

"I thought she would have caught a flight home on Friday."

"I think she couldn't miss one of her Friday classes."

"Hmmmm. That girl could have stayed in school. That's a lot of expense on Darryl and Francine. They will have to fly her back to California again."

"I guess money wasn't the object."

Darlene looked at Tonya as she put the next batch of chicken in the pan. *"She doesn't have a clue."*

"I asked did she have to take a leave from college, and they said she would be going back at the end of the week."

"She could have stayed at school. That was an unnecessary expense."

Tonya looked at Darlene.

"Why would you say unnecessary? Don't you think she should be at her Uncle's funeral?"

"Tonya, that girl is in college. We all know that. If she didn't come it wouldn't be, as though she didn't want to be here. I'm just saying that's a couple of hundred dollars they could have saved and paid for books or supplies for her next semester."

They both went into the living room to sit. Tonya used the remote to turn on the television to no particular show.

"So you agree with Dershai and Derek?"

"Agree with them about what?"

"They won't be at the early wake."

"Maybe it would be too much for them to be at both wakes."

"Then they should come to the early wake and leave."

"What difference does it make Tonya? Besides, doesn't Derek have his job orientation on Monday?"

"Their father is dead. Does that mean anything to them or you?"

"Tonya, calm down. First of all, he was my brother, so, yes, it means a lot to me. Life goes on though, sweetie. Derek has been waiting for this job offer for the past few weeks. It's unfortunate that it came through now. Dershai and Derek are a comforting support to each other. At a time like this neither of them wants the other to go through this alone. So they will come together. Tonya, it's not like they will miss the funeral."

Tonya gave Darlene's words some thought. *"Here we go with the bull again. They've got you all wrapped around their fingers. I will be glad when all of you see what a piece of shit D.Q. was."*

"Darlene they have lost their father. I am the other parent. The only parent they have left. Who is my support during all of this? I don't think when we're faced with the reality and grief of D.Q.'s passing, there will be a set of open arms for me."

Darlene waited before commenting. She wanted to say, *"You reap what you sow."* But she held it as a thought.

"Tonya, I don't understand you. D.Q. left you two years ago. Granted, you may still have some feelings for the man. You may even love him still. But what did you expect people to do? Let's face it, you were separated. Everyone knows that. You may get a nod or two out of respect, but you're not the typical grieving wife. If D.Q. had died, say, three months from now you would have been an ex-wife."

"I am Mrs. Derek Quincy Mince and no one can change that!"

"Tonya no one doubts your name. You just don't have that status. You were separated for two-year honey. You and D.Q. weren't even speaking, for the most part. You talked through your lawyers. You got money and property as your statement that you had separated yourself from him. You dropped his friends, and his family. As his sister I tried to stay in touch with you because I will always be Dershai and Derek's aunt. We all felt that way. We are connected to D.Q.'s children. Not to you. You never welcomed us. Let's be real Tonya. You accepted us because D.Q. made you accept us. You didn't fool us. You're reaching out now because there is a will to be read. Tonya, it is signed by D.Q. What it is, it is."

"I know you don't think I invited you here to form some kind of alliance?" Tonya's game had been revealed. Darlene knew exactly what she wanted.

"Tonya, anytime you call me, it's for your own purposes. I ain't mad at you. I just want you to know we know your game. I want you to have a relationship with your children so that you can live the rest of your life in peace. Your relationship with them is what needs support. I'm here to tell you as their family, my mother and I will help you and them through this mess. They will need you as a mother, their only parent, to get through this funeral and the reading of the will."

"So you're helping them, not me?"

"Helping them does help you. I've been their ears for years. That won't stop because you cut your ties with us. But they will need someone to talk to, someone who will answer their questions without anger or hate toward their father."

"Do you want some wine? I need some."

Tonya got up to get the ice bucket. She went in the kitchen getting the ice and glasses. She kept her eyes on Darlene thinking she would comment on her saying she needed a drink.

"Tonya, I know this is making you uncomfortable and that's the last thing I want to do. I can leave if you like, but I needed to let you know that D.Q.'s situation has affected all of us."

"So you know that this mess has affected all of us? Where were you all when D.Q. was sleeping with that bitch? It was a mess then. It affected my family, my children and I then, but no one stopped it. I told D.Q. to stop it, but he claimed he loved that tramp. After she got pregnant he wanted to leave. I held on to what I loved and vowed to be with until death due us part. Well, he's dead and I am his wife. Now everyone is concerned about what has affected them. Bullshit! It affected me for thirty years or more. Do you know that tramp and her bastard son?"

"No, I never met her or Rell. I told D.Q. what I felt about it. I told him when it started. I also decided it was his life and we all have a right to do as we choose with our lives. It would be easy for me to say it didn't have anything to do with me, but that would be a lie. I have kept a secret from my daughters for thirty years or more about a cousin they don't know. I started to tell them today. I have that type of relationship with my children. But I thought about you and your children, my niece and nephew. How would they feel about their remaining parent if they heard the secret of their father, the other woman, and their son? How would they feel to know that he wanted to leave you before they were born? How would they feel to know you held on and helped to create this mess? You chose to stay. You chose to hold on to your husband despite the fact that he didn't want you! Damn, Tonya! How selfish is that? Now you want what? More money as though he had to pay you to be his wife?"

Tonya had never heard Darlene be this passionate about D.Q. and his mess. In the past Darlene wouldn't even talk about it. She understood her feelings but Tonya was looking forward to getting revenge any way she could, even if he was dead. She poured more wine in her glass.

"Darlene, it is what it is. If you want to tell your daughters go right ahead. I told Dershai that if she and Derek couldn't be with me from the beginning don't show up. Darlene, I mean it. They have treated me like shit for more than two years now because D.Q. didn't want to be with me. I have tried to sit them down and talk and his angelic nature disguised the truth. I'm going to get what a wife is due. After that, you and your mother can support Dershai and Derek in their father's mess. I don't owe them a thing. Their father does and he's dead!"

Darlene stood up. She was through. It wasn't worth the effort to talk to Tonya. She was scorned and had her own agenda.

"Well baby, good luck. Good luck with your kids and trying to get my brother's money. 'Cause just like me and my mother know what you hung on for, so did he. I'll let myself out. Enjoy the wine."

Darlene walked out the door and never looked back.

Chapter 45

Marci couldn't stop laughing at Dershai's narration of her fantastic date. Mia just kept repeating, "I know that's right!" They never left Mia's apartment. They sat in her living room drinking soda, eating chips and enjoying Dershai's memories.

"Girl, you got your wish this time." Marci laughed again. She found it amusing that Dershai never got a chance to lead in her sexual escapade.

"Marci, I can't help but think his girl must be crazy! This man is NICE! He has just the right sized package and is fine. His manner and attitude are so different than the brothers I have dealt with. Girl, I wanted to say thank you, out loud at least one hundred times."

"Well at least you don't have to worry about him feeling insecure because your dad is D.Q. Mince." Mia chimed in. That was one of Mia's pet peeves. Men that she met always wondered what she could get from her uncle. She never understood what they thought she was going to get being his niece. They thought there was a road to his money if they dated his niece.

"You're right Mia. He never even asked about my parents or who my parents were?"

"What's his last name Shai?" Marci asked the question and laughed. "You still don't know. You'll be walking down the aisle ready to marry the man and won't know his last name."

"Shut up, Marci. I would ask him by then. I forgot my damn name after he laid me down."

"Doesn't his name show up on your cell phone?" Mia asked a question even Marci hadn't asked.

"You know, I never paid it any mind. I don't think so. I think it says, hmm, I don't know. I'll have to pay attention when he calls again. I think I may have programmed it to just say Rell. His has a jazz ring to it."

"If you set it to a certain ring then I think it just goes to the name you programmed it to."

"Yea, Mia you're right. That's what it does."

"So, you still don't know the mystery man's last name."

"He holds his own; that's what I know. He's definitely on my level, financially. I won't have to worry about him bugging because I spend my money the way I want to. Those brothers I dated were upset 'cause, I spent my money. I used to tell them, "You didn't buy this why are you bugging?""

"I think all guys bug out when a woman buys what they want with their own money. I think it makes them feel like they fell short." Mia laughed. She knew what Marci was going to say.

"Mia, those brothers couldn't buy you anything anyway. Shit, we can't buy you anything. Your taste is beyond expensive. I don't know how you keep a boyfriend. I would feel intimidated too."

"Mia, say it ain't so. Tell Marci what your man bought for you over the weekend."

"Shai, she can't. She picked up the pocketbook and the salesman said one hundred and ten dollars. She pulled out one hundred. Her so called man pulled out ten and said Baby I got it."

They all started laughing again. Shai's phone rang. She smiled, got up and went in the kitchen to get her cell phone from her purse.

"Hello."

"Hey Babe. How are you?" It was Rell. Dershai looked at her watch.

"Wow. I thought you said eleven?"

"I was thinking about you. I'm on my way to my mother's house. I will be back at the suite by ten."

"Hmm. And you thought you would let me know that now?"

"Yeah, I just wanted you to know."

"I see. What happened to your friend?"

"Shai, I don't know. Call me later okay?"

"Rell are you okay?"

"Yeah, I'm fine. We'll talk about it."

"I can talk now. You don't sound right."

"I'm caught between emotions I guess being around family. I'll be alright. So what's up with you, did you meet your cousins."

"Yeah I did. We're just clowning around."

"That's all good. I hope I didn't interrupt."

"No, not at all. You'll be done and back by ten?"

"Yeah I don't have to make anymore stops after my mother's house. I think I'll take it down after that."

"Well, you can call me. I'll probably still be here."

"I guess you'll be busy at ten?"

"No, I don't think so. I'll be either here or at home. I would invite you over, but it's in Richmond, remember."

"I'll get the address later."

"I'll call you later."

"Later, Shai."

Shai returned to the living room smiling and blushing.

"So Mister Mysterious is still a mystery huh?" Marci looked at Shai and smiled.

"Yeah, in more ways than one. I think he broke up with his girlfriend. I'm not sure he was ready to though."

"If I had sex with you last night and this morning and had a problem with my girlfriend that may help me to end my relationship with her." Mia spoke and then waited for comments.

"I hope he didn't, I mean not for me. I want him to break up with her because it's over. I don't want him debating later about where they could have been. They were together for five years. They have a history."

"Well you're off to a great start Shai. I think you set a record of your own last night and maybe this morning too."

"Shut up Marci." They laughed again.

"Hey let's get some movies for the night. We're not going anywhere. Who knows maybe we'll see the mystery man in our travels."

Both Marci and Shai looked at Mia and laughed. They gathered their purses and headed out for videos.

Chapter 46

Nana's house was getting crowded with members of the church and neighbors. Rell said his hellos and good-byes promising Nana he would see her the next day. She reminded him that she would be riding with him to the wake. Rell assured her he would be at her house by one o'clock in the afternoon. Darryl saw Rell coming out of the front door as he pulled his car into the driveway.

"Hey nephew, you leaving?" Darryl yelled from the car window.

"Yeah, hey Aunt Francine. I told my mom I would eat dinner with her. It's almost seven, so I figured I better get over there before she starts blowing my phone up."

"Rell you sure are looking good. You got a special workout or something? Give some tips to your Uncle."

Francine made this comment often. She admired how Rell kept up his appearance. She and Darryl got out of the car.

"Nothing much, Aunt Francine. I haven't even been to the gym in at least two weeks. I play a lot of racquet ball though. I guess that keeps me in shape." Rell answered and tapped his uncle in the stomach. Darryl tagged him back and they exchanged playful punches.

"So what time will we see you tomorrow?"

"I told Nana I would be here about one."

"That's early enough for her. You know she would want you to be here. Well, I don't have to tell you. You deal with her more than I do."

Darryl stepped back and leaned getting a full view of Rell's car parked in front of the house.

"Is that what you sporting now? I like that one."

Francine kissed him on his cheek saying goodbye and went into the house. Darryl and Rell walked closer to the car. Rell opened the door so Darryl could sit on the passenger's side and look in the car.

"This is nice. What did you do with your truck?"

"It's at home. I don't drive this that much. This is just something I wanted and decided to buy it for myself."

"Go head, big baller. You're doing your thing. How's the job?"

"Great, I have my own division and a couple of people under me. I still have my clients, and I mix and mingle with a few of the big shots. It's all good."

"I'm glad for you."

"How's your company? The last time we talked you were making some major decisions. How did it work out?"

Darryl saw his turn. He didn't want to pass up the opportunity, but he wasn't sure he should unload his problem now. He decided to test the waters.

"Money wasn't right. I made some mistakes. I took some bad advice. I'm hoping I can fix it when I get home."

"I'm sorry to hear that. I don't know what I can do but if I can help you, I mean, I don't know what the situation is but I can look at your paperwork and figure some things out to better your finances."

"Yeah that might help. I think I'm going to have to hire a financial consultant anyway. It might as well be you."

"Uncle Darryl I don't know if I can take all that on, but I would be willing to look at things to see if we can't patch them up until you can get back in the green."

"Maybe after all this is over with your father's business.... I mean before I go home. I can have someone at the office fax me the papers you may need to look at. Also, I 'll be happy to show you the company dividends on the computer site."

"Yeah, let's sit down before you leave to go home."

"Do you know when you'll be calling Mr. Simpson? Your grandmother said you would be making the appointment."

"Mr. Simpson left it on me. I want to get it over with as soon as possible. I need to get back to my job."

"Rell you might not be going back to your job. Your father's company may be yours."

"I still need to go back. I'm not sure what the status of his company is. Uncle Darryl to be truthful with you, I haven't thought about it. I'll talk with Mr. Simpson the day after the funeral to set up the appointment. I don't want to delay it, the sooner the better."

Darryl got out of the car. He smiled to himself. Rell wouldn't let him down. If Nana didn't tell him about the gambling, he would be set. He could truly walk away in the green.

"Well nephew, tell your mom, I said hello, and I'll see her tomorrow. Do you know if she's going to the early wake?"

"I didn't ask her. She will probably go with us in the afternoon. I don't think she would want to be at the later one without us being there."

"You're right. I'll see you later then."

Rell pulled off thinking about his uncle's statement about his father's business. He had more than enough on his plate. Monique was right. It was enough to be scared about. He would call the lawyer and talk to him before setting a date for the reading.

Chapter 47

Reverend Wilcox rang the bell promptly at seven o'clock. Deacon Smalls and the other members of the church had left fifteen minutes before he arrived. Darryl and Francine laughed and whispered to each other about Nana's expected guest as they left the living room and went into the den. Nana gave them a sharp look and laughed to herself.

"Come on in Reverend. I'm glad you could make it."

"Sister Mince, anytime."

"Would you like something to eat or drink? What can I get you?"

"I'm fine Sister Mince, maybe a little later."

Nana thought to herself, *"If he thinks he's going to be here all night, he's got another thing coming."*

"We can go into the sitting room and talk. How was the rest of your day?"

Nana led Reverend Wilcox to the sitting room talking as they took their seats. Nana sat in the winged back chair across from the couch. She only sat in her recliner for relaxation and this was business.

Reverend Wilcox waited for her to sit before he took his seat. Nana smiled recognizing the gentleman in him.

"It was as well as to be expected. I had a few calls to make. A couple of our members are sick. I called their families to check on them. I do that every Sunday and at least once a week. A few of them seemed to be coming around. I prayed with the families before hanging up."

"How nice, I know that must have been a comfort to them."

"Yes, well Sister Mince, I know you must have something important to talk about. You usually talk to me at the church office. What could it be that you have invited me to your lovely home?"

The Reverend had taken the time to view the room in its entirety. Nana's touch was obvious throughout the house. Reverend Wilcox felt the love it held and became very comfortable.

"Reverend Wilcox, you know every funeral brings its own family drama."

Nana started at the beginning. She explained D.Q. and Tonya's marriage, his love for Nikki and the birth of Darrell. She added Tonya's greed getting in the way of her love for herself, the birth of Dershai and Derek, and the beginning of the secrets and lies. Reverend Wilcox listened, nodding his head and agreeing with Nana's personal observations. Nana told him of her concern with the wake, funeral and the reading of the will. She wasn't sure what problems may develop before the reading of the will, but she felt things would peak and erupt at the funeral.

"What do you think may happen Sister Mince?"

"I'm not sure. It's something that I feel. I can't say that I condoned what D.Q. did. Reverend I watched him as he went through those thirty years trying to keep his marriage with Tonya while having a love for Nikki. I watched him be a devoted father for his children in two separate homes. I watched as he lost the woman he loved and his first born because of the secrets and lies.

Reverend Wilcox I watched my son die slowly for two years because he waited too late to find his own peace."

"I think I understand your concerns. Have you talked to your family about the concerns you have?"

"Reverend if I could talk to them, and it would solve this animosity, I would have done it. I am talking about two women who will stand their ground, and I don't know that either of them should back down."

"Well Sister Mince, they will have to see that this problem didn't start when D.Q. died. From what you are telling me it happened over thirty years ago. You can't fix that in a couple of days. If they can't come to a compromise it may take your grandchildren to bridge the gap."

"The children don't know about each other Reverend. They've never met. I'm worried about that too. I don't want them to think we kept it a secret from them. That was D.Q. and Tonya's doing. Nikki didn't even know about the children until she and D.Q. broke up."

"Now, Sister Mince, Nikki is Darrell's mother."

"Yes, and Dershai and Derek belong to Tonya. They are siblings. Rell is the oldest. The program will be their first knowledge that the other exist."

"Aren't the names in the program?"

"No, we just stated three children. Tonya didn't want Rell's name mentioned at all in the program. We compromised to listing D.Q. had three children."

"You're right, now I see the problem. Well, we will have to deal with it in prayer until the reading of the will. Prayer that God will handle it in His time."

"Reverend I have prayed day in and day out. It's not that I don't trust His will, but I don't want those children to resent any of the family who has tried to protect them in all of this."

"I understand Sister Mince. I wish you or D.Q. had brought this to me sooner. We could have arranged family sessions to break the news to them in a loving setting. You may consider getting all of your family together after the will is read."

"Reverend Wilcox, that's exactly what I suggested to my daughter Darlene. She's worried about her two not knowing. They are real close to Dershai, and she was worried they would tell her before her mother did. Darlene didn't tell them either. It's a mess, just a mess."

"Sister Mince, it will be fine. The Lord works in mysterious ways. Maybe you can talk to your grandchildren before the funeral. Think about it. They all trust you to tell them the truth. Through their anger, they will trust you."

"I don't know if I can do it tomorrow, with the viewing and all. I understand what you are saying but each of us has to deal with tomorrow. I would hate for them to have to deal with the death, family secrets and lies."

"Sister Mince, I know you think it may be like stabbing them in their hearts, but it doesn't dull the pain to wait a few days. It will still hurt."

"You are right Reverend. I don't know what to do. I just wanted to vent, I guess. D.Q. has set up a will to be done by video, but I don't know what he says and his lawyer won't tell me. I sure hope it comes with an explanation for all this mess."

Reverend Wilcox began to survey the room while he listened. Thoughts ran through his mind about asking her age, what did she do in her spare time and could he visit her more often? Since Nana's family problems would take some time to clear, Reverend Wilcox saw an opportunity to get as close to Sister Mince as he could.

"Can I trouble you Sister Mince for something cold to drink?"

"Certainly, Reverend, what would you like? I have iced tea, lemonade and soda."

"Lemonade would be fine."

Nana headed for the kitchen. She thought about what the Reverend said about the pain. She didn't want to cause anyone pain so maybe she would wait to have the family meeting after the reading of the will. She would let Mr. Simpson know they would need to use his conference room after the reading of the will. Everyone would be in shock. Nana thought if she asked them to come to her house later they might not show up. Nana returned with a tall glass of lemonade. Reverend Wilcox was standing looking out of the window.

"I hope I haven't taken up too much of your time Reverend."

"No, Ma'am, you don't need to worry about that. My time is yours whenever you need it."

"I am going to take your advice. I will have a family meeting immediately after the reading of the will. They all will attend the reading, and I won't have to worry about them not coming to my house."

"I hope that works for you. If you need my support before, then or after, don't hesitate to call me."

"I won't Reverend. You helped me clear my mind and my heart."

Reverend Wilcox handed Nana her glass and smiled. His hand touched hers and they both smiled moving them away slowly.

"I will see you tomorrow. I'm going to set up my readings for the wake. Is there any particular scripture you would like to have read?"

"Whatever you choose will be fine. D.Q. loved the gospel choir. They will be singing on Tuesday at the funeral right?"

"Yes, I talked with the director, and they are ready to sing at the wake and the service."

"Oh how nice Reverend, thank you so much."

"I would like to check on you after the wake tomorrow evening if that's okay with you."

"That's fine Reverend. I won't be at the second viewing. Are you sure I can't get you something to eat?"

"Not tonight Sister Mince. I won't be able to move after I eat."

Nana laughed. "Okay, have it your way Reverend."

Reverend Wilcox hugged Nana and told her he would call and check on her in the morning.

As Nana closed the door she told herself courting a Reverend might not be that bad. *"He slipped that checking on me in the morning in without me paying attention to it."* She smiled as she locked her doors and headed for her bedroom.

Chapter 48

Simone brought the ice bucket into the den for Rell to make drinks. She kept repeating how excited she was about seeing him although it was due to his father's funeral. Rell told her about his new job, his condo and his reservations regarding the reading of the will. Simone was comfortable talking with Rell, and he loved being in her presence. When he was younger he would visit her often. Simone didn't have any children, then and shared Rell with his mother, as though he was hers. Rell was ten when she had her son. By then Rell had new interests in his childhood activities and friends. Nikki and Rell visited off and on. They stayed in touch more often by phone.

Nikki came in the room with a tray of fruit, celery crackers and cheese. They had enjoyed their dinner earlier, and she promised the tray of after dinner snacks.

"Rell, I didn't know you bought a new car? How is the ride? I heard it was better than the other models."

Nikki loved all Mercedes models; she wouldn't look at other cars. D.Q. wouldn't let her settle for less after seeing her reaction to her first one. Now she had a 2007 CL 600 Coupe and vowed it would be her last.

"I bought it last month. I haven't driven it much. I usually drive my truck."

"What kind of truck do you have?" Simone was making mental notes.

"A Cadillac Escalade. I love my truck but I didn't want Nana and everybody to have to climb in to ride with me."

"Well I say you have done well for yourself in the past two years. Are you thinking about moving back to Richmond?"

"I haven't given it much thought. Maybe I'll venture up north with you. New York can be interesting to an accountant."

"A lot of competition though."

"Simone, what are you going to do about your job?" Nikki saw the opening and jumped in.

"I really don't know. I'm using the time to think. I thought I would keep you company a while and redirect my goals. The cable company doesn't hold much of a future. I thought it did when I took the job, but they've been laying people off and the job positions that were available have been micro managed."

"How's your job coming, Nikki? Aren't you about ready to retire?"

"Girl I have bills. This house has a mortgage to be paid, and I love my car but it has a car note. Not to mention I am accustomed to a certain way of living. D.Q. is gone. I don't know how my salary will be able to handle it all. I was smart enough to save over the years because he wouldn't let me use my money for anything. I have a nice nest egg. My rainy day funds, I guess the rain has started."

"D.Q. paid all your bills?"

"Every one of them. I told him he wasn't obligated to pay them. He said he would always take care of me. I stopped talking to him about it. The bills would be paid before I could put a stamp on an envelope."

"Nikki, it must have been a blessing to have a man like that."

The door bell rang and Rell gestured for his mother to sit. He would get the door. The conversation was getting heavy. He didn't know how long he could have sat there listening to what his father did for his mother. The bell rang again and Rell wondered what the emergency was. He opened the door and Monique turned around as she heard the door opening.

Chapter 49

"Hello, Rell. I know I didn't call. I wanted to know if we could talk about this afternoon."

"Come in." Rell answered allowing Monique to enter the house.

Rell didn't respond to her question. He led her into the den. Simone and Nikki stopped talking. Rell had told them what happened on the phone between him and Monique.

"Hey Monique, do you want a drink? Can I get you something to eat?"

Nikki didn't want her to feel out of place. The instant silence when she entered the room let Monique know they knew what went on earlier.

"No thank you. I wanted to talk to Rell a moment if I could."

"Let's go in the living room. Excuse us."

Rell didn't feel much like talking, but he would listen. The reality of the days to come had begun to rattle his nerves.

"Have a seat." Rell sat opposite Monique on an ottoman.

"Rell I think we both rushed into decisions that were made this afternoon. I think you misunderstood my intentions when I told you I had checked the internet for your father's business and your new position. My girlfriend told me she saw the site, and I wanted to look at it too. I was shocked because you never told me how your promotion put you in such a prestigious position. I knew about your father, but I didn't realize how much of a financial icon he was in the state. I guess I thought you felt you had to hide it because you didn't want me to know. That led me to other insecurities I shouldn't have had."

"Are you sure you don't want a drink? I left my beer in the den, I'll be right back."

"I'm sure."

"Excuse me a minute."

Rell left the room thinking. *"She must be crazy if she thinks I'm going to buy this shit. Damn. What happened to trust? Money changes everyone."*

Nikki looked up from a magazine she was looking through.

"Are you okay, Rell? Where's Monique?"

"Simone can you hand me my beer by you? She's still in the other room. I'm okay, I forgot my beer."

He left the room returning to Monique in the living room. She was looking frantically through her purse.

"I'm sorry. Please continue with your thoughts."

"Rell why are you talking like this doesn't include you?"

"Monique, you know me. You know me better than all my friends and most of my family. You should know that I care for you. I love you. I can't allow my love for you to blind me to the point of not seeing what has

242

become a serious problem between us. If my father had not died, I don't think your friend would have called you about my firm's web site or his. That is, if a friend called you. I don't like playing games when emotions are involved. My mother hurt for a long time playing similar games. I learned a valued lesson. You need to know who I am without the price tag. When I left two years ago, I didn't know who I was. You helped me see I had inner value."

"That's what I mean Rell. I saw your value and your value to me before you had this position and before your father died. I think you misunderstood what I meant."

"Monique you wanted to know our future. Why would our future change because of my position, or what I may inherit?"

"It doesn't Rell. I guess I was scared you wouldn't want me. I mean since you live in Maryland and all. Who's to say you wouldn't take over your father's business and be so wrapped up there wouldn't be a place in your life for me?"

"Monique. I always had a place for you. Even when I didn't have time for me, I made time for you. Think about it. I had a promotion, and an obligation to that position. I still made sure I saw you. We don't need to rehash this. You know what we have done together in the past two years. I am not ready to make any commitments, if that's what you are looking for. After this afternoon, I think we can be friends. I want us to be friends. I want us to stay in contact. I need to handle this business. It is no different than when I left two years ago. You need to give me room to settle what's going on in my life. I don't want you to have to deal with my problems. It's fine if you don't want to deal with me at all.

I can understand that too. I may have to move back to Richmond, but I want to make the right decision. My father worked hard to build his company, and if it is left to me, I am going to continue to make it lucrative."

"Rell, it isn't about the company or your position. Where do we stand?"

"Monique, what you said left me with a bad feeling. There is no need to apologize, you said what you felt. I can accept that. I still love you but if there is anything to salvage from our relationship we need to part as friends for now."

"Rell, can we talk after the funeral or the reading of the will? Maybe once the air clears of the other issues you can see past this."

"Maybe, Monique but I don't see the difference. You implied you didn't know who I would be after all of these issues were handled, or as I was handling them. I don't want a relationship that is attached to my wallet."

"Rell I don't want to argue about it. I just want you to understand you took it the wrong way."

"I took it the way you said it."

Rell's phone interrupted Monique's response.

"Hello"

"Hey Rell, it's Shai. Are you still at your mother's?"

"Yeah, I'm still here. I was talking to her and my cousin. I should be leaving in about say an hour. Are you still at your cousin's?"

"We rented some videos. I was going home but my brother is the only one there. You know what I mean?"

Rell laughed and glanced over at Monique. He stood up to walk across the room for a little privacy. Monique was steaming. She got up to leave. Rell put out his arm to stop her.

"Rell are you okay? Call me back when you are leaving your moms."

"I will. I'll call you in about an hour then."

Rell hung up his phone. Monique stood looking him in his eyes.

"So Rell, this is a first. You usually let the phone ring when we're together."

"We usually have limited time. I'll be around a while, at least a few weeks or more."

"So the call was that important."

"Yes, to me, it was. That's what I am talking about, you questioning my every move. There's no need for that. What's going to be, will be. We need to leave it where it is baby before we destroy what we have."

"So that call was a little test or something?"

"How could it be a test? I knew I was going to get the call about this time. I didn't know you would be here. Besides I don't need to test you. You answered what I wanted to know this afternoon. You're worried about being scared for us because of the changes in my life. I'm relieving you of the worry. Time goes on. If we're to be together again it will happen. For now we need to just be friends."

"Alright Rell, I'm not going to be your fool."

"What are you talking about?"

Monique headed for the door.

"Goodnight Mrs. Robbins, goodnight Simone. Monique paused at the door. Rell, that bitch I told you about, the one I knew you would meet, tell her I said hi when you call her back!"

Monique walked out the door. Rell shook his head. *"Drama."*

Nikki and Simone never asked Rell what Monique's unannounced visit was about. Their conversation picked up where it left off before the door bell rang. Nikki and Simone continued to talk about D.Q. and the memories they had. Rell soon tired of the memories and felt the urge to talk to Shai.

Rell called Shai as he was leaving his mother's house. It was close to eleven o'clock. His visit was longer than he planned. Rell didn't tell Nikki or Simone about Shai. He decided to wait to see if she would follow Monique with the love for his wallet. If she acted like Monique there would beno need to introduce her to his family. He would keep her to himself for a while. Rell dialed Shai's number while he walked to his car.

"Hey Shai."

"Hi, later than you thought, huh?"

"Yeah, unexpected guest; you know how houses are during funerals."

"How could I forget? I stayed away from my mother's house and my grandmother's for the same reason. I can't say I regret it though."

"Well I was going to stop by and see you on my way to the suite, but it's later than I thought. Are you going to work tomorrow?"

"I haven't decided yet. I need to prepare myself mentally for this funeral. Maybe I'll stay home and read my bible."

"Well I'll call you tomorrow. I doubt if I will see you with us both running to funerals. If you need to talk, just call."

"You too."

"Not a problem."

"Rell, what about your girlfriend?"

"What about her?"

"You sounded as though there was something going on earlier. I was just wondering,"

"Girl you need to do something about that ESP you have. We, rather I, decided we needed to continue our relationship as friends."

"That serious huh?"

"Yeah, that serious. The only thing that is permanent is change. Some of the things that are going on in my life are bringing about change."

"Okay, promise to let me know if there is a change between us before I fall in love with you."

"Can't promise that babe."

"And why not?"

"I'll keep that to myself."

"So that's why you said you would get my address later. You knew you would be breaking up with her."

"It was already done by then. What is the address?"

"I'll text message it to you. That way you won't forget it and I know you can't write it while you're driving."

"Thanks. That will help me. I probably would have asked you again by the end of the week."

"So we'll talk during the week for sure?"

"For sure. I'll pick you up for drinks on Friday night and dinner."

"Nothing fancy, I don't want you to think I need that treatment always."

"Nothing fancy."

"Be safe. I'll talk with you later."

"You too lady. Have a good night's rest."

Rell pulled into the parking lot of the Ramada Inn Suites mentally worn out. Monique had his heart and mind battling. He got out of the car and his phone vibrated indicating he had a text message. Shai's address. He read it off. *"Nice area near the college. She is pretty stable."* Maybe it will work. Since he had talked to her over two years he knew they had a lot in common and shared similar goals. They connected sexually. Things seemed to be going well. He would take it a step at a time. Just in case.

Chapter 50

The church was decorated with beautiful flowers from places all over the world. D.Q. was laid to rest in an expensive mahogany coffin with gold handles. It was lined in cream satin with his initials were embroidered on the folded edge. Reverend Wilcox monitored the funeral home setting up the flowers and the coffin. He thanked them and assured them the family would be pleased. As the choir members started arriving he greeted them with thanks and praise. Within an hour the church was prepared to receive visitors for the viewing of Mr. Derek Quincy Mince.

Tonya was the first of D.Q.'s family to arrive. Business associates, neighbors and casual friends were softly talking in the pews. As Tonya passed they looked up and nodded their heads respectfully. Tonya heard a few whispers asking who she was as others asked where were D.Q.'s children. She hadn't waited for Dershai or Derek to call and most of her family sent cards and phoned saying they wouldn't make the wake but would attend the funeral. Tonya thought they would call her to see how she was making out on the day of his wake. No one called.

She kept her promise about Dershai and Derek. She hadn't called them and she left hoping they took her seriously. She searched over the church pews and noted that they were not in the church, its foyer or the parking lot. She found her seat in the first row in front of the opened coffin. Tonya prayed silently for courage to look in his face. She wanted people to feel she was truly grieving, but she was happy it all was over. She was interrupted by a few of his coworkers touching her shoulder to speak. Tonya looked up as solemn as she could and whispered hello and thank you. Reverend Wilcox was at the end of the line of people waiting to give their condolences.

"Mrs. Mince, how are you sister?"

"Reverend Wilcox. Everything is beautiful thank you so much."

"Do you need anything? Is there something I can do for you?"

"No I can't think of anything. Are the prayer cards and guest book out? I didn't see them."

"They're in the back on the pedestal. If you should need anything just let one of the ushers know."

"Reverend, thank you."

Tonya stood and walked to the coffin. She looked in the coffin and closed her eyes. She touched his sleeve feeling for his hand. It was cold to the touch. She tried to force herself to look at his face. She couldn't do it. She had no prayer, no last words. Tonya patted his hand as tears ran down her cheek. An usher came behind her to support her stance. She turned toward her seat and walked slowly guided by the usher. The usher stood by assuring Tonya she was okay. Tonya nodded thanks as he handed her a tissues; she took her seat holding back her tears. Rell pulled into the parking spot marked reserved as he was instructed by Nana. Nana waited for Rell to open the door on her side of the car. Once he did they walked into the church together. Reverend Wilcox greeted them at the door to the sanctuary.

"Sister Mince, how are you?"

"I'm just fine Reverend, just fine. You remember Darrell, my grandson, don't you?"

"I sure do. You sure have matured son."

"Thank you sir. We appreciate all you have done during these times. We really do."

"Sister Mince, you will stop by before you leave, won't you?"

"Yes Reverend, I'll have Rell bring me to your office."

"That will be fine."

The two of them looked at each other differently. Reverend Wilcox had called Nana earlier that morning. He told her that his call was to make sure she was up to the proceedings of the day. Although his call was comforting, Nana knew he was trying his hand. She let him play it out. She told him that she would be with her grandson and all would be well. It was the nights that were unbearable, and she knew only time would ease her lost. Reverend Wilcox couldn't refrain from telling her if she allowed him, he wanted to help her through this because he had grown fond of her and wanted to know her. Nana agreed to them talking about it at another time.

Rell and his grandmother entered the church which had a fairly large crowd sitting and standing, talking softly. Rell escorted her to the front to view her son, his father. They both knelt down together holding hands. They reached and touched his hands and lowered their head in prayer. Nana began to sob and Rell felt a piercing in his heart. He had never heard his grandmother cry. Tears

filled his eyes but he knew he had to be her strength. She rose slowly. Nana was a strong woman, she was seventy two and didn't look a day over sixty-five. Her character could be read long
before her personality was revealed. Today she was numb. She couldn't feel the stares. She couldn't hear the whispers. She didn't care. Rell walked her to her seat and the two cried in each other's arms.

Tonya watched from her seat across the aisle. She had never seen this young man who had attached himself to Mrs. Mince. Then again, he reminded her of someone she had seen at a glance or maybe in a picture. It came to her, it was Darrell Mince. He was the outside child. Rell sat up straight wiping his grandmother's tears. He handed her a tissue and pulled his handkerchief out for himself. He began looking over their pew scanning the room. Tonya watched in awe. She couldn't believe how much he looked like D.Q. when he was younger, during the early days of their marriage. There was no denying it. He was a Mince.

Rell whispered to his grandmother, and she nodded her head. He walked to the back of the church where he was approached by the D.Q.'s business associates and coworkers. Tonya couldn't believe her eyes. They knew him. They were introducing him to others that didn't know him. She got up from her space and came over to where Nana sat humming and rocking.

"Mrs. Mince. How are you holding out?"

"Hi Tonya. I'm doing as well as to be expected. What about you?"

"Well, you know I don't have to tell you. The young man that escorted you in, is that Rell?"

"Yes, Tonya, that is him."

"My God, he looks just like D.Q. I mean Derek and Dershai are his children too, but they don't resemble their father as much as he does."

"Yes he looks as though D.Q. spit him out. I don't think it would be appropriate to introduce you though. It shouldn't be done here or now. It's not the place."

"Well when do you think he should find out?"

"Tonya this should have been done years ago. Does it really matter if he finds out here or at the reading? The pain will be the same."

"Mrs. Mince, everyone who sees him knows he's a Mince. How could they not know?"

Tonya didn't wait for her to answer. She returned to her seat and watched Rell from a distance. She wanted to hear him speak. He was D.Q. in all his perfections. Good looking, sociable, educated, well dressed and just like his father, he was a wealthy CPA.

Nikki walked into the church with Simone. They both hugged Rell as Tonya tried the guessing game. *"Which one is the mother?"* They both were beautiful. Tonya felt her insecurities hitting her from all sides. Nikki and Simone came to the front of the church and looked at D.Q.'s body. Nikki smiled and touched D.Q's face while tears flowed from Simone's eyes. They held each other's hands and sat on the pew next to Nana. Nana kissed both of them, and they passed the tissues between them.

Mitch, Craig and Byron came into the church together viewed the body and spoke to Nana, Nikki and Simone. They returned to the back of the church where Rell had taken a seat trying to get it together. They asked about Monique and Rell told them to walk with him outside.

Darlene walked in slowly approaching her brother's coffin with Darryl and Francine closely behind her. Darlene turned and saw her mother sitting with two women who she didn't know. As they got closer Darryl spoke to both women and Francine gave each of them a hug. Darryl introduced them.

"Nikki and Simone, this is my sister Darlene."

Nikki extended her hand, "Pleased to meet you. I am sorry it's at such an inconvenient time for introductions."

"Yes something that should have been done years ago. Pleased to meet you to. Simone, are you Nikki's sister?"

"No, I'm her cousin. Pleased to meet you also."

"Where is this handsome son of yours I hear so much about?"

"I believe he went outside. A few of his coworkers showed up, and he was talking to them in the back."

"Darlene, I forgot to show him to you. We passed him on the way in."

"I don't want you to show me. I want to meet the young man."

"That's a good start." Nana replied as she looked across the aisle and noticed Tonya had started talking to a few of her coworkers and friends. Darlene had followed her mother's eyes and spotted Tonya. She walked across the aisle to say hello.

"Hello everyone. Hi Tonya, how are you doing?"

"I'm fine Darlene. I will be fine. I see she showed up."

"She who?"

Tonya turned her back to the coworkers and friends signaling she was only talking to Darlene.

"You know who. Some women have more nerve than brains. Why would she sit in the front like it was her right?"

"Tonya, don't start she's speaking to my mother. I don't think she will sit there all night or tomorrow."

"We'll see. Did you see her son though Darlene?"

"No Darryl said he went outside."

"Darlene, I can't say he's not D.Q.'s child. They look like twins. It's scary. He looks like D.Q. when he was his age."

"Really, wow. Well there's no need for you to be asking for any tests huh?"

"You're going straight to hell Darlene."

Darlene stood, "If you can't swallow your pride. You'll be there with me." Darlene went back to the opposite side where her family was seated. She put her arms around Nana and kissed her cheek.

"Where is Mia and Marci?"

"They're coming in the evening with Dershai and Derek."

Rell walked up and sat in the pew behind his grandmother next to his mother. Nana put her hand up for him to put his face on her palm. Rell knew what she wanted and placed his face in her palm as he had done many times as a child. The thought of the gesture brought tears to his eyes.

"Baby come up here for Nana."

Rell got up and excused himself pass Darlene to sit on the other side of his grandmother. Darlene watched his movement after she had gotten over his resemblance to his father. She was stunned. His voice was the beautiful tenor voice that D.Q. had. She thought to herself, *"Good Lord D.Q., he is handsome. He is you all over."*

"Rell I want you to meet someone. Don't ask any questions it will all be explained later. This is your Aunt Darlene, your father's sister. She is older than your Uncle Darryl and your father."

Rell stood up and gave her a hug. Darlene was shocked.

"I'm glad to meet you. Do you prefer Aunt or Auntie or Darlene?"

"Whatever makes you comfortable, I know it's going to be awkward for a moment. But I think we can work at it."

"Sure we can."

"You sure look just like your father."

"So I've been told. I think most of the people that knew him when he was young are saying that."

"Well at least you know what you may look like as an old man." Darryl loved to dig at Rell.

"Well I could think of who I won't look like."

They all laughed. Nana gave them a stern look and Darlene sat in the second row with Nikki and Simone. They talked for the balance of the time they were there.

"Rell where is that gal of yours?"

"Nana I don't know if she went to work or not."

"Why you don't?"

"Nana, I ..."

"Y'all done broke up? I thought you would be talking about the problems you're having.

"I don't think talking would help Nana."

"Boy, you and your father."

They all laughed again, and again Nana gave them a stern look.

Reverend Wilcox entered the altar and the church went silent. The choir sang "I will fly away" and the people in the church joined in. Reverend Wilcox said a few words and an encouraging prayer to close out the first viewing. He reminded the people the second viewing would begin at six o'clock.

Nana stood and walked toward the altar and beckoned Reverend Wilcox to her side. The Reverend stood at her side with his ear near Nana's face, so she didn't have to talk loudly to be heard.

"Reverend, I think you were right. The introduction of Darlene went over well. I hope it's this easy for the rest of the introductions."

"Sister Mince, the power of prayer is an amazing thing. Are you alright?"

"Yes, I'm fine. I'm going to the house and get my food ready for anyone who may stop by. Will I see you at the house later?"

"Yes Sister Mince, I will make it my business to come by later this evening."

"Thank you again Reverend."

"Anytime Sister Mince."

Tonya watched as the family left together. Nikki and Simone left prior to the Minces' telling them all good bye. Nana told Nikki they would see her in the morning. Tonya wanted to stir the calm and create a storm. It was going to well for them. They had ignored her and she wasn't pleased. She needed to speak to Rell. Tonya wouldn't be silenced or ignored. *"I will be noticed before this is over."* If Tonya had her way, she would have had Reverend Wilcox announce her thought during his closing words.

Chapter 51

Nikki was standing at Rell's car when he and Nana got there. Two of D.Q.'s business partners in DQ Enterprises, Alan Scott and Robert Franklin had stopped to talk with Nikki. Rell spoke to them assuring them he would be calling as soon as things settled down. They told him they would be available when he was ready. They also told Nikki to call them if she needed their assistance. Tonya watched from the top of the church steps. She recognized the business partners and wondered what they could be talking with Nikki about. She quickened her pace to catch them in the parking lot of the church. Nana was getting in Rell's car and didn't see Tonya as she hurried to catch the men before they left.

"Alan, Rob, I wanted to say thank you for coming. I didn't have a chance to speak to you in the church."

"Tonya, how are you?"

Tonya decided to ask them about the business before questioning them about Nikki and Rell.

"I'm as well as to be expected. I came by the offices last week to get my husband's belongings. I didn't have a chance to stop in to see either of you."

"I don't think we were there." Alan answered as Rob walked around the car to get in on the passenger's side.

"Well, I was wondering when we could sit and talk. I'm quite sure there is some business matters D.Q. left undone. I could have my lawyer contact you say, next week."

"Tonya, I don't think there is anything to be done until after the reading of D.Q.'s will. His lawyer called our corporate lawyer and gave him the information we needed. We will have to wait until the executor of the will contacts the office."

"So D.Q.'s lawyer contacted you?"

"No, he contacted our corporate lawyer. Tonya, D.Q. took care of all business ends before he died. It will all be handled through the lawyers. They will contact you when everything is settled. We will be glad to talk to you then if you still need our assistance."

"Okay, thanks."

Alan and Rob drove out of the parking lot leaving Tonya standing, looking at Nikki, Rell and the Mince family get in their vehicles.

Chapter 52

Rell took Nana home and promised he would call her later. Rell drove to his mother's, buried in his thoughts and memories of D.Q. Nikki told him she needed to talk with him before he went and got lost with Mitch and his other friends. He didn't think much of her request when she asked him to stop by, but he did have questions about Nana's comment, "It *all would be explained later.*" Maybe his mother would be explaining what Nana meant or what was in the will. He really didn't want to be surprised again by Mr. Simpson. Rell decided he couldn't beat himself up with questions. He would simply go by his mother's house.

Mitch and his other friends had booked rooms in the Ramada Suites where he was staying so it wouldn't be a problem to catch up with them there. He gave them his room number and the extra key. They could order food and get drinks by the time he got there. Rell noticed his Uncle Darryl's car in his mother's driveway. He was wondering what was going on. He hoped it wouldn't be drama; he just wasn't up to it.

"Here he is, come on in Rell." Darryl answered the door with a glass in his hand. Rell could tell it wasn't his first drink.

"Mama must have kept you longer than we thought."

"No, I was talking with some friends who came in from Maryland. I didn't know you were waiting for me."

"It's okay. Your mother wanted Darlene and I to come by for a minute just in case you had any questions."

"Questions about what?" Rell didn't understand what his Uncle was talking about.

"Your aunt or why you didn't meet her earlier."

"Uncle Darryl, that is minor. I don't really need to know all about that. I'm sure it's attached to my father's ongoing drama. I don't want to be in a foul mood tomorrow at the funeral, so I don't want to dig into this now."

"There's something you need to know before the funeral Darrell." Nikki only used his full name in serious situations.

Rell sat down and braced himself. *"I knew this shit would start sooner or later."* His thoughts began to race again.

"Okay, I'm sitting."

"Nikki, maybe Rell is right, maybe it is better that he knows there will be some issues arising and let it go at that. He shouldn't be angered with drama on the day of the funeral."

Darlene spoke up just before Nikki got ready to sit at Rell's side. Nikki ignored Darlene's comment. She had held on to this secret too long. "Rell I need you to know what happened that the day you overheard your father and I talking. Your father and I continued our talk, well disagreement when you left. It led into our worst argument, and we ended our relationship that evening. At least it ended for me. He called often after that and then the calls dwindled to weekly calls just to find out about you. I tried to sever my love for your father, but it never changed. I loved him and always will. D.Q. told me that the reason he couldn't marry me was because of his marriage. Rell I knew he was married, but I thought he would leave her because of his devotion and commitment to our relationship and to you. We were together just after he was married, and he didn't know how to get out of his marriage.

"He was married all those years?"

"Yes, he was. What I didn't know was that he had two children by his wife. They were born after you. That would make you the oldest. But she claimed she couldn't have children and that led to your father pursuing a relationship with me. He said she married him because she saw the direction his life was headed. She wanted to be a CEO's wife."

Rell was silent. Darlene and Darryl looked at Nikki for a sign that they needed to say something. Darryl spoke up.

"It was hard enough for you to find out he wasn't married to your mother. Your father didn't want to hurt you at all, so he made me swear not to tell you at all. He said he would tell you in his own way and time. I respected that. After all he was your father."

Darlene saw her opportunity to explain her position. Rell hadn't reacted to either his uncle or his mother.

"I didn't want to be a part of the lies at all Rell. That's why I stayed out of you and your mom's life. I had a relationship like that, and I didn't want what I believed to influence your mother or destroy my relationship with your father. I couldn't bear the thought of pretending to the two of you, so I didn't put myself in your life at all. I thought it was the right thing to do. Today, after seeing you and finally meeting your mom, I am so sorry. I regret it, every minute of it."

Rell sat in silence. He was overwhelmed. He wanted to scream, shout and cry. *What other secrets could be hidden?* Nikki began to sob. Darlene comforted her while Simone got a box of tissues for her.

"Children?" Rell asked as though he woke from a trance.

Darryl and Darlene told Nikki about the program. Nikki wanted Rell to know before he read the program what to expect.

"Yes, children. The program will state he had a wife and three children. I wanted you to be aware of that before you saw it tomorrow."

"Thanks. I guess I will need a stiff drink by the time we get with this lawyer."

"Seriously Rell, we didn't know how you would take it, reading it like that." Darryl went to the bar. "Do you want a drink now?"

"Just a beer is fine. I'm okay. I guess. I don't suppose they were at the wake this afternoon."

"Just Tonya, his would have been ex-wife." Darlene put a sarcastic tone on the answer.

"Would have been?"

"He filed for divorce. They were legally separated shortly after he and your mother broke up. The divorce was due to be finalized next month."

Nikki had excused herself and went into her bedroom. She was more upset than she wanted anyone to know. He had finally decided to divorce her. That thought hurt her more each time she heard it. She closed the bedroom door and sat on the vanity stool in her private bathroom, off from her bedroom, crying.

"Rell your mother thinks you will hold this against her and your father. Think about it before you cast judgment."

"Simone, you know me better than that. Who am I to judge anyone? I guess they did what they thought was right? By the time it got out that they weren't married, all kinds of things ran across my mind. I kinda figured he may have been married. I just thought he hadn't done the divorce thing. I had no idea they were still living together. I never would have thought he had other children."

"Well before it's all over you will meet my two daughters and your brother and sister."

Darlene felt relief just knowing they had told Rell prior to the funeral. Darlene knew Shai and Derek would appreciate the same gesture from their mother but Tonya didn't seem to care. Rell's phone rang.

"Excuse me."

Darlene went over to the bar and Simone followed giving Rell a little room to talk.

"Do you think he's okay with this?" Darryl was worried.

He didn't want Rell to leave town before the reading of the will. He needed time to talk with him about his business and the future of D.Q. Enterprises. He wanted to remain in good standings with him. They had always had a closerelationship, and he needed him on his side now.

"I think it will work itself out. Rell is not one for drama. He avoids it at all cost. I guess he got that from

D.Q. too. It will be okay. I'm sure of it." Simone could usually tell when Rell was pissed. This had not affected him as she thought it would. Darlene looked at Rell.

"I'm so glad I met him and his mother. They are what I imagined they would be and more. Beautiful people and again I will say it Darryl, I don't know what was on D.Q.'s mind."

"Well I guess we'll hear it in the reading of this will."

Nikki returned. She had changed her clothes and brushed her hair back. She looked like she had had a good cry. No one mentioned it.

"Darryl, pour me a drink please. I'll need it to relax. This is rough. Thank you guys for your support."

Everyone chimed in with, "no problem". Rell walked slowly toward the group.

"Well family, I have to go. I have a situation that arose at my job that must be dealt with. My papers are in my hotel room. I need them to answer some of the client's questions. Mom I will call you later, and if I don't catch you up tonight, I will be here about ten in the morning."

"Is your Nana looking for you to ride with her?"

"She didn't say. I doubt it though. I'll be riding in my car. It may be rough tomorrow. Thanks for the warning. It will save me the embarrassment. I'm sure I am one of the few that don't know about this."

"It will be fine. I'll see to that." Darryl shook Rell's hand and gave him a manly hug.

"Thanks Uncle Darryl. My father would appreciate you looking out for my mother the way you have. Aunt Darlene, I'll see you in the morning, Simone, you too."

Everyone said their goodbyes. Darlene and Darryl stayed with Nikki and Simone until eight o'clock, they left

Nikki's headed their separate ways. Simone and Nikki ate popcorn while watching the television and discussing the possibilities of the next day until sleep hit them both.

Chapter 53

t was close to six thirty when Dershai and Derek walked into the church. Neither of them went to church often. They attended special events at the church by their grandmother's invitations. Reverend Wilcox recognized Dershai and approached them as they were coming down the center aisle. Dershai assumed he was Reverend Wilcox and began to smile.

"Dershai, how are you my dear?"

"I'm just fine Reverend and you?"

"And you must be Derek. It has been years since I've seen you. How are you young man?"

"Fine sir."

"If there is anything you need while you are here just ask one of the ushers."

Dershai and Derek thanked him and scanned the pews for familiar faces. A lot of their friends and coworkers were in attendance and a few of their mother's friends spoke when they realized who they were.

Marci and Mia were seated in the front row with Michael, Alesha and the rest of their Uncle Darryl's offspring.

"So, it's the younger half of the family attending the evening wake. What's up family?" Dershai was glad to see them.

They all stood to hug and greet their cousins. Marci leaned over the pew to whisper to Dershai.

"Your mother just stomped out. I think she got mad because you weren't here promptly at six."

"Marci she'll get over it. I can't please her anyway. I refuse to keep trying. Derek, let's go up and see dad."

Derek looked toward the coffin and reached for Dershai's hand. They walked to the coffin together. Dershai leaned over and kissed her father gently on the cheek. Derek did the same. They knelt together and said a silent prayer. Dershai got up first and admired the flowers around the coffin. He was known by so many people, through business and socializing. There were flowers from Jamaica, Puerto Rico, Canada and California. She was amazed, *"He was well loved."*

She looked down at Derek, he broke down. He was crying into his arm, which was resting on the edge of the coffin. Shai tried to help him stand. Michael and Ronnie came to her assistance. Derek cried louder. Shai began to cry too. Marci and Mia came to her side. Dershai let go, she couldn't hold Derek any longer. Marci led her to the pew as Michael guided Derek. The ushers came with water and tissues. Dershai closed her eyes to get herself together. *"How will I make it through tomorrow? How will Derek make it? Where is my mother?"*

Marci left the group and walked to the back of the church. She hoped her aunt hadn't been so cold as to leave the church totally. She checked the foyer and the ladies' room. She saw Deacon Smalls.

"Deacon, have you seen my Aunt Tonya?"

"Baby she was just in the parking lot. Go out this door, you'll see her car."

"Thank you." Marci hurried hoping Tonya hadn't left. She spotted Tonya standing at her car smoking a cigarette. Marci thought it was strange. She never saw Tonya smoke before.

"Aunt Tonya, I came to tell you Dershai and Derek are here and they…."

Tonya didn't let her finish.

"They what? They didn't come out here looking for me, you did. Where were they this afternoon when I was looking for them? I told them I wanted them to be here for me then. We would have been here for each other. Now you came to say what? They need their mother?"

Marci was stunned. She couldn't say the words that came to mind. She summed it up the best she could.

"There is no need for you to be a mother now. It's not like they haven't needed you before, and you turned your back. It's okay, they'll be fine. I just thought you would be concerned. They're not my children and I'm not your therapist."

"You need to mind your mouth, and remember who you're talking to!"

"Whatever!"

Marci turned her back and went back in the church not hearing the rest of Tonya's scolding. She couldn't believe her aunt's reaction. Shai said she was a trip but Marci had never seen that side of her. She returned to the front of the church and found Dershai and Mia talking. Everyone else was gone.

"Where's Derek, Michael and the crew?"

"Derek couldn't take it. He said he needed air, and he would see us at Nana's in the morning. They all left with him."

"Wow, Dershai are you okay? Do you want to leave too?"

"No, I'm okay, besides someone from the family should be here.

Marci wouldn't tell Dershai she attempted to find Tonya and what took place in the parking lot. She would definitely tell her mother and Mia later.

Tonya entered the church hoping to find Dershai and Derek. She spotted Marci and Mia sitting in the front pew while Dershai was standing walking along the altar looking at all the flowers across the front of the church.

Marci tapped Mia for her to watch Tonya as she walked up behind Dershai. Tonya stood next to Dershai not saying a word. Dershai continued to read the cards attached to the flowers.

"Where's your brother?"

"Well, hello to you too. He left, he needed air, and he left."

"Hmmm, just like that?"

"Just like that. He'll be here for the funeral tomorrow."

"Why didn't you leave with him?"

"Because I am spending a few moments with my father in prayer, that's the purpose of wakes. One spends the time remembering moments with the deceased."

"Don't forget those of us who are living."

"Some walk around because God gives them breath, but their heart and souls are dead."

Dershai walked away leaving Tonya where she stood. The reality of what her daughter said sent chills throughout her body. She wondered if Dershai truly felt that way. Dershai returned to her seat after greeting some of her father's coworkers.

Mia and Marci watched both Dershai and their Aunt. Tonya walked to the back of the church and left.

"Marci, I didn't know if you had plans, but I told Dershai we would stay with her."

"That's fine Mia. That's what families are for."

Chapter 54

"I don't understand why my father felt it was necessary to hide his true feelings or his family from my mother. He treated the situation like his wife and family didn't exist."

Rell went to the refrigerator in the suite and got the cranberry juice out. He placed it on the bar and looked at Mitchell and Byron for an answer.

"You're not asking us for a comment are you?" Mitchell got up from the couch and came over to the bar to join Rell.

"He can't be asking us. If it had been done in our era, your mother and the wife would have known from the door what was up. I mean, men of today don't usually stay with their wife just because. It sounds like your dad took everyone's feelings into consideration except his own." Byron waited for Mitchell or Rell to agree. Neither of them responded.

"How did he take my mother's feelings or mine into consideration? I left them together arguing that day. If I had stayed, I would have found out some deep shit. Two children and a wife for thirty years and he didn't tell my mother. Byron, he claimed he loved her. Why didn't he tell her? She knew he was married. She had accepted that but he didn't give her the option to accept the complete package."

"Maybe he knew she wouldn't accept it. I mean he told her, and although they had the thirty years, she left him."

Byron didn't know what else to say, but he knew he made a good point because both Rell and Mitchell were attentive as he spoke.

"Not that I'm saying it would have made a big difference. No, I will say it would have made a big difference. Suppose your dad would have told your mom that his wife was pregnant. She would have been mad that he was sleeping with her when he was with your mother everyday. You know women get caught up in that shit. I mean once somebody says they're married you know there's some bedroom play some of the time."

Bryon looked to Mitchell for a response.

"Rell, man, he's right. You know that is what happens. Women get all caught up with what's going on in the guy's home with him and his wife. It ruins the relationship they have with each other." Mitchell passed Byron a beer.

"So you just live a lie for thirty years? Man, that's bull. Byron, I know you couldn't have done it. None of us could. You find a woman that you love and are willing to leave your wife for, what do you do?"

They responded together. "You leave."

"You're damn right you do. Baby, here's your half of what we have. Here's my house key. Keep the car and I'm gone. From what my mom said I was at least two before my dad's first child with his wife was born. That would have been two years of getting my legal papers and divorce together."

"Man, you're right. If your old man had done that you would have known his people and the children they had. What do you have? I mean a sister, a brother or what?"

Mitchell handed Rell another beer and made himself a drink.

"Man, a sister and a brother. I don't know their names though. Mr. Moore called for that paperwork while we were talking. That reminds me, I handled the call, but you have to take the paperwork back to the office for the final review."

"No problem, we're not leaving until Wednesday morning."

"He gave you guys three days?"

Byron laughed, "We wish. Craig and Keith are holding it down. We are leaving here going straight to work on Wednesday. You know things don't run if all of us are out."

"I'm really glad you guys are here. My mother seems to be holding her own, but I know her. She's going to snap soon. That's why I think Simone decided to stay with her a while."

"So how long before you see the lawyer?" Mitchell asked the question knowing Rell wouldn't wait long to start handling business.

"I figured I would make an appointment to see him maybe Thursday or Friday of this week. That will give the family time to recoup from the funeral. I'll schedule the reading for the early part of next week. My uncle will probably need to get back to his business in Detroit. I don't want to hold him here or make him return for the reading."

"So is it supposed to be your uncle, aunt, his wife your grandmother, your mom and you at the reading? Do you think there will be problems with them all together?"

Byron knew if it was his family, it wouldn't happen. They would need the police for escorts.

"Yeah, those are the attendees. I never met anyone other than my Aunt. She seems pretty cool though. I don't know anything about his wife or how anyone reacts to her. I don't think my mother has ever met her."

"Man, that's drama written in bold ink. You'll need a vacation after it's all over. I'll put in a request for you when I get back." Mitchell laughed and waited for Rell to tell him different.

"Rell, man, will you go to your father's company if it's an option?" Byron didn't know that Rell and Mitch had talked about this since college.

"I hope so man. My father was the top man of DQ Enterprises. His partner's relationship with him is similar to ours; they met right after college. The three of them were close. They'll tell me where I fit in the future of the company."

"Do they have family that may be a part of their decisions?" Mitch hadn't thought about their decisions and the effects it would have on whether Rell could bring them in the company.

"I think one has two sons, and I know the other has all girls. None of them are in the business field. I'm sure they have stock investments but that's it. My father looked out for them when they were young. I've talked to my dad's business partners from time to time about

Sheldon Finance, and what it held for me. My father would laugh and say stick with it. He never told me to join his company, and I guess it was for the good. I saw them today at the wake. They told me to call them when I was ready. I'm sure they know what my father set up for me."

Byron got the remote and turned on the television. "The reading of the will should be detailed with that information too."

"Now there's more on the table, a wife and two more children." Mitchell shook his head. "It will be interesting."

"I'll be alright; you guys just hang in there with me. We'll all be rich."

Chapter 55

The funeral director approached Nana as family and friends headed toward their cars to proceed to the church for D.Q.'s service.

"Mrs. Mince, can we have everyone for the family car?"

"Mr. Watson, do you want them outside?"

"No, they can gather in your living room for a departing prayer. Only the immediate family of the deceased, all others can get in their cars now."

"Darlene, you and Darryl come on now. Get Dershai and Derek, Mr. Watson is ready for us to leave."

Darlene followed Nana into her bedroom.

"Mama, Tonya's outside, is she riding with us?"

"Lord, please get me through this day. Darlene, tell her to come into the living room for prayer. I'll ask Mr. Watson where she is supposed to ride."

Tonya was in the living room when Darlene came out of her mother's bedroom. She waited for Darlene to enter the room before she made her announcement.

"I just wanted you all to know I will be riding in my car. I don't want to be a part of a discussion about the separated wife's place. Today is not a day for the Mince family nonsense. So keep it to yourself."

Tonya went out the front door and almost knocked Mr. Watson off the top step. He entered the living room and called for Nana again.

"We're all here Mr. Watson," answered Nana as she entered the room, "Whoever is not here will ride in their cars."

Reverend Wilcox said a prayer while they all held hands. Upon the word 'Amen' they filed out of the house and got in the family car. Darlene sat between her mother and brother. Dershai and Derek sat on the opposite side. The limo had plenty of room for more passengers.

"Nana, why did they give us such a big limo? Derek figured it could hold at least four more people.

"I told them to decide what size. I think I may have included your Aunt Francine, Mia and Marci. I also included your mother who insists on making herself the center of attention."

"What was she talking about Aunt Darlene? She started acting up yesterday in the church after Derek left."

"She was there?" Dershai hadn't told Derek what happened in the church.

"Yea, she tried her mess with me right at the altar and that's where I left it."

"Your mother has issues and that's all I'm going to say about it."

"Aunt Darlene, we all know that's not all it is. She is beyond having issues. She wants to poison me and Derek's mind, for some reason. She can say and do what she wants; I will always love my father."

"Well today we're going to avoid drama. That includes your momma's issues."

Everyone knew that meant Nana didn't want to talk about it anymore. They were getting close to the church. People were standing outside waiting for the line to move so they could be seated. The line was not waiting to view D.Q. Nana had made prior arrangements for the coffin to be opened later in the service but not before. The church was filled with what seemed to be any and everyone who knew D.Q. through business or personal relationships.

"There's a lot of people going in there. You would think he was someone big in the media." Shai wanted to get out of the car. She decided against it and put on her hat. The black hat had its own veil around the brim. It fell softly over her face so no one could see her crying. She added her black shades.

"You look like someone who would be working with the Men In Black."

Everyone had to laugh. Even Nana found the humor in what Derek said. She reached in her purse to check for her handkerchief and adjusted her hat. The line was gone and Mr. Watson stood at their door.

"If you are ready I would like you and the family members that followed you to line up in twos so you may enter the church."

They all followed his direction. Tonya found her way through the crowd.

"Where do I sit Mr. Watson? Is there a special spot for me so I won't stick out like a sore thumb?"

"Mrs. Mince you can get in the line before or after your children."

Before Tonya could object, Mr. Watson continued down the line making sure everyone had formed two lines. They proceeded into the church. Everyone stood waiting for the family to sit; the choir sung all of D.Q.'s favorites.

There were proclamations, thank you and sympathy cards, acknowledgments, poetry and other tributes made in D.Q's name and memory. Nikki was seated on the opposite side of the family, three pews from the front of the church. She seemed to have lost Rell, although they came to the church together. She scanned the church slowly trying not to make it look as though she was looking for someone. Nikki spotted Monique, Mitchell and Byron. She knew Rell wouldn't be far from them. Just as she suspected, Rell was sitting on the other side of Byron in the back of the church. Nikki would ask him later why he sat so far back.

Mr. Watson and his staff prepared the body for the final viewing. The ushers started on Nikki's side of the church. A few people were returning to their seats using their tissue and consoling one another. Nikki's row stood, they exited at the opposite end of their aisle, walked to the back of the church and approached the coffin down the center aisle. Nikki stopped at Nana and kissed her gently on her cheek. She went to the coffin. Nikki held D.Q.'s hand, she rubbed his arm and began to sob softly. She reached across to the opposite shoulder. Nikki leaned into the coffin and kissed D.Q. long and softly. She started crying loudly as she rested her head on his chest.

Tonya jumped up from her seat. She crossed over Darryl and Francine yelling and screaming.

"Get the hell off my husband. Get the hell off of him. He's not your husband bitch, he never was."

Rell looked up from his program when he heard his mother cry. He froze and couldn't move. He started crying in his seat. Byron put his arms around his shoulder. When Nikki laid her head in D.Q.'s chest and cried louder so did Rell. Mitch and Byron took Rell out of the sanctuary when Tonya jumped up screaming and cursing. Rell starting fighting his friends to get out of their hold, he could hear Tonya's words through the closed doors. Dershai and Derek watched their mother as she was carried away from the coffin by the ushers. They sat her on the first pew talking to her softly. Tonya was still yelling at Nikki.

"It's over, he's dead. You don't have him and I don't either. It's over. Live with it. I did. I dealt with you and your bastard son all these years. It's over now! Sleep on D.Q.; you left shit behind. Sleep on you dog, that's if your conscious will let you!"

Mitchell and Byron tussled with Rell until they were on the front steps of the church. Monique went to the front of the church to help Simone with Nikki, who was crying hysterically from the front pew opposite Tonya. Other church members came forward to offer their assistance.

The ushers took Tonya out of the sanctuary to one of the offices. Darlene held on to her mother as the viewing continued. They all walked to the coffin together holding hands and praying silently. Darlene and Darryl returned to their seats crying softly. Dershai, Derek and Nana remained at the coffin to give D.Q. a final kiss. The coffin was closed and a wail of cries let out from the Mince family as the reality set in.

The obituary was read aloud as the choir hummed 'Amazing Grace' during the reading. Dershai and Derek held hands. They squeezed each other's hand when the reader read who Derek Quincy Mince left to mourn. They broke into tears when the reader read, there were three children. Nana tapped them both on the legs. When they looked at her trusting face she winked and smiled. Although they didn't quite understand they knew she would explain the situation later. At the conclusion of the reading, the choir sang another selection.

Reverend Wilcox did a fantastic Eulogy about repenting, and family ties. In his ability to preach and teach he continued D.Q.'s service before it became a distasteful memory for the people in the church. Nana nodded in agreement with his words and was appreciative that Reverend Wilcox used it as a basis for his eulogy.

"Not all things done by man can be explained. Their acts, during the course of their lives, are not to be judged by any of us. Only God knows their heart. Only God can determine if they are of a pure soul. Only God can save them. Here lies our son, our brother, our father, our friend, someone we loved. The man we knew is no longer with us, but I'm here to tell you, Derek Quincy Mince came to God with his confessions. And on that day, his heart was opened to God, his soul was committed to God. His walk changed, his talk changed, how he loved himself and God changed. I'm here to tell you today church, you've got to change. Can you be saved? Derek is okay. Derek is resting well. Derek has no issues to confront. But you have to make a change in your life. You have to make a commitment to yourself and God….."

Dershai and Derek cried softly. They knew who the sermon was for and they prayed for the change. The services concluded and the cars loaded for the ride to the cemetery. Rell saw Darryl and stopped him.

"Uncle Darryl, I'm going to my mother's. She's not going to the cemetery. I'm going to be with her for a while. Can you let Nana her know for me please?"

"Sure, I'll call you when we get to the house. Are you going to be okay?

"Simone is with us and so are Mitch, Byron and Monique. I think we'll be fine."

"Okay, call me if you need anything."

"Alright Uncle Darryl thanks."

Mr. Watson told all the drivers to put on their headlights. The procession began. Rell sat in his car and waited. He cried as he watched the family car and the hearse drive away.

Chapter 56

Nikki didn't say much on the way home. Simone and Rell followed her lead. They were all reliving the last moments of D.Q.'s service. Each of them had held on to their anger while praying they would have another opportunity to confront Mrs. Tonya Mince. They arrived at the house and Nikki found her keys and opened the door. Simone went into the kitchen and put on a pot of coffee while Nikki went and sat in the living room. Rell and Monique stopped at the front door.

"Thank you for helping my mother. It seems like you're always around to clean up my mess for me."

"Rell, there's no need to thank me and besides it's not your mess. I love your mother and I would hate to go through what she just went through."

"Well, I wanted to say thank you."

"Rell, is this the way it's going to be between us, formal and uncomfortable? Our friendship is beyond that, or at least I thought it was."

"You're right." Rell didn't want to lead Monique on. He didn't want to rekindle their relationship until he was sure about her intentions. "C'mon in, we can eat and talk. Mitch and Byron should be here shortly."

Monique smiled. She knew she would have to start reuniting with Rell on his terms and at his pace. Being there when he needed someone was to her advantage. She would give it a month or two and move on if Rell wasn't ready for a serious commitment. Monique was looking to be financially stable. They went in the house and sat in the kitchen with Simone.

"Do either of you want a cup of coffee?

"No, thank you. I'll get a glass of juice. Monique do you want something from the refrigerator."

"Juice is fine, thanks."

"Well Mr. Mince you got your work cut out for you with that Mrs. Mince."

"Simone, that woman is a bit much."

"She caught your mother on a good day. Any other time your mother might have beat her ass and laid her next to D.Q."

Rell smiled. He knew his cousin was right. His mother wasn't the type to keep things going, but she could put a stop to them quickly. Nikki didn't argue much and she couldn't stand women who talked loud and cursed.

"Monique, my mother was quick to fight, so they tell me."

"Rell your mother was quick to fight for someone else. She loved fighting. Then she grew up. It seemed like it was overnight, she began to walk away, you know, avoiding the drama. It was as though fighting was a waste of her time. Yeah, that Mrs. Mince lucked up today."

"I don't know Simone; the way she acted, I think I would have to find a way to let her know God was on her side."

Monique didn't think ignoring a woman like her would help the situation. Simone laughed at Monique's comment. Rell left the kitchen and went into the living room where his mother sat in silence.

"Hey lady, you okay?"

"What happened to you? Why did you sit in the back of the church?"

"Mitch and Byron arrived right after I went to the bathroom. I came out of the bathroom and saw them in the foyer. Everyone was standing for the family procession, and we just ducked into the back row where Monique was sitting. There was no special reason other than I didn't want everyone looking at me coming up the aisle to the row you were in. I saw you and Simone."

"I thought maybe you felt you didn't belong up front."

"Ma, don't get caught up in that nonsense that woman said. I don't need a banner printed that says who I am, or what I am entitled to."

"Nikki, do you think she knew who you and Rell were before you got up?" Simone brought a tray into the living room with two cups of coffee, cream, sugar and napkins for her and Nikki. Monique sat across the room and handed Rell his glass of juice.

"I believe she did Simone. I also think she was waiting for me to go up for the last viewing. If she was at the wake she didn't move. I held his hand,I prayed over him, and touched his face last night. She waited for today to pull that shit."

"Well you were the better woman. She made a spectacle of herself. How many sugars do you want?"

"Three is good, thanks Simone. I can't wait until Mama Mince gets a hold of her ass. You know this ain't over."

"Rell, is she supposed to be at the reading of the will?"

Simone handed Nikki her cup of coffee and began fixing hers.

"Her name was on the letter I got. I don't think all the letters have all the names. I know mine does and so does Nana's. Does yours Ma?"

"It does. It's not stated in the body of the letter it's at the bottom. It tells you all who got a carbon copy. Her initials are there."

"Mitch and Byron were right. That meeting with the lawyer is going to be interesting."

Rell looked over at Monique and smiled. She smiled in return but her smile made him think her mind was somewhere else.

"What happened to Craig and Keith?"

Monique's expression seemed to show more interest as she waited for Rell to answer his mother's question.

"Craig came to the wake. Keith couldn't make it. I think he had some personal problems yesterday to take care of. Anyway since we work on the same financial team at the job all of us couldn't be away at the same time. Craig volunteered to work so Byron and Mitch could come. Keith won't be back until the end of the week."

"Is he okay? I mean he's not sick is he?"

"No ma, I think his mother or grandmother is not well. He went to see about them."

"I haven't seen Craig in a year. Is he still with his girlfriend?"

"No, they broke up a few months ago. They talk off and on, but I think the relationship is over."

"Well as long as he's okay."

Monique listened as Rell and his mother talked about Mitch and Byron in the same manner. How they were doing on the job and how their relationships were holding up. She wondered what they said about her and Rell when she wasn't around. Monique didn't feel comfortable.

"Monique are you hungry? Can I get you something?"

Simone's questions brought Monique from the dark walls in her mind.

"No, I can't stay much longer. I was trying to wait for Mitch and Byron to come, but it looks like they must have stopped off somewhere."

"You're probably right. You don't have to stay. I can call you later and all of us can get together. They're leaving in the morning."

Rell was hoping she wouldn't ask if he would stop by later.

"You can call if you want to. They may have other plans. We'll play it by ear. Simone, Mrs. Robbins I'm going to leave now. I will talk with you during the week Mrs. Robbins.

"Well thank you Monique for your support. Don't forget to call me now and then."

That comment confirmed that Simone and Nikki knew that she and Rell had decided to just be friends. Monique's thoughts went deeper. *"Rell must have told them everything. I hope he doesn't think I'll be as desperate as that woman was in the church. There were too many men for that. I'm not going to chase him for a relationship."*

Rell walked Monique to the door. She stopped at the door and told him he didn't have to walk her out. They said goodbye and Monique went to her car.

Chapter 57

erek and Dershai told Marci and Mia to meet them at Nana's house after they left the repast at the church. They all agreed that would be the last place Tonya would be. There was little conversation on the ride to Nana's house. Mr. Watson let them out and told everyone to take care. A few of Nana's friends from the church had prepared food for the family to have when they returned; none of them really ate at the church. Darlene and Francine went in the kitchen to bring the prepared dishes into the dining room. Michael and Alesha went with their sisters and brothers to claim their seats outside on the deck. Darryl changed his clothes and went to the store for more ice.

"Dershai go check on your grandmother. She's been quiet ever since we got back from the cemetery."

"Derek is in the room with her Aunt Darlene. I think they're talking."

"Oh I didn't know. That's good then."

Mia, Marci and Dershai went out to the deck. The weather was beautiful. It had reached seventy-five degrees. The summer weather was beginning to set in. They sat down and relaxed. No one said a word. Derek had followed Nana into her bedroom. She told him to come with her when they got out of the limo.

"Derek, how old are you now?"

"I'm twenty-eight, Nana."

"Well, I'm gonna put a heavy load on you as the son of D.Q. You know your father left a lot of unfinished business. A lot of it, he should have taken care of years ago. As his son, I'm expecting you to help take care of his unfinished personal business. Now as you heard today, your father had three children. You and your sister have an older brother that you will meet some time this week I would imagine. Your father left the company business for him to handle, that's why I'm giving you the delicate parts of this mess."

"Nana, where was this so called brother during the service? I didn't see any signs of a son. I saw his mother."

"Baby, he was there. Now there are some things you and your sister are going to have to understand as just being what your father decided to do. You can't have an attitude about his decisions or the results they have caused. Where is Dershai? Go get her, so I can explain this to the both of you."

"Dershai, Nana wants you." Derek went to the kitchen to get something to drink. He called Dershai as he walked back to Nana's room. Shai sat in one of the two chairs in the room. Derek sat in the other while Nana sat on the edge of her bed.

"Shai I told your brother to call you, so I could attempt to explain your father's unfinished personal business. I am expecting both of you to handle this situation as mature adults. No one is to blame for this situation but your parents and I'm not here to decide who was more at fault, and I don't expect you to blame them either. They did what they thought was best at the time."

Nana explained what she knew from the time D.Q. and Tonya married until his death. She told them about Tonya's drinking and her denial of having a problem. She told them about the appointments for marriage counseling. She told them how many times their father asked for a divorce or threatened to leave.

She told them that D.Q. took care of Nikki and her son over the years. Nana explained how their father never told Nikki about them. She mentioned how Nikki knew he was married and begged him to end his dual way of life. She never mentioned Rell's name.

"What I want you to do Derek is promise me you will do everything you can possibly do to develop a relationship with your brother. He is a fine young man."

Dershai started crying. She told them she couldn't understand how her father lived that way for years. She shouted and screamed that she hated her mother.

"She's always causing someone pain. We don't even know how Daddy felt all those years. That had to be lifelong pain. How could she do that to him? What is the woman's name Nana and her son, what is his name?"

"The woman, the woman your father loved until his death is named Nikki Robbins. Her son, who you will meet soon probably at the reading of the will, is Darrell Quinton Mince."

Dershai started breathing hard. She could feel her heart racing. Dershai fainted.

"Darlene! Francine! Y'all get in here quick. This gal done fell out. Oh my God in heaven! Derek go and get a towel; wet it with cold water. Dershai, Dershai, can you hear me child?"

Mia and Marci helped Nana get Dershai to the bed. They placed the towel on her forehead. Shai started to stir.

"Dershai, you alright baby? She seems to be coming around. Give her some air. Lord, what else is going to happen on this day."

Nana took the towel from Mia and fanned them away from the bed as she sat close to Shai.

"Somebody get her some water. Ain't this something! I am so sorry baby. I didn't know this would affect you this way. Derek are you okay?"

"Nana, I'm good. Is Shai gonna be alright?"

"She'll be fine. Let her rest a while. This has been an ordeal

for all of us. Mama let Marci stay with her. You come on and sit in the living room with us. We all need to just calm down and relax."

Darlene gave her mother a reassuring pat on the back and helped her to her feet.

They all agreed. Marci stayed with Dershai talking softly to her until she opened her eyes.

"Girl, are you alright. You scared us to death."

"Marci, where is everybody?"

"They're in the living room. You lay here a minute. You passed out. Are you feeling dizzy?"

"I think I'm okay. I don't know what came over me. Nana said our brother's name and Marci, I hope he's not who I think it may be."

"What are you talking about?"

"Nana said his name is Darrell Quinton Mince."

"Darrell? Not mystery man Darrell?"

"She didn't say he called himself Rell but Da Rell? How many men are named Da Rell? Marci, I think I'm in

"Well, I am going to talk with him when he calls. If he asks to see me, I will see him, and we'll talk. Maybe he'll bring it up. Marci I asked him who died, and he just answered a relative. He never said his father."

"You were on your first date. I don't think he wanted you to know his business, plus look at who his father was. He has the same apprehensions as you when it comes to mentioning his father's name. He would have said his father, and you would have asked for a name. Especially since your father had passed. Did you tell him the funeral you were attending was your father?"

"No, I guess you're right. Anyway I'll play it by ear, and if it doesn't come up, it will, at the meeting with the lawyer."

"Shai, you're not going to sleep with him again, right?"

"If we have sex again what damage can it do? We already had sex. Marci, I just don't know what to do. I think I really love him, and I don't consider him my brother. I don't know anything about him as a child and our history began as us being friends for two years and taking it further."

"Shai, I'm not trying to change your mind, but I want you to think of the problems it may cause."

"It won't cause any if no one knows but you, me and him."

"He may have said something to his friends."

"He'll handle that, I'm sure. He doesn't seem to have a large group of friends he would tell his personal information or intimacies. He only mentions two all the time. That's Mitch and Byron. I think there's two more that work with him. He doesn't seem to be that close to them though. He'll handle it."

"Well girl you know as usual, I'm by your side."

Thanks. I promise I will try to stay away from the Ramada Inn."

"No don't promise cause I'll hold you to it. Just think about the consequences."

"Alright, let's go eat, I'm starving."

Chapter 58

onya spent the balance of her day crying while drinking Vodka and grapefruit juice. None of Darryl's family stayed with her as previously arranged. They called saying they would be staying with other relatives. She knew that was Mrs. Minces' doing. They stayed with Tonya every time they came into town. Ronnie, Michael and Derek would sit up half the night. The gap had widened since D.Q. passed, and she knew it would get wider. Those in Tonya's family, that came to the funeral left from the cemetery without a word of goodbye. She called them on their cell phones and no one answered her call. When Tonya thought about it, she concluded, *"The hell with them."*

Tonya's conscious was cleared. She told D.Q.'s tramp what she wanted to say to her for years, and she told D.Q. what she should have said years ago. She knew it wouldn't sit well with Derek and Dershai, but she was sure D.Q.'s mother would explain it to them. Tonya didn't care who told them, she was tired of them too. She sat down to her computer. She went to the home page of D.Q. Enterprises.

"Stocks and Investments, that's what I want to see."

Tonya had stock in the company and as a member could see the other investors and the amount of their shares. She scrolled down the page alphabetically looking for 'Robbins'.

"Nikki Robbins. That bitch has stock investments too. I'll be damned."

She continued her investment search. Tonya found out that Nikki Robbins had been an investor since 1976.

"That was the year the company was established. Damn! That bitch has money."

Tonya picked up her phone and dialed D.Q. Enterprises.

"Hello, D.Q. Enterprises, may I help you?"

"Yes, may I speak with Mr. Franklin or Mr. Scott, please?"

"I'm sorry Ma'am there's no one in the office now. May I take a message? If it is urgent I can page them for you."

"No thank you sweetie, I can page them myself."

Tonya slammed the phone down. She went back to the home page on the computer and clicked properties. She scrolled down to property owners. They were listed in alphabetical order also. Tonya clicked on Nikki's name. The screen read. 'For information contact the property manager at D.Q. Enterprises.' It gave the number and the extension. Tonya dialed the number.

"Hello D.Q. Enterprises."

"Good Afternoon. I was looking at your vacation properties. I am extremely interested in staying in one of the spots owned by Ms. Robbins. There is no information to contact her."

"Yes, some of our owners prefer the office handle all reservations or sales. Which of her properties did you want to inquire about?"

"I'm sorry. I only saw one. How many does she have on your site?"

"There are at least three. I don't know if she has them all listed. The other two may not be available to the general public."

"Can I access them on the company's home page?"

"Yes Ma'am, if you click on the vacation link after you pull up our home page. Look for her name under vacation links. All the areas she owns will come up with the information for each. It will do that under any of the names if you don't see anything of interest in her sites."

"Thank you. I will call back if I see any I like."

"Have a good day Ma'am."

Tonya went back to the home page and followed his instructions. She got up to refresh her drink before she started her search of Nikki's properties.

"He set her ass up pretty, properties, a house, and a car. Damn what was I paying attention to?"

Tonya spent two hours or more writing information about the properties listed under Nikki's name. She made notes about her being a stock holder. She also looked for Rell's name under property, stocks and investments. She didn't find his name.

"D.Q. this is a battle I won't let you win. I'll fight this until I die. That bitch won't get what should be mine."

Tonya logged off the computer and decided to get something to eat. She ate leftovers from her dinner the night before. She turned on her television and got comfortable. Her phone rang just as she was beginning to fall to sleep.

"Hello, Ma." It was Derek.

"Yes."

"How are you making out?"

"Who wants to know? Where are you calling from?"

"I'm home. I was going to stop by, but I still have on my clothes from the funeral. I wanted to get comfortable."

"I see. Well, where is your sister? I know you weren't thinking of coming over here by yourself."

"If I had to I was. Are you okay? You sound funny?"

"Nothing a few drinks won't take care of."

"Ma, drinking won't take care of anything. Are you lying down? You need to rest."

"Derek, say what you want. If you're coming over to say it, then bring your ass here. All of this pretending to care is sickening. Your father is dead. We all can talk truth. You don't have to worry if it will hurt my feelings."

"Ma, I know you think the world is against Tonya Mince. Your attitude and sarcastic remarks don't make the circum-

stances any better. You turn people away from you. Then you say no one cares. Let's start with you. You have to care. You don't need to be drinking and smoking to hide your hurt. I know you're hurting. I am too and so is Dershai. We can get through this if you stop looking at us as the enemy. No matter what you do or say, we will always love our father. Now leave it at that and let us love you."

"Derek that all sounds good but I am living proof, loving your father takes away from your soul. I don't want to talk now Derek. Goodnight."

"Ma, Ma, wait let me..."

The phone went dead in his ear.

Chapter 59

Dershai looked at her clock in her bedroom. It was close to nine, she wondered if Rell was still at his mother's. She went into the living room and saw Derek sitting on the couch looking at the phone.

"Is there something wrong with the telephone?"

"No, it's your mother. I called her to see how she was. Well, you know how that went. I'm worried about her Shai. I know she has issues, but she's drowning her sorrows in alcohol and blaming the world for her and dad's problems."

"Derek, I don't think that's her problem. Dad ended their problems two years ago. He left her. She should have gotten over that by now. They had all those years together, and it seems from what Nana was saying Dad spent most of them telling her it was over. I wonder what she did that led him outside of their marriage."

"Yeah, Nana didn't know what she said or did. I can imagine though. She's got a bad spirit about the whole thing. I don't know whether she married him for love or money."

"That could be it. I mean if you think about it, that's the same problem we have when we date. We always hook up with men or women looking to love us for the financial advantage, like we're they're financial support. If we fell in love with them, we would have the same type relationship Dad and Mom had."

"But Shai, Dad didn't have the business then."

"I think he had a solid plan though. Mom's not dumb either, she saw the bigger picture, and she set out to be a part of it."

"Okay, so they were dating, and she saw a future. What's wrong with that? Shai, they were in love and they both knew where they were headed. She had to do more than just want to be a part of his finances. He met Nikki five years later and started dating her. Why would he want to start a family outside of his marriage? If he wanted a family why not start it with Mom before he met Nikki?"

"I don't know. Maybe she didn't want a family right away. Who knows, there was a reason though. Maybe Aunt Darlene knows."

"Well they kept it a secret like Dad wanted though."

"That's the other thing. Not only did they keep it a secret Nana didn't turn her back on Nikki and her son. Derek, they accepted it like they understood why."

"Maybe you're right. I mean, suppose Mom said she didn't want a family. A man who is in business and sees it's profitable would want to leave it to his family to keep it going after he's gone. Maybe the money was important to her but the family was important to him."

"That does make sense. Nikki gets pregnant. Dad tells Mom that after all the problems they're having with her drinking and whatever that Nikki was having his child. Mom tells him she won't give him a divorce, and he figured it would be financially sound to stay. Now think about it. How could she get him to stay? What did he want the most? A family, she gets pregnant and you were born. He still wanted to leave, and I was born. When she saw it didn't matter, you know that he still wanted Nikki, she went back to her drinking."

"Shai what you're saying makes a lot of sense. That explains something else too."

"What's that?"

"Why she hated the fact that we loved Dad so much. That also explains why she didn't shower us with a lot of love and attention. I don't think she wanted kids. She wanted to keep Dad, and he wanted kids, so she had us."

"Wow, Derek that's some deep shit."

"Yeah, now that he's dead, and we're grown, she really doesn't need to pretend that she wanted us."

"Derek, I would hate to think that, but I think you're right."

"Shai this meeting with the lawyer is going to be ugly."

Shai thought to herself, *"Derek you don't know how ugly it's going to be."*

Chapter 60

"Mitch I need to talk to you man. Can you come up? Come by yourself. Tell Byron you'll be right back. Thanks"

Rell hung up the phone in his suite. He went to the refrigerator and got the ice for the ice bucket. He needed to talk and knew Mitch would be his ear. He opened the door so Mitch could walk in, and he made them both a drink. Mitch came through the door with a worried look on his face.

"Rell, man, what's up? Are you okay?"

"I think so man. This shit is wearing on me though."

"Okay, so what is it?"

"Did you read the obituary? I mean did you read it through?"

"Yeah, I think I did. But obviously I missed something you want me to know."

"What about the fact that my father leaves to mourn three children, and we weren't named?"

"Uh, yeah, I saw that. I thought it was something the family agreed to. Maybe they don't know about you either."

"Right, Mitch, it seems like I'm always finding out secrets …no lies, covered by him. If it wasn't for my mother telling me last night, look how it read. How can I trust his business and his decisions for the business if his personal life is a mess?"

"Rell I really don't know if you can decide whether a man can run a business, by the way, he runs his life. It usually doesn't work that way. Your father has a tight business. It will always be profitable, and he built it that way with the help of good partners. His marriage didn't have a good partner, if you want to compare the two. I think he should have sold and bought more stock in Nikki Robbins."

They both laughed. Rell knew Mitch was trying to make light of the situation, but he had a serious problem understanding all the lies and secrets.

"Mitch, I guess you are right. I just don't understand. I don't even know who these siblings are. Suppose I already met my sister and don't know it."

"Don't tell anyone." Mitch laughed.

"Shit. Man, this is a mess."

"Rell, I think you're putting more on yourself than you need to. It's your father's mess. You go to the reading of his will, meet your brother and sister, and handle the business like your father wanted you to. You'll see it won't be that hard. The partners will guide you along. Don't let that personal shit be your problem. The wife is whacked though. She may be a problem."

"You're telling me. My mom will step to her at the lawyer's office though. She won't get that off twice."

"Your mother handled herself well. She was and is the better woman and that counts."

"Mitch, I was thinking of calling the lawyer to find out if he knows what my father put in the will. You know, so I would be a couple of steps ahead of the game."

"To tell you the truth, I don't think he can tell you that legally. I think it's something that binds him to reading it with everyone or at least the principal people being present."

"Hmmm, maybe you're right. I don't know. I just thought he and I could get acquainted before he calls the others to his office."

"You can still do that. I just don't think he will reveal any of the will to you."

"I still have to call him to make the appointment. I'll talk to him on the phone and see if I can get him to open up a little."

"You haven't talked to him, since he sent you the letter?"

"No, other than replying to him saying I would be available to meet after the funeral. He left the date and time to me."

"It's worth a try. I just don't understand what you want to know."

"I don't know what I want to know either Mitch. I guess I want to make sense of all of this. What was my father expecting if he got the chance to tell us? How did he think we would feel?"

"Man, no one can answer that except him."

"And he ain't talking."

"Yeah, and no one else wants to. Rell if I were you, my friend, I would let it go. Go into the meeting knowing what you know now. Let the chips fall where they may. How does that song go? When you've done all you can, just stand."

"You're right. Hey, how's Craig making out at the office?"

"I didn't talk to him today so I'm assuming all is well. You know I meant to ask you, what's up with him and Monique?"

"What do you mean?"

"They talk frequently, I thought you knew. She called the office for you, and he took the call. We were together Saturday and she called him, just thought I would mention it."

"Well, we've decided to be friends. I guess that would leave her available. I wonder if she's calling him to keep tabs on me."

"Don't know man. I'll keep my left ear listening though. Listen we're leaving about six in the morning. I need to stop at home before going to the office. Do you need anything at the office faxed to you? I know you were handling the Weston's account yesterday."

"No, it's okay. I gave the secretary the information they needed. Listen get home safe and call me. Tell Byron I'll talk to him later. Hey, did Keith call you?"

"Yeah, everything is fine. They're keeping his grand-mother in the hospital for some test, nothing major. His mom is staying with her. He'll be in the office by Thursday."

"That's good. Okay, one, brother."

"One."

Rell looked around for his cell phone. He wondered if Shai had gone through as much drama as he had. When he found the phone he decided to wait until the morning to call her. He turned on the television and found a comfortable spot on the couch. When he woke up it was three in the morning. He went to the bedroom to finish his nights sleep.

Chapter 61

*T*onya got up with a nasty hangover. Nothing a few pain pills wouldn't cure. She downed the pills and got dressed for business. She told her job she needed a leave of absence due to the funeral, but she had no intention of returning to that job or any job. The business of the day would take her to the offices of Simpson and Simon Attorney's at Law. Mr. Simpson didn't know it yet but Mrs. Mince wanted a one on one with him before the reading of Derek Quincy Minces' will.

Tonya drank her coffee and grabbed her keys. She tore the sheet off the writing pad with all the information about Nikki's properties and investments. She got in her car and headed downtown. The traffic was moving well since it was after the morning rush hour. Tonya decided to get to Mr. Simpson's office about ten thirty. She assumed he would just be getting in. After parking her car in the lot, she looked at the directory for his office. She got on the elevator and got off at the second floor. The entrance was a large glass door, the lettering read Simpson and Simon Attorneys at Law in gold lettering.

"Good Morning, may I help you?"

"Good Morning, I don't have an appointment, but I would like to speak with Mr. Simpson if I may."

"Please have a seat. May I say who you are?"

"Oh, I'm sorry, Mrs. Derek Mince."

"Please be seated Ma'am."

The receptionist went into two large mahogany doors. When she returned Tonya was thumbing through the magazines that were on the table in the reception area.

"He'll be with you in a moment, Mrs. Mince."

Tonya had been waiting about ten minutes when she heard a voice come over the intercom.

"Tracy, send in Mrs. Mince please."

"Mrs. Mince, Mr. Simpson will see you now."

"Thank you."

Tonya followed Tracy to his office. There were people walking in and out of the offices in the hall that the large doors in the reception area opened to. Tonya knew the lawyers were expensive just by the office design. Tracy opened the door and told Tonya to have a seat Mr. Simpson would be right out. Tonya didn't have to wait long.

"Good morning Mrs. Mince. I'm Mr. Simpson. How can I be of service to you?"

"I'm here, Mr. Simpson, to see exactly what this meeting is about. I know it is the reading of my husband's will, but I don't understand how some of the other people are a part of the reading."

"Who would that be Mrs. Mince? I mean what other people are you speaking about?"

"Mr. Simpson, I know you're a busy man. I didn't come here to take up your time. You know there are people who will be in attendance at the reading of this will that are not related to my deceased husband."

"Mrs. Mince, people don't have to be related, they only need to be named as recipients of funds or property to be in attendance."

"So these people are named by my husband."

"Mrs. Mince, I assure you if your husband had not asked for them to be here I would not have invited them to the reading."

"Mr. Simpson, I don't understand what they could possibly get from my husband. He doesn't owe them anything. Why would he give them anything?"

"I'm quite sure the reading will clarify what and why they are included."

"I found information on this woman Nikki Robbins. I assume you know who she is."

"Yes, I do."

"Well she has stock and is an investor in D.Q. Enterprises. She even owns property and uses the company to lease the property for vacations. I'm sure she has other financial ties to my husband. What could he possibly be leaving her?"

"Mrs. Mince what she owns or invests in has nothing to do with your husband or his will. I am not at liberty to tell you what he has left her until the will has been read."

"And when will that be?"

"I am awaiting a call to set the date and time. I will contact you when I know that. I am hoping it will be within the next two weeks."

"Why didn't you set the date? It should have been done right away."

"Mr. Mince requested the appointed executor set the date and the time that best suited them."

"Who is that his mother?"

"Mrs. Mince, I can't discuss that with you."

"I'm his wife Mrs. Simpson. That information is pertaining to the man I married. I would think that mattered to a man who deals in the law."

"The law says once you are legally separated you lose some of those rights. I am aware of the law."

"Mr. Simpson, I don't think I can bear leaving this office knowing that woman got more than I did."

"Mrs. Mince, your husband left a will, a legal will. He was of sound mind and body when he wrote the will and signed it. You will have to attend the reading of the will to know what was left to everyone. If you decide you can't handle the reading and don't attend, my office will send you a copy of what has been left to you."

"I'll be here Mr. Simpson, you can bet on that. I'll be here."

Tonya got up to leave. Mr. Simpson rose from his chair. He pressed a button on his phone. His door opened and a young man stepped inside.

"See that Mrs. Mince makes it to the front door. Good day Mrs. Mince. I will have my office call you with the date and time of the reading."

Tonya didn't acknowledge his statement. She walked out and the young man followed her.

Chapter 62

"Hello, Mr. Simpson, this is Darrell Mince."

"Hello, Darrell, how are you? I'm glad you called."

"Why is that sir? Did you think I wouldn't?"

"Let's just say your father said I shouldn't be surprised if you didn't."

"Well, my father didn't know too much about the business man in me."

"I don't know Darrell, I think he did."

"Well sir, I'm calling to set a date for the reading of the will."

"Good, good, let me get a pen in hand. Okay, what day is good for you?"

"What about Monday or Tuesday of next week?"

"Tuesday is fine, what time?"

"Let's set it for one o'clock?"

"Can we meet about three? I have a lunch appointment, and they tend to run late."

"Three is fine."

"Okay, Tuesday at three is fine. Is there anything else I can help you with?"

"I wanted to talk to you about some of the business matters, but I guess that can wait."

"Darrell, you should know, I was your father's personal lawyer. There is a corporate lawyer for his business matters."

"So you handled his stocks and investments? Or did the corporate lawyers handle those for him as well?"

"Anything that was under the name D.Q. Enterprises was handled through the corporate lawyer. They will want to sit with you and the partners after the reading of the will. They will guide you through the business matters and the part your father played in the company. It was a rather large part as you can imagine. He was the owner of the company, and he oversaw the operations of each division. They will help you with that. Everyone is prepared for you to step into his shoes. I handled anything under the name of Derek Quincy Mince. It is my job to take you through all of his assets and belongings. Should you decide you don't need my service, I will surrender the job to any lawyer of your choice. You will need a lawyer to handle those dealings though."

"I see. Well, I don't have a personal lawyer that handles my matters, so I guess the job is yours. You'll have to give me your rate though."

They both laughed. Rell liked the way Mr. Simpson handled himself. He had no doubt they would work well together.

"I was paid a yearly salary. My payments are quarterly. You may decide to pay me differently but my fee will remain the same for you as it was for your father. I will not take more, although there will be times you may offer it. As a CEO of D.Q. Enterprises your father found himself behind the eight ball in litigations often. I would imagine it will be the same for you. Trust me, trust the partnership your father has in place, and you will be fine. They are loyal friends of your father's and they won't steer you wrong. We all owe our financial growth to your father and our loyalty is a small payment for that growth."

"Okay, I'm glad to see I am welcomed. Now is there room for other partners to come in?"

"That would be your friends and coworkers Mitchell Carter, Byron Washington, Craig Masters and Keith Larson?"

"Yes, it would. I must say you have done your homework."

"That's what you will pay me for sir. There has been a discussion about them coming aboard. The partners are not fond of Craig Masters or Keith Larson. You will have to bargain for them to come aboard."

"I see. Well, that can be discussed at a later time."

"Yes, they will tell you the reason for their decisions. Darrell, may I call you Rell?"

"Sure, if it makes you comfortable."

"Your father referred to you as Rell. They will not make a ruling or a decision that they cannot explain. If at any time you don't quite understand, call me or one of the corporate lawyers. Don't discuss it with any one out of your circle. That means your father's partners, Alan Scott and Robert Franklin or Mitchell and Byron. It makes it easier for the lawyers to work for you."

"Thank you for the advice. I will see you on Tuesday at three o'clock."

"Yes, it will be my pleasure. Don't hesitate to call if you have any questions prior to our meeting."

Rell hung up the phone. He had a smile on his face. He knew he was in the big league. His father had made sure he was well taken care of.

Chapter 63

Nana was in the kitchen preparing breakfast for herself and Darryl. Francine and the rest of the family had left for the airport earlier that morning. Darryl was sitting at the table reading the newspaper.

"Darryl, why did Francine leave this morning? I thought she would be staying with you?"

"Mama she got the notion to go home last night. She said she didn't think Michael would be able to handle things, so she would go home to help him."

"Michael has been working with you in that company, since he was fourteen. I thought he was only going back to answer the phone and file the orders. Didn't you have someone handling things while you were gone?"

"Mama I don't think Francine felt comfortable being around the family business that had to be handled."

"Well that's what she should have said. She didn't have to lie to me. I would have found out sooner or later."

"I guess she didn't want you to know the truth. Anyway she said she would feel better keeping an eye on things at home."

"Well suits me fine. I just didn't want her to feel that we forced her to go home."

"No, I don't think she feels that way."

The phone rang and Darryl picked it up.

"Hello. Yes, she's here. Hold on please. Mama, it's Mr. Simpson."

"Hello Mr. Simpson. How are you?"

"No, you didn't interrupt anything. I'm just fixing a little breakfast, brunch you might as well say. Yes, I understand. That will be fine. Thank you, Mr. Simpson. You too."

"Is everything okay Mama?"

"Yes, Rell called and set the date for the reading. It will be Tuesday at three o'clock. That won't be too late for you will it?"

"No, that's what I was about to tell you. Francine actually helped by going home. I have two jobs that are being worked on. The workers won't be ready for inspection on them for at least another two weeks. I want to be home for the inspections. Tuesday is fine."

"Well it could have been tomorrow for me. I will be glad when this mess is over, too much drama for me. I don't want no more family secrets. If you can't tell your family you shouldn't do it."

"I hope D.Q.'s will won't complicate things. I hope it explains more than we know."

"Rell is on top of things though. He didn't wait long at all. I hope Nikki is okay. I'll call her later on. Maybe she'll come over and sit awhile."

"Yeah, that should make her feel comfortable. Tell her to make sure Simone is with her."

"Darryl, your wife just left here. There ain't gonna be no messing around in my house."

"I know, I know. I was just agreeing about Nikki visiting with you; they both need to visit."

Darryl smiled in spite of himself. He always flirted with Simone and enjoyed her company. Nana was aware of his feelings toward pretty women. Nana gave Darryl her stern stare and they both laughed.

"Did Reverend Wilcox call?" Darryl was deliberately prying.

"No, he didn't. He's probably busy this morning."

"Wednesday morning? What's going on at the church on Wednesday morning?"

"Darryl, he may have some personal things to take care of. He does have his life you know."

"Well, I just noticed he watches you a lot. He's been watching you a while."

"Here's your food. Maybe if you stuff your mouth you won't just say anything."

Nana walked to the sliding doors which led to the backyard; she stood gazing, silently thinking of how she would pass another day. Loneliness had begun to set in. Although Darryl was in her home with her, she missed D.Q. Nana wanted to work in her garden later in the day. She had seedlings to plant and promised herself she would plant them before the week was out. She could have Darryl dig the holes for a few of them, and she would manage with the rest. Planting helped her think. She remembered planting with D.Q. He would stay in the yard and talk with her while she planted and cared for her flowers. She would miss those times with him. When Darryl left, she would be alone and those days would repeat repeatedly. Nana decided to plant the seedlings another day.

Chapter 64

"What's up lady?"

Rell had kept his promise. It was close to two o'clock. Shai had went to work for a few hours that morning and asked for the balance of the day off. Her supervisor gave her the rest of the week off. She had attended the funeral and told Shai she understood the stress she was under. Shai had the time to take off with pay, so she took the offer and suggestion from her supervisor. Shai told her she would call her at the end of the week.

"What's up with you? I'm glad to hear your voice."

"Well I wanted to hear yours, so I called. Are you at work? Can you talk a minute?"

"I can talk as long as you would like to. I took the rest of the day off. I think the funeral wore me out. You know black family drama."

Shai knew he understood. He was there. She wouldn't mention it again. She thought about her conversation with Marci. She knew that once he found out she was his sister, the relationship she dreamed of would fade. She didn't know how he would react. But if he knew she knew ahead of time he would be mad.

"Yeah, I dealt with a bit of that too. Listen, I want to see you. You've been on my mind. Can we meet up, maybe grab something to eat? If you still have family in town, I'll under-stand."

"I don't know if anyone is here other than my uncle's family. My cousins live here in Richmond. Those are the only family members I deal with. You know how that goes, you see the others only during times of mourning or celebration; funerals or weddings."

They both laughed. Rell knew it was that way in his family. He really wanted to show Shai she wasn't just someone he enjoyed in the bedroom.

"Okay, I was thinking we could ride to the park. We could walk and talk, just something simple."

"That will be fine. Where are you now? Do you want me to meet you?"

"Let's do this the way I like it. How about I pick you up?"

Shai thought about it. Derek was at the apartment. His new job didn't start for two weeks. He took a leave from the job he was on. She didn't want them to meet. Marci wasn't home but she didn't want him to know where she lived either. *"Damn, what do I say?"*

"Rell, I'm near the mall. I was going window shopping. Can we meet there?"

"Sure, how long before you get there?"

"Are you coming from the hotel?"

"No, my mother's, I went to see her this morning."

"Okay so you're in Richmond?"

"Shai what's wrong, you sound shaky?"

"I'm okay just trying to time you. I don't want you waiting for me."

"Baby, I'll wait. Tell me where."

"In front of Old Navy. I'll meet you there."

"No problem, I'll see you in a few."

The phone clicked off. Shai thought it would be easier than it was. *"How am I going to look at him, knowing he's my brother? Shit, I don't want another brother, I need him as my man!"*

Shai made the next left turn and headed for the mall.

Chapter 65

Dershai's phone rang just as she was parking in the mall's lot. She looked at the number to see if it was Rell. It was Marci.

"What's up girl?"

"I called your job, they said you left and wouldn't be in the rest of the week."

"Yeah, Ms. Paul suggested I use the time to relieve the stress from the funeral. I agree. Marci I kept thinking about my mother and the way she acted. I haven't spoken to her but Derek called her. He thinks she has a serious drinking problem just to touch on one of her issues. Derek thinks she has a problem with us because she only had us to keep my father. I don't know girl, it just threw me off. I couldn't stay focused. Ms. Paul was at the funeral. She said she could understand and gave me the week off. I guess she saw the "Tonya Mince Show". I told her I would call Friday to let her know what my plans were for next week."

"Cool, so what are you doing?"

"I'm at the mall. Rell called and asked me to meet him. I chose the mall as the meeting spot."

"Shai, think of the consequences; that's all I'm going to say. You know how you get. All wound up emotionally. Don't sink your own ship girl. He's your father's son."

"I hear you. I'm going to check if a stepchild is considered a blood relative. It could be like that fourth and fifth cousin, shit. Marci you have to see this man, or be around him to understand."

"Okay so you're at the mall. Where are you guys going from there?"

"He said he wanted to eat and walk through a park or something. I mean we can eat and walk through the mall for all I care."

"Yeah the mall is safer than the park. You'll do a brother in the park. This time it would literally be your brother."

"You got jokes. Listen, I see him standing at the store entrance."

"Shai, what is he wearing?"

"Girl, he's your cousin!"

"To hell with the dumb shit, what's he wearing?"

"Black jeans and a black shirt, damn, women are walking by whispering and smiling. Girl let me walk up on this man, so they'll know."

"It just ain't no stopping you. Call me later."

"Later."

Rell spotted Dershai and smiled. He walked toward her to greet her with a tender kiss. Shai kissed him and forgot all about him being her brother.

They agreed on window shopping in the mall. Rell even told her if she saw something she liked go ahead and get it. He would pay for it. Shai was fighting all her temptations. Rell was making it hard. They went into a restaurant to eat.

"What are you having?"

Rell looked at the menu. "I don't know what I want. I do, but I promised myself I would be good."

Shai smiled, she knew what he was referring to. She had the same wants.

"Rell we're talking about the food on the menu."

"You're right. I'll have the shrimp with garlic sauce over pasta."

"I think I'll have that too."

They sat waiting for the waitress. Rell reached across the table to hold Shai's hand. He massaged her fingers and smiled when she pretended to get weak. Rell looked from the window where they were seated to the people walking in the mall. He spotted Craig and Monique.

"Wow."

"Wow, what?" Shai turned her head in the direction Rell was looking.

"The guy and the lady he's with, see them at the candy shop window?"

"Yeah, I see them."

"Well that's Craig, my co-worker. And the girl he's with is my ex, Monique."

"You're joking."

"Nah wow, I thought she was going through changes for a reason."

"You said he's a co-worker. Why isn't he at work?"

"I don't know but I'll find out. He may have a meeting in town tonight with a client. A lot of our clients are in the Rich-mond area. Our company has an office here also."

"Did the two of you officially call it off?"

"I told her I didn't want someone who was constantly in my wallet. I guess she'll be in his wallet now. Maybe she was in both wallets at the same time."

"But where's his loyalty to you as a friend?"

Rell heard that statement for the second time. Mr. Simpson said the partners weren't sure about Craig and Keith. Maybe they knew he was seeing Monique. That would put a damper in Rell and Craig's relationship.

"I'm glad I saw them. It answers some questions I had."

"So you're not upset that she's with your friend."

"No, I think if I dug into it, I may get upset. But I'm not going to dig. I see that they have some sort of relationship, and I'm leaving it at that. I won't be dealing with her any more, and I can keep my relationship with him as a co-worker only. They'll figure it out sooner or later."

"Wow, I would expect you to call him and her and tell them you don't appreciate them using your friendship like that."

"Like what? They don't owe it to me to tell me they're seeing each other. I'm no longer her man."

"Hmmm. I guess you're right. But you and I both know them seeing each other didn't start today."

"You're probably right."

"And you're cool with that?"

"Yeah, I'm moving on. So how have you been since we were last together? I know you had to deal with family, the funeral and all but otherwise how are you?"

"I've been stressed to no end. I've been waiting to see you again."

"I'm glad. I wanted to see you too. So how long are you on leave, just for the day or what?"

"No, I took the rest of the week off."

"What a coincidence? I guess you don't have plans?"

"No, I can't say that I do."

Shai was getting nervous. *Suppose this man asks me to stay with him a while at the suite. How will I turn him down?*

"So, can I make some plans for the both of us?"

"Depends, I don't want you to think I'm taking up all of your time."

"That's fair; we'll play it by ear."

They ate and had drinks. They finished their window shopping laughing and talking about family traditions, problems and issues. Rell enjoyed her company and Shai didn't want the afternoon to end.

"Are you spending time with your family before you leave?"

"I don't think I will see most of them again until Tuesday."

"I see, I thought you had family business to handle."

"Yeah, that part of the trip will begin on Tuesday."

"Begin, I thought you would be finishing it in a couple of weeks."

"That's why I kept the suite. I don't know how long it will take. It's pretty extensive."

"So you'll be leaving after you handle it all?"

"Shai, you're asking a lot of questions? What do you want to know?"

"When will you be leaving me? I mean I think I'm falling in love with you and when your family business is done, will we be done too?"

"That won't happen, unless we decide it will be done. I don't want you to be in a long distance relationship though.

We'll have to talk about that when the time comes. Let's just take it a day at a time."

"It just seems that we will only have a little time together. Next week you'll be dealing with your family and when that's done, you'll be gone."

"There will be time for you. I don't mix personal pleasure with business. I make sure I am pleased with both separately. Although now my business may change a few things for me personally, you'll be the first to know. I wouldn't just run off and leave."

"That sounds good but we don't know what your family business may be."

"Let me worry about that. Listen today is Wednesday. We have almost a week before that stuff begins. I promise to show you who I am in all aspects by Tuesday. If we don't feel comfortable with each other by then, we'll agree to be friends. If all works out, we'll be lovers."

Dershai thought to herself, *"Shit, I have six days to work on him. I have to keep him away from Nana though. She'll throw my name out just like she told me and Derek. I'll keep him too busy to visit anyone. I will have to convince him that the relationship is worth it, even if we are somewhat related."*

"So what do you have on your agenda until Tuesday?"

"That's up to you. I'm yours until Tuesday."

They walked out of the mall discussing outings for the next few days. They laughed saying by Tuesday, they would be sick of each other. Smiling they both said *"No, not a chance."* They got to Dershai's car, and she opened the door.

"So, my lady, where are you headed?"

"I'm following you. Lead the way and I'll follow."

"Shai, it's not nice to tease a man who is weak for you."

"I'm sorry. But I couldn't help it."

"So then follow me. No, better than that, come by the suite tonight. Let me cook dinner for you. Stay with me until you're ready to leave."

Shai just smiled. She couldn't think of anything she would love to do more.

Chapter 66

Rell called Nana and his mother letting them both know the appointment had been set for Tuesday at three in the afternoon. He told them he would be at his suite working if they needed him for anything. He was relieved to know that Aunt Francine and his cousins had left. Without them there he wouldn't be pressured to entertain his younger cousins. His Uncle Darryl sent the message through Nana that he still needed to meet with him. Rell agreed to see him after the reading of the will. His next call was to Mitch.

"Hey man, how's the office?"

"It's all good. How are you making out?"

"It's as good as to be expected. I spoke with the lawyer this morning. You and Byron are a shoe in. This company is thorough. They must have run a check on you guys. The lawyer knew that I would want you to come on board. They also didn't like the idea of Craig and Keith being brought in. Man, I wanted to argue with him and something just said hold it for another day and time."

"Wow, I wonder what they got on them?"

"Check this, man, me and Shai went to the mall for lunch. We're sitting where we can see the people passing by. Who passes by the window? Craig and Monique, hand in hand. Man that's enough for me not to include Craig. I don't know what they may have on Keith, but if they tagged Craig and he was with my ex before the ex dried, they probably got some true shit on Keith too."

"Damn man. I thought he stayed in town to see a client at six tonight in Richmond. He also has an appointment for two clients in the morning."

"I guess he'll be with her tonight. I should call her ass about ten and tell her I want to stop by so she can fall the hell out."

They both laughed. "Rell man, I had no idea. I thought they were talking a lot though. I guess it goes further than talk."

"Man, I told you Monique was bugging. I guess she wanted to make sure I wasn't planning to make her Mrs. Mince first before she did Craig up."

"Damn, that's foul. Craig knew what was going on with you and her and just waited you out."

"It's all good. She's not wife material if she'll do this. So there's no returning to her. I can move on."

"So, how are things coming along with you and Shai?"

"Man, I'm trying to take it slow. My emotions and my physical desires won't let me. I think I'm falling fast. I hope not though."

"Why, you said you're done with Monique? Why not fall in with Dershai?"

"Mitch you know every time I fall fast, there's something wrong with the girl."

"Yeah, but you said yourself she seems stable. Able to hold her own and has preset goals."

"You're right. Man, I just hope so. I got to tell you something. This is for your ears only."

"What just tell me man?"

"We've had sex three times. Mitch, it's the best I've had. I was totally relaxed. There was one problem."

"What? Not another one who complained about your size?"

"No not at all. I said we had sex three times. I didn't use a condom."

"Whew, that's taking a chance my brother. Of course she said she was on the pill or something."

"Yeah, but Mitch, you know usually when a woman says that you get a little nervous and make sure the next time you use protection. I'm not upset. If she's pregnant we'll deal with it."

"Rell, you must be kidding. You never said that before. It was always, 'I don't have time for a wife and family'. You must really like this girl."

"I do Mitch. I would want her to be the mother of my children and my wife. I'm not telling her that of course but that's how I feel man. I guess the relationship went the way a prerequisite for marriage would go. You know you meet, become friends, then date and have sex. We met two years ago man, she didn't even push for a relationship during the two years. Now, I don't think I can put my feelings on the back burner, but I'm still taking my time."

"Well, good luck man. So what are you doing until the meeting with the lawyer?"

"I'm going to the suite. I'm gonna take it down for a few days, lounging around with Shai."

"Well, expect to be a father if you keep it going without a condom."

"I got some. Can't say I'll use them though. She said it was all good, she is on birth control."

"Okay, big baller, I would use the condom anyway. Listen, call me later."

"Later man."

Chapter 67

Derek heard Dershai put her keys into the door. He had spent most of the day hanging up the phone on their mother.

"Call mom Dershai."

"Call her for what?"

"She keeps calling, crying in the phone that she needs to talk to you."

"What's wrong with her? I don't have time for her shit."

"I don't know what's wrong. Listen I gave you the message. Call her and tell her anything you like. I did my part. I gave you the message."

Dershai knew that meant that she would feel guilty later if something was wrong with their mother. She went into her bedroom and picked up the phone. While her mother's phone rang Dershai began to pack her weekend suitcase.

"Hello, Dershai?"

"Yes mother, it's me. What's wrong? What do you want?"

"I don't want you to be mad at me. I did what I had to do for you and your brother. I want you to understand me. Your father kept that woman and her son over my head as a threat. I loved your father."

"Ma, I really don't want to hear this now. I'm busy. That stuff is in the past. Get over it. I did. I don't blame either of you."

"You should hold your father accountable for his wrong doings Dershai. How can you forgive him and me in the same breath? He caused this drama and left it for me to clean up."

"Ma, no one can change what has happened. We can't ask Daddy why, so, leave it alone."

"Then what about our relationship. If you're not mad why don't you and Derek like me?"

"Ma, Not now! Our relationship has nothing to do with Daddy and his issues. You stopped being our mother years ago. Maybe at birth, who knows? You can't undo what you damaged. You showed your ass at the funeral. The whole town watched you fall from your high horse. Now you want us to pick you up. You caused yourself to fall. And if you hurt, so be it. I love you mom. I guess it's just the fate of a child. They always love their parents. I just don't like you much. I don't like your ways of handling this situation. I don't like the fact that you choose when you want to deal with me and Derek. Unlike Derek, I'm not looking for answers to your problems anymore. I'm moving on with my life."

"Dershai, you're upset. Why don't you come over so we all can talk about this?"

"You had time to talk. You had over thirty years to prepare for the talk. I don't want to talk. You told me if we couldn't be there in the beginning don't come at all. Ma, pretend we didn't come."

Shai hung up the phone. Surprisingly she wasn't upset. She continued to pack her bag.

"Derek, I'll be back on Monday. I'm going away to relax and enjoy another atmosphere. If you need me call my cell or call Marci."

"Shai, someone needs to know where you are."

"I'm fine Derek. Your mother doesn't faze me anymore. Marci knows exactly where I'll be. I love you."

Derek knew her comments meant the discussion was over. It became clear to him that Dershai wasn't worried about his mother's actions. Derek went back into the living room and his favorite chaise chair. He picked up the book he had been reading earlier, it was as though he never put it down. Shai came out of her bedroom shortly after she kissed Derek on his forehead as she said good-bye.

Once Dershai got into her car, she called Marci. There was no answer on her cell so she left a message for her to call back when she could. Shai called Nana and told her she would be out of town until Monday with a friend. Nana told her about the meeting with the lawyer, and she told her she would be there. Shai promised to call Derek and let him know about the meeting. Shai called Rell and told him she was on her way.

Chapter 68

Reverend Wilcox left his office at seven o'clock. He was certain Julie Mince was supposed to be at the meeting that started at five thirty. He wanted to be sure she was okay. The drama from the day before was enough to stress the average person. He didn't want her to feel that the church members looked at her differently. He decided to stop by her house. Once he got in the car he thought twice about it and thought it best to call her first.

"Hello."

"Yes."

"Sister Mince?"

"Yes."

"Reverend Wilcox, I was calling to check on you. I noticed you weren't at the meeting for new members today. Are you alright?"

"Yes, Reverend, I guess I forgot about the meeting. I think I may have my days confused. I thought the meeting was tomorrow."

"Well, no Sister Mince, it's okay. Do you mind if I stop by to visit you?"

"No Reverend, not at all. Darryl is here with me now, but I'm sure he won't mind the company."

"I won't stay long. I just want to talk with you a while."

"Well I'll be looking forward to your visit."

Nana hurried through the house moving things that were out of place. She went into the kitchen and made a pitcher of lemonade. She went into her room and changed her clothes from her old house dress to a two piece pant suit. Darryl watched her with a puzzling look.

"Mama what are you doing? Why did you change clothes it's almost eight o'clock?"

"Reverend Wilcox is stopping by."

"Oh, I see and you changed clothes, straightened up and whatever for the Reverend?"

"No, I don't want to go to bed with the house being a mess. Anyway I just wanted you to know he was coming."

"Well I think that's nice. You make a nice couple."

"We ain't no couple Darryl. Don't start no mess now. That man's a man of the cloth. He ain't about no mess and don't you start none."

Darryl laughed and walked away. "No problem Mama, everyone has someone they love."

"Lord knows Darryl, you make me sick sometime."

The bell rang. Nana looked at the clock wondering, *"He must have been on his way when he called."*

"Good evening Reverend, please, come in."

"Thank you Sister Mince."

"Have a seat in the living room. I was watching television when you called. Would you like a glass of lemonade?"

"Is it sweet?"

"That's how I make my lemonade and my iced tea."

"I like it sweet. Thank you, I'll have a glass."

"Did you have dinner Reverend?"

"I ate at the church. Thank you. They had fried chicken, corn and string beans with cornbread. They're selling them for the student education fund."

"Well since you ate, I can't offer you dinner."

"I didn't stop by for you to feed me. I was concerned about not seeing you this evening at the meeting."

"To tell you the truth Reverend, I was a little tired today. I guess these last few days are catching up to me. I still got to deal with this reading. It's scheduled for Tuesday. Then when all that's said and done, I have to face the fact that my son is truly gone. Darryl will be going home shortly after the reading. You know he lives in Detroit. Rell will be busy dealing with his father's business. Those are my closest. The others visit but they don't see about me like D.Q., Darryl and Rell. Well now just Darryl and Rell."

"Well, maybe it's time someone else came around to see about you."

Nana smiled. She knew what Reverend Wilcox was talking about. It was fine with her. The thought of loneliness had broken down the walls. They talked for two more hours before Reverend Wilcox told her he wanted her to get her rest.

"Reverend, I truly enjoyed your company."

"And I yours. Can I ask a favor of you?"

"Sure, Reverend."

"Can you call me Wallace when we're together such as this? It sounds so formal to call me Reverend."

Nana smiled. "Wallace it is. Don't get upset now if I call you Rev every now and then. And in return you call me Julie."

"That's a beautiful name. Jewels, that is what you are, Jewels. Well, good night, Jewels. I'll call you tomorrow from the office if that's alright with you."

"I'll look forward to your call. Goodnight Wallace."

Nana closed her door and thanked the Lord for sending her a friend in Reverend Wallace. She couldn't believe how much they had in common. *That wasn't as bad as I thought. I could become accustomed to his company.*

"Mama, did your company leave?" Darryl entered the room smiling. He too was pleased his mother could talk with Reverend Wallace.

"He sure did, said he would call me tomorrow."

"Who said dating gets old? Do your thing Ma. He seems to be really nice."

"Time will tell Darryl. He still got on his good clothes when he comes. You know y'all men don't show yourself until you pull those clothes off and put on your every day wear."

They laughed and locked the doors preparing for their night's rest.

Chapter 69

It was Sunday morning. Rell was in the shower. Dershai was cooking breakfast for the two of them. She prepared the plates and put them on the counter. As she entered the bedroom Rell was drying off. Shai wrapped her arms around him from behind. Neither of them had tried to ignite the passion they had for each other. They both put each other to the test. After spending four nights and three days together they couldn't hold back the physical attraction any longer. They had made love to each other mentally during the past days. They teased each other but never took it beyond kissing and touching. That was a new experience for them both. They spoke about their love for each other. The future they could imagine they would have. Shai almost cried as she realized none of what they wanted would work. However, this Sunday morning, Shai put aside the fact that Darrell was her brother.

Rell told Shai that his mother told him he had siblings, and they didn't know he or his mother existed until recently. He told her his family values ran deep. They both agreed that family was important, and that they didn't understand why people did the things they did. Then Rell told her his father must have loved his mother

342

and his family to torture himself for years being devoted to both. Rell kissed her saying he probably would do the same for her, if they were in a similar situation.

Shai wanted to make love to him for what she felt would possibly be the last time. They would have this last day and night together as lovers. She had decided to go to work on Monday. After talking to Marci, she agreed her fairytale would have to end.

Rell turned around in her arms and faced her naked in the bedroom. Shai kissed his lips and mouthed. "I love you."

Rell took her to the bed and took off her gown leaving her bare except for a black lace thong.

"I love you too Shai."

Their ecstasy began. They made love repeatedly. Rell gave her pleasure, pleasure that she knew she wouldn't get anywhere else. She loved his sensitivity and his desire to please her as long as she wanted. Shai had orgasm after orgasm. She knew she wouldn't love this way with anyone again. She cried. Rell set a different pace and exploded. He laid his head on her breast before he noticed her tears.

"Baby, what's wrong? Are you okay?"

"I'm fine Rell."

"Why the tears? Did I hurt you?"

"No baby, women, cry when they are in love. I guess now I know why."

"Being in love is supposed to make you happy, not sad. I don't want to make you cry."

"These are happy tears Rell. I am finally in love. Now I know what it feels like. I don't want to live without you in my life. I truly love you."

"Wow, okay, but why the tears Shai? We can be together. I love you too. I think as much as you love me. You're talking as though I'm going somewhere. Baby, I'm yours. I have no desire to leave you."

"I don't know Rell. It's just a feeling I have. I've never loved anyone like this before. I've told guys I loved them, but I know different now. It was a temporary thing, maybe just good sex."

"I can understand that. You're more than that to me. I wanted you to know that. I love you; just the thought of you gives me chills. Baby, I'm not giving you up. Nothing can come in the way of me loving you. Stop crying Shai. I'm a man of my word. I will always be here for you."

"Rell, did you tell Monique that?"

"Funny you should ask that. No, I didn't. I told her I loved her. But I was scared to say I would be there for her, or that I never would go anywhere. I told you she wanted my wallet, my money. She didn't know Darrell. She just knew what I could afford to give her. You're different Shai. I'll give you my money. I just want you to love me in return."

"Rell, I love you without your money."

They kissed and Shai stopped crying. Rell took pleasure with her body massaging her breast until the nipples hardened. He began to caress her, holding her close to his body. Shai wanted him to enter her again. She massaged his penis slowly until Rell began to moan. He mounted her and slowly penetrated her with a full load. Their bodies moved as though they were dancing to a love song played by a saxophone. They both moaned together as they reached a climax. Rell smiled.

"Why wouldn't I love you?"

"I don't know. I never want you to stop though."

The warmth of their juices made her smile.

"Can I meet you here again say, about eleven this evening?"

"I wouldn't miss it for the world."

Chapter 70

Nana called Darlene, Mia and Marci to invite them to join her at the eleven o'clock Sunday service. Darryl told Darlene about Reverend Wilcox and Nana's past few days. They had been to dinner and the movies on Friday, and bingo on Saturday. Darryl laughed when Darlene teased Nana calling her First Lady of the church. Darryl and Nana got to the church fifteen minutes before the service. Darlene saw them in the parking lot and waved to get their attention.

"Good morning Mr. Mince. Good morning First Lady."

Darryl laughed along with Darlene.

"The two of you, don't start no mess now. You know how these hens are. They'll hear you and start a scandal."

"Mama, do you care what they say?"

"No, but I don't want the Reverend to have problems with those biddies."

"They're going to give him a problem when they find out you're dating the Reverend."

As they went to the front of the church Mia and Marci greeted them. They all found seats in the front pews where Nana sat each week. Nana went to Reverend Wilcox's office.

"Good morning Jewels. How are you sweetie?"

"Wallace, I'm fine. Do you need anything done before service?"

"Those envelopes were given to me this morning. Can you take them with you? Put them in your purse. I'll get them from you later this afternoon when I come to the house. I was going to put them in the safe, but I can deposit them in my account tomorrow."

"These are your personal envelopes?"

"Yes, my pay for ministry and counseling during the week. That's why I don't want them in the safe. I don't want the secretary to deposit them in the church funds. They have done that since I've been here. Then when I ask they don't know how much of the deposit was mine."

"Wallace, they ain't been giving you your money?"

"Jewels, it's okay. I get my pay from this church, the college where I teach and counseling. I just don't want the checks to cross again. This time I intercepted them. I already told the school to send my checks to my house. My ministry and counseling fees still come here though, but they aren't that large of an amount. Listen it will be alright. Fasten this button in the back. Go take your seat sweetie and prepare yourself for the word."

"I'll see you after the service, Rev."

Nana walked the halls leading to the sanctuary shaking her head as she thought of the so called "saved" members of the church. Nana took her seat looking around. *"Thieves in the midst, Lord have mercy."*

The service was uplifting. As they walked to the back of the church some of the congregation greeted them with condolences and warm wishes. Nana nodded her head thanking people as she headed to the door. They reached Reverend

Wilcox. He hugged Mia, Marci, and Darlene and shook Darryl's hand. Nana smiled when she got in front of him.

"I'll be at the house in about an hour or two."

Nana was shocked. She looked around to see who may have overheard his comment. He took her hand and kissed it gently.

"In an hour Jewels." Reverend Wilcox wouldn't allow Nana to comment. Nana understood. Reverend Wilcox wasn't worried about who knew he was visiting her.

"Okay, take your time. Call if you'll be later."

Darlene and Darryl waited for her at the bottom of the steps. "Mama, it's all good. He's a man of the cloth."

"Y'all stop your foolishness. These women don't need to know my business. That's all they looking for is someone to talk about."

"Mama Mince. Hey, how you doing?"

"Hey Nikki."

They all greeted Nikki with a hug.

"Nikki these are my daughters Mia and Marci. This is Rell's mother."

Darlene told Mia and Marci about Nikki and Rell after the funeral. She also told them that no one had seen Rell since the funeral. Marci looked at Nikki and tried to imagine what Rell would look like. Shai said he was fine. Nikki was an attractive woman. She had a beautiful smile. Marci kept her promise to Shai and didn't tell Mia, who he was. Mia was none the wiser.

"Nikki where is Rell? Did he come to service with you?" Darlene was anxious for Marci and Mia to meet him.

"No Darlene, he's at his hotel suite. He said he wouldn't see us until Tuesday. He wanted to keep up with his business matters at his firm in Maryland. He called though. Didn't he call you Mama Mince?"

"He called, I think Wednesday or Thursday. Darryl spoke with him Saturday. He's okay."

"Well Nikki, it's good to see you."

"Yes, I'm glad I met your ladies too. They're beautiful. I just wanted to speak. I usually attend the eight o'clock service. I overslept this morning."

"There was a reason for it. We needed to get together other than for a funeral or a will."

"I know that's right."

"Nikki, where's Simone? She didn't come this morning?"

"Mama Mince. I don't have to tell you about family. She thought she was a part of the reading of the will."

"What?"

"Yeah, she had mapped out how we were going to spend the money. She said she was drunk when she said it. I had her bags ready the next morning. I put her on the next thing smoking to New York. You know they say you tell the truth when you're drunk. I don't need that drama."

"Well, what did she expect you to do? Share your money with her?"

"What money, Darlene? I don't have a clue as to what D.Q. left me. I never gave it a second thought. I even asked your mother why I was listed to be there. Rell is grown, he can handle this business and finance stuff better than me. That's what D.Q. put him through school for. Simone thought there was big money coming my way, and I would be buying property. Anyway, I told her how to get to New York quickly. I'll call her later. She'll talk better after she realizes what she said."

"So you're by yourself in that big house?"

"Yeah, I was gonna call Rell and tell him he could stay with me instead of spending money on a suite. Then I thought about it, he probably wants his privacy. I mean we haven't lived together in almost three years. So I dumped that thought. I'll be okay."

"Well if you don't mind, I'll stop by and visit. We don't have to end our relationship at the reading of the will."

"Darlene, I'll look forward to that. Really, I would."

"Well y'all say your goodbyes and exchange numbers, I have food waiting. Some of it has to go in the oven. Y'all coming by to eat right?"

"Mama I hadn't planned on it. Are you all gonna be at Mama's at about four o'clock? I have a stop to make."

"Well come when you're ready there's plenty to eat. I cooked for Reverend Wilcox and Deacon Smalls."

"Is Deacon Smalls that nice looking man that's always with the Reverend?"

"Yeah, Nikki, now I know you know who Deacon Smalls is."

"Now I do. I will be there on time. What time is he coming?"

They all laughed. Both Mia and Marci said they would join them. They got in their cars promising to see each other at Nana's house.

Chapter 71

"Mitch I really don't think meeting with this guy is going to benefit us in the long run. I mean if he is going to sue, then let him sue. We did what we were legally obligated to do. There's nothing else we can do for him. Yeah, I understand. Well, I'll speak to Craig. You said he's in this hotel right. Okay I'll call you back. Maybe Monique's here with him. No, I'm just joking. Anyway I'll call him and get it straight. He'll be at the office to get his things. I'm sure by tomorrow he won't have a job."

"What's up Rell?" Shai overheard the end of their call.

"Remember the guy we saw in the mall. Well, apparently he tried to get the client to build an alliance with him and another firm. He offered him a better contract through the other firm. Now the client wants to sue saying we swindled him out of his money over the years he has been with us."

"Wow first your girl, then your firm?"

"Not my firm. I'm just a team leader."

"Oh but it seems like he's digging at you. Why would he do that with a client of yours that knows you and Mitch?"

"I don't know. But the funny thing is he's staying in this hotel."

"You're not thinking of inviting him here are you?"

Shai didn't want anyone to know who she was until they decided what they would do on Tuesday. She didn't want anyone to know they were seeing each other and later find out they were sister and brother.

"No baby, I'm going to his room. If Monique is there oh well, he knows I'm staying here."

Rell called the front desk and got Craig's room number. He asked if he was presently in his room. The desk clerk said he just came in. He thanked him and headed for Craig's room.

Rell knocked on the door. Craig didn't even look to see who it was. He opened the door. Rell walked in and sitting on the couch relaxing was Monique.

"I'm sorry. I don't mean to intrude but Craig, we need to discuss the Madison account."

"Oh shit! Craig! Rell I'm sorry." Monique didn't see Rell walk in, but she recognized his voice.

"Sorry for what Monique. It's all good. Getting Craig's wallet is better than getting mine. Listen man, the Madison's lawyers, hey, can we sit down? I mean, I don't want to have to talk to you again."

"Uh, sure Rell, sit at the table. Do you want to see the file?"

"No, I don't need the file. Listen the lawyers want to sue Sheldon Finance because you sold them on some bull that Sheldon Finance is extorting them for their money. Who is this new company you're balling with?"

"Rell, man, let me explain. They hired me to fish out Sheldon's dead contracts. Madison said they were looking to pull out so I shot them the other company's name and their contract."

"Wow. So we loose the contracts, but you make your money by giving them to our competition. Your job title must be snake. The Madison contract isn't heavy enough for me to hurt your reputation, where you couldn't work. Besides the girl you got, likes men with bank. So I'm going to do you a favor. Pack your shit at Sheldon. Tell your boys you're theirs full time. Don't let me hear your name again on anything that I am tied to. That includes my personal life. Do you understand my terms? If you don't and you cross me again, I will ruin you."

"Rell, man, it isn't like you think."

"Craig, I don't give a shit. I'm going by what I see. You're a snake. Goodnight Monique, I'm glad to know you've hooked another fool."

Rell left smiling. He felt good knowing he didn't have to have eyes in back of him watching Craig. Now he had to find out what was going on with Keith. He returned to his suite. Shai was on her phone. He went into the bedroom and called Mitchell. He let him know everything was taken care of. Rell returned to the bar, Shai had prepared a drink for him.

"Thanks baby. You know people are funny. I walked in that room, and they immediately started apologizing like I came to talk to them about their relationship."

"What did they think you were going to say?"

"I don't know. I didn't give them a chance. I told Craig what I wanted him to know. I could care less about him and Monique and that's how I acted. She looked like she was about to cry."

Rell's cell phone rang.

"Hello."

"Rell, can I talk to you a minute?"

"What is there to talk about? I only came to speak to Craig. It had nothing to do with you."

"I know but I don't want you to take our involvement and use it against his business career."

"I just said it had nothing to do with you. Is he trying to blame his extorting a client in the company's name on you? That punk ass."

"Rell, please, he doesn't even know I'm calling you. I don't know what he did, but it must be serious for you to fire him."

"Monique, he's a snake. I can't work with him. When I tell Mr. Moore why, he will fire him. He might as well pack his shit and leave. That's business. He shook the dice and lost. What are you calling me for? That's your man, or going to be your man, you should be dealing with his shit."

"Rell, you're angry about us."

"No, Monique you're wrong. Craig did this to Craig. This has nothing to do with you. I saw the two of you Wednesday at the mall. If it was about you, I would have called him then or called you, for that matter. I am over you. I am over the bull. I have moved on. I am okay. You need to move on. Just do me a favor Monique. Don't turn back."

Rell hung up the phone. Shai took his glass.

"You want more ice."

"No thanks, look in the refrigerator and see if there is any beer."

"There's two left. Do you want me to call room service?"

"They'll fill it in the morning. Thanks. Hand me one of them please."

"So what's next? They'll be coming to the room."

Rell smiled at the thought.

"They better not. I have plans for this room tonight. Monique might see some things that she can't handle. She will be crying then."

Shai smiled. She went and sat back on the chaise lounge chair where they first made love. Rell had other tricks in store for her. He turned on the radio to the smooth jazz station.

"Hey Shai, come here girl."

Shai walked toward Rell, who stood in the middle of the floor. He put his arms around her, as though he was ready to slow dance.

"You ever made love in a hot tub?"

"I can't say I have."

"Well you won't say that in the morning."

He picked her up and began kissing her. Their night of pleasure began in the hot tub.

Chapter 72

$\mathcal{M}$r. Simpson told his receptionist to set up the conference room and television for a video conference. He told her the principal players and said each would be assigned seats according to his diagram. Each would have a pad, pen, glass and coffee cup in front of them. Coffee, tea and water would be on a serving table in the corner of the room. There would also be a box of tissue at each end of the table. He would need Mr. Derek Q. Minces' file at the head of the table. He would be sitting there. He told her the meeting was to begin at three o'clock and no one was to enter the conference room until that time. Mr. Simpson left for lunch after he confirmed Tracy understood his requests.

Tracy prepared the room as she was told. She was glad she would be in the room for the reading. Tracy usually enjoyed the reading of the will for Mr. Simpson's clients. It brought on entertaining drama. She had prepared some of the forms for Mr. Mince and she could see that everything was in order. There was no room for disputes or misunderstandings. Mr. Mince had prepared for this reading prior to his death and Tracy liked his style. She placed the name cards as shown in the diagram and shook her head when she noted Tonya Mince was at the far end near Mr. Simpson. The television monitor was set at the head of the table opposite Mr. Simpson. Clockwise from the set was the following seating arrangement; Mrs. Mince, Darlene, Dershai, Tonya, Mr. Simpson, Derek, Darryl, Nikki and Darrell, they all were seated where they could see the television from their seats. The room was ready. Tracy hoped the principals were ready as well.

It was two-thirty when Nana and Darryl arrived. Tracy asked them to have a seat and offered them a glass of water while they waited. Nana told her yes. Tracy brought a tray of glasses with a pitcher of water in the middle. At two forty-five, Darlene, Derek and Dershai arrived. Nikki came in at two fifty. At three o'clock they were escorted into the conference room and sat where they found their name cards.

"This office is beautiful. Ma would you like more water?"

"Yes, Darlene. I would. What time is it?"

Nana had developed a nervous thirst.

"It's five after three."

"Nikki have you met Dershai and Derek?"

"No I haven't." Nikki stood to shake their hands.

Tonya walked in. She looked for her seat and sat in it without a word of hello. Everyone looked at her in disgust.

"Well, Ms. Thang. Hello to you."

Nana had a few choice words for Tonya. She was waiting for the opportunity to be alone with her.

"Hello Mrs. Mince, how are you? This is not the best of occasions to be social. Why are we waiting?"

Mr. Simpson entered the room prepared to answer her question.

"We're waiting for Mr. Mince. He's in traffic. He should be here shortly."

"He's a Mince for sure. Can't get nowhere on time."

"Mrs. Mince, I must warn you, any sign of hostility that I deem may interrupt these proceedings is grounds to have you escorted out. That goes for anyone in the room."

"I see. I want to get this over with, the sooner the better. I think we'll find out who is on the outside then."

The room got quiet. They waited for Darrell Mince.

Darrell walked into the room at three fifteen. He excused himself as he looked around the table. There were only two faces he didn't know, Tonya's and Derek's. He saw Dershai and held on to his emotions and thoughts. *"Say this woman is not my sister. Shit, say this woman is not my sister."* He looked to make eye contact with her. She looked at him hoping he wouldn't think she knew about their relationship prior to the meeting. Rell thought he was dreaming. He sat in his chair across from Nana. He kept his eyes on Shai.

"Excuse me Mr. Simpson, before we start, can I speak to the young lady across the table a minute."

"Sure Mr. Mince you can use my office. Ms. Mince is that okay with you?"

"Sure sir."

They excused themselves stepping into a private office where Traci stood gesturing for them to enter.

"Shai, what's up? Why are you here?"

"Tonya is my mother. She said we are here for the reading of my father's will. I had no idea until I got to the conference room and saw your name. Even then I wasn't sure. I thought maybe the guy's name was Darrell like my Uncle Darryl's just spell differently. Rell they can't know. I mean, how can we tell them? What will we do?"

"We'll get through this first. Are you okay?"

"Rell, I don't know. I'm scared, I just lost my father, and now I know I'm going to lose you." Tears rolled down Shai's face.

"Shai, baby, don't start crying. We'll talk when this is over. Listen no matter what when this is done. Meet me at the suite. It's gonna be alright, Shai."

"Alright. Rell I love you."

"I love you too, but don't say that out there."

Shai smiled. She felt better. She wiped her eyes. *"He didn't blow up. They could get through it. Maybe they would still remain lovers."* They returned to their seats. Everyone, especially Nana looked at them questioning the reason for their private meeting.

"I'm sorry I interviewed Dershai some time ago at Sheldon Finance, and she had given me another name. I just wanted to be clear about her reason for the lie or mistake at the time. We're fine"

"Mr. Mince, are you sure sir."

"Yes, Mr. Simpson, proceed. Rell thought about it. *"If the firm checked Craig and the others, they checked me and Shai. Do they know I am dealing with Shai, my sister? Shit, I need to talk to Mr. Simpson."*

Chapter 73

"As you all know, this meeting was called for the formal reading of Mr. Derek Quincy Minces' last will and testament. This is a taped proceeding for record keeping purposes only. Before the reading, I will need you all to verify attendance by stating your name and relationship to the deceased. This will be done clockwise, starting with you, the elder Mrs. Mince."

"Oh, okay. I am Mrs. Julie Mince, mother of the deceased."

"I'm Darlene Nichelle Mince, sister of the deceased."

"I'm Dershai Quinelle Mince, daughter of the deceased."

"I'm Mrs. Tonya Mince, wife of the deceased."

"I'm Mr. Stanley Simpson, Attorney for the deceased."

"I'm Mr. Derek Quinton Mince, son of the deceased."

"I'm Mr. Darryl Lamont Mince, brother of the deceased."

"I'm Nikki Robbins, friend of the deceased."

"I'm Darrell Quincy Mince, son of the deceased."

The lights in the room dimmed and the television came on with D.Q. sitting in a chair similar to the ones they were in.

"I'm Derek Quincy Mince, the deceased, I'm glad you all are here."

There was total silence in the room. It was though D.Q. waited for a response of some sort. He turned his head and looked right at his mother.

"Mama, I don't know what to tell you. You were right, there's nothing more sacred in life than one's peace of mind. I found peace when I admitted what I always knew, I loved Nikki. Mama, I know now how much a heart can endure. It killed me. Just as you said it would. Not being able to love her as I should have, killed me. Mama I love you and I always will. Everyone at the table today will need your love and support. I don't have to tell you to continue to be steadfast in our family. I have paid off your home. I leave you with stocks and an investment that will roll over each year. Mr. Simpson will explain to you how it works. At the end of each year you will yield funds that will match the bank account I have set up for you. This cannot begin to repay you for being the woman and mother you are."

D.Q.'s television image took a sip from a glass of water in front of him. He paused and smiled, looking at Darlene.

"Lene, baby girl. I miss you already and you don't even know it. You couldn't have said it better. Stay away from drama. I don't know why I have put you in this mess. I know it caught you off guard, but you accepted me with all my bull. Accept Nikki, she's a wonderful person. She should have been your sister-n-law. You will love her as I have over the years because her being is pure and loving. Accept our son, your nephew. He's strong Darlene. He reminds me of you. He hates drama. He made me grow up though. In the thick of things I grew up. I know it was wrong to hide my love for Nikki and Rell. I know I should have stood up and shouted, I love them with all my heart. But you loved them first. You wouldn't pretend to accept my actions toward them or Dershai and Derek. Darlene I didn't understand it then but I understand it now. I thank you. I have left you fifty thousand dollars and that summer home you always found a reason not to go to. Mr. Simpson has your ownership papers. Enjoy Lene. Live well."

Darlene excused herself crying into the bathroom. The receptionist followed her with tissues in her hand.

"Shai, Shai, my one and only daughter. Baby I owe you so many apologies. So many answers, I hope your Nana explained most of the details to you. Your mother and I married with my thought of having a business, a wife and children. Your mother married with the thought of having a business. There was no room in her life for me. When I needed her love and support, she turned her back until I became a financial leverage, by then I had looked for support elsewhere. I fell in love with Nikki. She got pregnant, I told your mother, we had no marriage and no children, I wanted a divorce. She had said she couldn't bear children, and I couldn't hold that against her. I had the grounds to divorce her. She said she would ruin me. She would say I abused her, and I feared she would. We tried to love each other, but it was purely sexual pleasure. You and your brother were conceived. I wanted the two of you and a divorce. She agreed to the divorce but told me I would never see you again. I stayed. I loved Nikki every year I lived with your mother.

I know it is hard for you to see me in this light. But I am a mere man; a man who needed to love someone who loved him. Your mother loved no one. I can only imagine what you and Derek are going through. Stay close to Nana and your Aunt Darlene. They will always be there for you. Get to know your brother Darrell, Rell. He is a fine man, a strong man and a brilliant businessman. You have the support you need to get you through. Get to know Nikki. She stood in the shadows for years. She has a marvelous glow. She will love you both, I know. To you baby girl. I have set you up in company stocks, and money investments. Mr. Simpson will tell you how it works. You've always wanted to finish your Medical training. When you decide, you will have the money to pay for it. I have given you two vacation properties. Do with them as you want. You can lease them, use them as summer spots or sell them. They are yours. Remember, I will always love you."

Darlene returned to her seat and Shai began to sob into her arms. D.Q. leaned forward looking directly at Tonya.

"Tonya, I was going to seat you at the other end of the table. Yes, I set up the seating arrangements. I wanted you here to hear what was going on. There is no reason for you to call my mother, my children, my sister, or brother. Don't call Mr. Simpson, D.Q. Enterprises or your lawyer. He has a copy of this will and testament. He got it today. You are a witness not a principal at today's proceedings. You got all you're going to get from me. There is nothing that is given here today in my name. It was given to them two years ago in related business deals done through the company. Oh, and the stock that you have been sold as of this morning. D.Q.

Enterprises has liquidated that stock line. You are no longer a vested member. You will not be allowed to view our stocks as a member. Your holdings were traded the day after my death. I do thank you for two beautiful children, that's all you did for me in thirty years."

Tonya got up from her seat. "Mr. Simpson you can put me out now. I don't want to know anything else. You fucked up D.Q. I will sue this bitch for all she gets."

Tracy stopped the tape and backed up. Nikki stood to her feet. "I ain't gonna be no more bitches. Enough is enough!

She ran over to where Tonya stood and punched her in her face.

"Call me another Bitch, see don't I tear your ass from its frame!"

The fight began. Tonya cursed at Nikki throwing her arms up to protect her face. Rell grabbed his mother and pulled her back into Mr. Simpson's office. Derek and Mr. Simpson escorted Tonya to the reception area where security escorted her out the building.

"Mama, you okay?"

"I'm fine. This is stressful enough without that foolish woman calling names. I am truly sorry Rell."

Mr. Simpson came to the door and told them to return to their seats. Nikki stood at her seat to apologize.

"I'm so sorry. I want to apologize to all of you. I have had enough of her. It's been coming a long time. Especially you Dershai and Derek, it's not about your father. Your mother has been, well let's just leave it at that, I am truly sorry."

"We understand Ms. Robbins. We have to deal with her too."

Shai answered looking at Derek. Derek didn't answer at all. He reached for Nikki's hand and squeezed it. Tracy started the tape from where it left off.

"Derek, there is no need to repeat the words, I said to your sister. They were meant for the both of you. You never were much of a businessman. You blow more money than I can record. I have a challenge for you. You now know your brother. He is an accountant, a damn good accountant. He's one of the best in the state, if Mr. Simpson's research is right. You will be given an open line of credit with D.Q. Enterprises. Rell will over see it. The better you manage your money the more you will have. You also have a vacation spot to do as you please. Derek, don't fuck it up. Rell won't play with you and the company funds."

Derek thought to himself. *"Rell looks like a softy. I'll run the money the way I want. By the time he gets to me, I'll have what I want and be done with it. Thanks Pops you answered my prayers."*

"Darryl, your dilemma is similar to your nephew's. You asked for two hundred thousand. I'm giving you one hundred thousand. Seek financial advice. See Rell if need be. When that's gone Darryl, it's gone."

"Nikki, did you hit Tonya yet." Everyone at the table laughed. "Nikki, baby I wanted us to be together. Did mama tell you I filed for a divorce? Don't take stress tabs, they'll give you an ulcer. You can quit that damn job. You can start your home décor business you always wanted. Rell and Mr. Simpson can help you set your business up. I don't know what you will do, but you don't need to work, and Rell will help me with that. Our house is paid for. Your car is paid for. All your vacation homes are paid for. You already know you have stocks and rollover investments for cash. Baby live well. If you find someone you love like you loved me, tell him to take care of your heart, soul, and mind. Those are the only things I can't handle from here. I love you girl. Be it right or wrong, I always loved you. If I had to do it again, knowing the end, I would take the chance to love you over and over."

Nikki was crying in her seat. Tears rolled from D.Q.'s eyes, he had started crying on the screen. Tracy cut off the screen and waited. They all reached for tissues, water and each other. Tracy turned the screen on after everyone got themselves together.

"I'm sorry, Nikki, remember I love you."

"Rell, when you were born, I started this mission of setting everyone up, so they would be above the norm when and if I passed before they did. It took devotion. It took good friends. You will find them waiting for your call. That's Alan Scott and Robert Franklin. It took a personal confidant, Mr. Simpson. He knew my dilemma from the time I met Nikki, until my death. He took care of us, so I wouldn't lose what I built. I leave you them and D.Q. Enterprises. You have land, money, and success. Take care of your mother. Take care of those remaining at the table. You will notice; I knew Tonya would leave."

They all snickered.

"Seriously Rell I have prepared you for this day. Don't fear the unseen. It's there, you have to know how to look for it. You have three good guides. They won't steer you wrong. Rell, Derek and Dershai, take these final words. When you find the person you love, love them with all your heart, soul and mind. Don't love them because it is what is expected of you or what everyone around you believes you should do. Love them because you would die if you couldn't love them. Love them as long as they love and respect you. Love them because you love yourself. Be true to yourself and you will always be true to those you love."

"Mr. Simpson, sir, it has been an honor. Take care of my family as you would your own. Thank you. I love you all take care."

The screen went black. The family sat in silence taking it all in.

Chapter 74

Mr. Simpson spent the next half hour setting up appointments for the family to come to his office to be briefed on their inheritance. Nana reminded him that she wanted to talk to the family in his conference room. Mr. Simpson told her it wouldn't be a problem.

"Can you all sit for a minute or two? I would like to talk with you before we all leave."

Everyone took the seats they had during the reading and listened as Nana spoke.

"D.Q. has explained most of what I wanted to say. We must move on as a family. I would expect that we can all conduct ourselves as adults. If you can't get along, stay away from me with the drama. My house is open to all of you. I won't close the door to one to spare the feelings of another. There will be no bickering about who got what or who does what with what they got in my home. I love you all and I want us to have strong family ties. We've learned a lot about the damage secrets can cause. It's been a lesson to us all. I want to congratulate Rell, you have worked hard and it paid off. I still can't call you D.Q. though it's just too damn many of you with those initials."

Everyone laughed. They agreed to get together from time to time. Everyone got Nikki and Rell's numbers and address information and gave them theirs. What would seem to be a disastrous meeting turned out to be a happy moment in their lives. Rell approached Shai and winked. She smiled.

"Rell, we really need to talk."

"I know. I still want you to meet me at the suite. Is that possible?"

"Nothings changed for me Rell. I will follow your lead."

Rell thought to himself. *"I'm in love with my sister. What the hell? Damn, I can't continue loving her this way."*

"Mr. Simpson, we're done here, may I talk with you sir?"

"Sure Mr. Mince. Let me tell Tracy to hold my calls."

Rell told everyone he would talk to them later. They said their goodbyes and Rell returned to Mr. Simpson's office.

"Mr. Simpson, I can't say I'm overwhelmed with the transactions of today. I think I was mentally prepared for it. I knew my father would be leaving his company and assets to me. I also know it will take time for me to learn all that D.Q. Enterprises is involved in. I have no doubt that you will be sure I am aware of all I need to know. But Mr. Simpson I need to know about investigations done by D.Q. Enterprises. I know what Craig was up to, Mitch and I caught him extorting a client. I would imagine that by now he has been terminated. I know you guys knew what he was up to before we did. Who decides what and who is investigated?"

"Rell, that's not your question. You are concerned about you and your situation, and you have good reason for that concern. We investigate to protect top management. Anyone and everything that may hurt you or one of the partners may hurt the company. All is not told or made public information but top management is aware of all investigations and their findings."

"So, you know about me and Dershai."

"Yes."

"Mr. Simpson we didn't know we were related. We've been talking for two years. We started being intimate when I came into town for this reading."

"Rell we know that the relationship just got heavy. Your father knew the two of you talked. We debated whether or not to step in and stop you from the beginning. We decided it was your father's secret all these years, he didn't tell you for a reason. We do know you fled to Maryland when you found out he wasn't married. We didn't want you to go any further. Your father passed before he got the chance to talk with you about his affairs and Dershai. We needed you to accept your position at D.Q. Enterprises. You are accepting the appointment aren't you?"

"Yeah, I 'm definitely accepting the position my father wanted me to have. I just don't know what to do about this situation with Dershai. It's not as easy as you think Mr. Simpson. I love her, and not as a sister. I have made love to her. How do I back up from a woman I don't know as a sister? I only know her as a lover. You can't just cut love off like that"

"You and your father have a way of having difficult love affairs. How are you going to keep this away from your family? Rell you can't possibly think that it's okay to love your sister this way? How does she feel?"

"Mr. Simpson, she's my half sister. She has become my complete lover. Dershai has expressed she loves me too. I don't know what we're going to do. She's meeting me later. You said you handled my dad's personal business. Now you will handle mine. No investigations about me and Dershai. Our personal business is off limits. I will tell you what we plan to do, if anything. If I should find out anyone other than the partners knows about Dershai and I, all of you will lose what you have grown to love."

"I understand Rell. You sound like your father when he told us about Nikki and you. We have done this before. Your secret is safe with the partnership."

"Mr. Simpson, I want to make sure she is taken care of. As I said, I will be seeing her this evening, and we will decide what to do from that point on. I don't want it to look like I am doing more for her than anyone else. Let it be that you and the partners are looking out for her because she is my father's daughter. She lives in a condo near the University with Derek. I will be talking with him this week. I want them both to have their own condos. They can choose where."

"Rell they have lived together since they left their mother's home."

"Mr. Simpson if I want to visit her, I don't want Derek living there."

"Understood. Is there anything else?"

"No sir, I will call you in the morning."

"Rell, I am your personal lawyer you can call me when you need to. We will also need to sit down after you are settled in and go through your father's belongings."

"Thanks, you're right but I know you're going to be more to me than a lawyer."

"Then call me Stan."

"Okay, Stan it is. Thank you for listening. Don't hesitate to question what I say from time to time."

"Rell. I'm ahead of you. It's all taken care of."

Mr. Simpson walked Rell to the outer office doors. Rell's head was pounding. He couldn't wait to lay down.

Chapter 75

R ell called his mother and Nana telling them he would see them before the end of the week. He told them he planned on going to D.Q. Enterprises to set things up, so he could be in the office within a month. He would stay at the suite until he found a home. He had to put in his resignation at Sheldon Finances, and he would be traveling between Maryland and Virginia moving his personal belongings. Rell told his mother, he didn't know if he really wanted to live in Richmond, and he would have Mr. Simpson looking for land to build on if he couldn't find what he wanted. Everyone began to see D.Q. in Rell, and it pleased them.

Rell put his key in the suite's door. He opened the door to the smell of food cooking, soft music and candles burning. He looked around the room and didn't see Shai.

"Shai, Shai?"

"I'm in the bedroom Rell."

"What's up with all of this?"

Rell entered the suite placing his briefcase on the chaise lounge. He decided against walking into the bedroom. He grabbed a beer from the refrigerator and returned to the chair and sat down. The evening was setting in and Rell felt as though he could sleep for two days. His body and mind were beginning to show the lack of rest.

"Are you upset?"

"No, babe. I just…. Shai we have to seriously talk about us."

"I didn't think you were mad about it."

"I'm not. I'm confused. I'm not okay with it at all. It hurts. I want to love you. I want…. baby this is hard as hell."

Shai entered the room with two wine glasses. Rell shook his head no slowly and Shai poured wine for herself leaving the other glass on the bar.

"Rell, I want what you want. If I have to move to west hell where no one knows us, I am willing to do that. I don't want us to stop loving each other because we're half blood. What is that anyway?"

"It's that secret shit. I don't want us to have to love each other in secret Shai. Love is beautiful. I want people to see us hold hands, kiss, get married, have children. Shai before today I saw that for us. Now, man, shit, I don't want you as a sister."

"Rell, I don't need you as a brother. It's what fate has determined. It's still up to us. We can't make this a problem. I don't want to date or love anyone else. I am committed to you."

"Shai, how is our family going to feel, seeing that we never have anyone around? No girlfriend or boyfriend, no lovers ever? How is that going to work? I am the CEO of D.Q. Enterprises. I go to a convention with my sister on my side, and we stay in the same room. How does that read in the entertainment news? Baby, how will we cover the fact that when I see you my body cries out to you?"

"I'm not a business world girl. I can always travel with you as the daughter of the late D.Q. Mince. We can always get suites that are joined but not visibly together, or I can stay in an entirely different hotel. I can live somewhere else. Rell, my attachment here is my job, and I can find an opening for my position at any hospital in America. Rell you love me, I know you do. I love you. That's all that matters. If it doesn't work, don't let it be because you think someone will talk. They will talk if I'm not around. They will say the outside child pushed the wife's kids out of the business. Derek is not going to handle that money right. That's why our father wants you to watch him. Derek is not going to let you dictate his every move. Derek won't be around for long. I love him but he has my mother's ways."

"So you wouldn't mind getting your own place? I can handle Derek and his business problems. But the two of you are close. How will he like the change?"

"That condo is mine. But I hear you. Yes, I will tell him he can stay in the one I own. I'll buy another."

"You won't have to. I've told Mr. Simpson to purchase one wherever you want. It will be paid for through the company."

"You told Mr. Simpson about us?"

"Shai, the partners and Mr. Simpson have an investigation team. They have been watching us for two years. They know we're in love. They will protect the company from scandals. I have to let him know what we want, and they will see to it, we are protected. But Shai, we have to understand how this will look to others. We have to be brother and sister in the eyes of everyone who knows us."

"Rell, Marci knows about us. I told her about you and our conversations, since we met. She also knows I love you, and we made love."

"Anyone else?"

"Mia her sister but she will think we broke up if I don't mention you around her. Marci's good at keeping secrets. I needed someone to know, just in case you were a stalker or something. I told them the day after you and I got together for our first weekend."

"Hmph, well I guess I told Mitch for the same reason. Okay, let's invite Mitch and Marci to eat dinner with us Saturday and explain the situation. Now, what do we do about us?"

"What do you mean? I thought we would continue our relationship as it is?"

"Shai, it doesn't bother you a little that I am your brother? I mean doesn't it make you hesitate?"

"Rell, you're not what I consider a brother. I look at you as the close friend that I swore was off limits and I fell in love with. I can't shout it out loud, at least not in this state, but I love you, and I am not afraid of anyone knowing."

"Whoa, we can't let anybody know. Marci and Mitch and the partnership team, that's it. Shai if it should get out and become gossip, I will deny it and leave you alone forever. This is going to be hard for me Shai. I love being open with my feelings."

"We'll work it out together. There's nothing wrong with a sister and brother getting acquainted as adults. What we do behind closed doors is our business."

"I hope we can keep it behind those doors."

"Okay, Rell. I understand. I cooked for you. Baby, let's eat."

Rell smiled. Shai looked at him bashfully.

"I didn't mean that. I cooked dinner. It's ready."

"Hmmm. So am I."

Chapter 76

Several weeks had passed since the reading of D.Q.'s will. Tonya had been to her lawyer's office three times and was denied access to talk with him. She refused to make an appointment. Through a written correspondence Mr. Monroe had sent her copies of D.Q.'s will and explained that she was not a beneficiary or an investor in D.Q. Enterprises. She called the offices to speak with Darrell and was told he would not be taking calls until after the first of August. That was a month away. Tonya called Derek and Dershai to have dinner with them but neither of them returned her call.

Derek got the money to invest in starting his web design company. He and Rell sat down and drew up the financial plans for the business. Darryl sent his architectural drawings for Derek's approval. Darryl agreed to hire the crew to build the building once Derek was ready. Derek quickly found out that Rell was a business whiz and was not the softy he thought him to be. Rell showed him how to make money hand over fist with his company. Derek found a friend in his brother.

Nikki spent her spare time in the church activities and outings with Deacon Smalls. After being formerly introduced by Nana and Reverend Wilcox, they truly enjoyed each other's company. Darlene and Nikki shopped and visited each other often.

Darryl gambled a good portion of his money away after paying off his debts. Francine immediately called Rell and told him he had a problem and needed his nephew to pull him out of it before he was in debt again. Rell decided he would make Darryl responsible for land development, as a consultant in D.Q. Enterprises. Darryl was too busy to gamble and the money that he made he could have never won at a black jack table.

Mitch and Marci really hit it off at the dinner that Shai and Rell gave. They started dating. Mitch and Byron were due to start as partners in D.Q. Enterprises in September. They both were looking forward to moving to Richmond.

Shai moved into a home in Chesterfield, outside of Richmond. The house was large, complete with a pool and an oversized yard. It was separated by trees and a brook from the property around it. Rell teased her saying she lived on her own little island.

Rell would be moving to Norfolk, he had his uncle design the home and the builders had begun the framework. Shai and Rell continued their love affair. Mr. Simpson kept his word, although he kept his eye on them himself.

Nana invited the family for dinner and told them she wanted everyone there by four o'clock sharp. It had been two months since D.Q.'s death and none of them had been to see Nana. They all had called but their schedules didn't give them much time to visit. Sunday was a date for all.

"Darlene, see if those greens are done. I think they're ready. The macaroni and cheese is done I took that out of the stove with the candied yams. I sure hope Wallace didn't nibble at the church."

"Mama he knew you were cooking all this food. Why would he eat at the church?"

"To keep them hens from talking, I told him they're gonna talk anyway."

"Is Deacon Smalls coming?"

"I guess him and Nikki will come by. You can't separate them two. They knew each other before and didn't care nothing about each other. Strangest thing, love sure is funny."

Mia entered the kitchen. She placed the bags of soda and chips she had on the counter.

"Hey, Nana. Hey, ma. Did Marci get here yet?"

"No, Mia. Hand me that big bowl in the cabinet by you. I think Marci is waiting for Mitch to pick her up. I didn't know they were seeing each other."

"Nana, they're just dating. I don't think it's serious."

"Ain't for you to decide. I think so. They can't stay away from each other just like.... Just like you and Reverend Wilcox I hear."

"Mia! Who told you that? Tell.

"Y'all set the table. Everyone should be here shortly."

The family started coming in. Mitch was with Marci. Deacon Smalls walked in with Nikki. Reverend Wilcox arrived earlier than expected. Derek and Byron drove together. Dershai came in five minutes before Rell.

"Well Rev, if you'll bless the food we can get started."

Reverend Wilcox blessed the food and the Mince family and friends ate until they all were ready to pass out.

"That sure was a good meal Jewels. I love when you want to cook. You put your heart into it. It tastes so good."

"Thanks Wallace. I guess I thought about you and being blessed with your company and our family." "Hmm, our family, I like the sound of that."

Epilogue

Rell stood in his office window looking over downtown Richmond. Fall was quickly settling in. It was late September and it was on the cool side. Everything was going well. His home was completed and the furniture had been delivered. Derek was settled in his own company, the building's construction had begun. It wasn't to far from D.Q. Enterprises. His Uncle Darryl wasn't gambling away his earnings. Nana had found a true companion in Reverend Wilcox. Rell was waiting for them to say they would be getting married. His mother was busy in the church and home decorating. She had quit her job as a Secretarial Assistant. She was going on dates with Deacon Smalls but wouldn't say it was more to it than that. Byron and Mitch were set up as partners in D.Q. Enterprises. They used their stock investments from Sheldon Finances to buy their shares into a company where they all could be partners. Their offices were down the hall, and they had begun working on in house accounts. The phone rang. Rell pushed the speaker button.

"Yes."

"It's Mrs. Tonya Mince."

"Transfer the call."

"I'm sorry Mr. Mince. She's here in the reception area."

"Well, send her in." The door to his office opened quicker than he expected.

"Good morning Ms. Mince."

"Morning, Rell."

"What can I do for you?"

"I want someone to look into this so called liquidated stock that your father left me during our separation. I can't seem to find the holding company. No one has any information on it."

Rell pushed the intercom.

"Mitch, can you step in my office please."

"Oh, aren't you the businessman? Did you know this was your father's office?"

"Yes, I spent many afternoons and Saturday's here."

Mitch came into the office not noticing Tonya walking around the office observing pictures from Rell's black art collection.

"Yeah, Rell what's up? Oh, I'm sorry. I didn't see you had a client."

"This is Mrs. Tonya Mince. Could you take this information from her? Find out what you can, so she can contact the proper holding company. Let me know how you make out Mrs. Mince. If there is anything else you need, Mitch will handle it for you."

"Oh, you don't handle this stuff. What do you handle? Do you treat Derek and Dershai like this or do you handle them personally?"

"Mrs. Mince if you follow me to my office, I'll handle your problem."

Rell stood in shock. *Did that mean that she knew something about him and Dershai?* He called Mr. Simpson.

Mr. Simpson told him he was in the building and would be in his office in a few minutes. Rell called Shai on his cell.

"Shai, hey baby, how are you?"

"Busy, but okay. I have classes tonight. Did you read the message I left on the refrigerator this morning?"

"Yeah, listen you mother just left here. Well, she's with Mitch. She's looking for the holding company her stock was sold to. But she just threw me for a loop. I asked Mitch to help her because I didn't think she would be comfortable with me. She asked did I handle you and Derek personally. Do you think she knows something?"

"No, babe. She knows you helped Derek get his company started, and she knows you helped me get my home. Don't be fooled by her. She'll pick until someone tells her what she wants to hear or can build her assumptions on. Rell dealing with her is like dealing with poison. You may need to tell Mitch to treat her with kid gloves. She knows he deals with Marci."

"Alright, but babe, she may be your mother, but I will get her off our backs."

"Rell you do what you have to do. I've got to go baby, love you."

"I love you too."

Rell turned around as Mr. Simpson knocked on the door and entered.

"What's the problem Rell?"

Rell explained what transpired and waited for Mr. Simpson to respond.

"Rell, what do you want us to do? We have a lot on her. Your father let her live knowing her dirt."

"I'm not my father."

"I understand.

Mr. Simpson left the office. Mitch spoke to him as he was leaving giving him the information he had passed on to Tonya. Mitch closed the office door and threw up his hands in disgust.

"Rell she is whacked. It's a good thing she can't be your mother-n-law."

"Shut up Mitch. Just shut up." They both laughed. "Man, she's done. Mr. Simpson is on it. She'll be finished and then the only time she'll have is to take care of her business.

"So it's good."

"Mitch, it is what it is."

Excerpt From The Sequel:

A Different Kind
of Love

Chapter 1

Mitch packed his briefcase with contracts he had to read before the morning. He hadn't heard from Marci, and he thought it was strange. He was falling in love with her. It had been four months since they got together. He planned on asking for her hand in marriage during the Christmas Holidays. Darlene told Mitch she couldn't wait for them to be married because Marci only talked of him and the things they did together. He was ready for the commitment. He hadn't told anyone yet of his intentions, and he decided he would spring it on Byron and Rell while they were at the sports bar this weekend. Football season had started and they had a date every other Sunday at the sports bar. The alternate Sundays they spent entertaining the females in their life. Byron was dating Tracey, a young lady who worked as a paralegal for Mr. Simpson, the lawyer for DQ Enterprises.

Mitch passed Rell's office and wondered what was going on. Rell never left early. He waited until he got to his car and called Rell's cell phone.

"What's up Rell? You never leave early."

"I left today to get my mother some flowers. It's her birthday tomorrow and she already said she would be going out of town, so I took off to spend some time with her. Is everything okay with you?"

"Yeah, have you heard from Shai or Marci today?"

"They're spending our money man. They went to the spa. Shai passed some exam that had her stressed out, and she's celebrating. I don't think Marci even knew she was coming by to get her. Call her on her cell man. You missing her like that?"

"Man, don't start? You can't talk. If Shai didn't call you, Rell, you know you would break down."

"It's a different kind of love man. We've been dealing with each other for almost three years. Well, I guess we can't count the first two."

"Yeah you can't count long distance phone calls. Anyway, I'll call her now. Thanks man."

Mitch looked at his phone. "Why didn't she call?"

Mitch's phone rang.

"Hello."

"Mitch? Hey baby. I know you guess I lost my mind."

"No, you made me lose my mind. I just wanted to know you were alright."

"I'll meet you at your place. This spa is closer to you. Shai drove so she'll drop me off at your house."

"Do you want me to pick anything up for dinner?"

"Okay, umm, pick up some Chinese Food. You know what to get right?"

"Yeah, baby I know. Marci, call me if you're going to be later than you think. Those roads to the house get dark."

"I will. Love you."

"Love you too."

Marci went back to the room where she and Shai were waiting to get a manicure and pedicure. She noticed Shai holding her head.

"Hey, what's wrong girl?"

"I think that Sauna heat got to me. I feel dizzy. My head is heavy."

"You probably need some air. We're not next. We can step out into the other room. I'll tell the girl where we'll be."

"Thanks." Shai had been feeling bad the past few days. It was a weird sick feeling, she didn't know what it was. Marci came back and sat near her.

"You look sick. Shai are you alright?"

"Girl, I feel like, damn, I feel sick."

"Maybe you got a touch of the flu."

"I'm going to the doctor's office tomorrow."

"We can skip the pedicure and the manicure. Let me tell her you're not feeling well."

"Get a refund, I paid for everything already."

Marci got the reimbursement and told Shai they would reschedule. She walked her to the car and told Shai to give her the keys.

"I'll drive you home and tell Mitch to pick me up at your house. Do you want me to call Rell for you?"

Marci helped Shai into the car. Shai let the seat back and closed her eyes. "No, don't call him Marci. He's going to his mother's today. Her birthday is tomorrow and she is leaving town for the weekend."

Marci drove while Shai tried to drift off to sleep. They pulled in her driveway twenty minutes later. Marci tapped Shai and they both got out the car.

"Do you feel better? Maybe you need some Ginger Ale to settle your stomach."

"I have some in the house. Rell usually drinks that. Marci, this is the strangest feeling. I don't think it's a cold."

Marci's phone rang. "Hello."

"Marci, are you still at the spa?"

"No, as a matter of a fact, I was going to call you. Can you pick me up at Shai's?"

"Well, it will be after seven. I have to stop at Rell's mom's house. He has a file I need."

"That's okay Shai doesn't feel well so we left the spa."

"What's wrong with her?"

"I don't know. She's going to take something for her head and stomach and lay down."

"Alright, I'll pick you up after I leave there."

"See you then."

Marci went into the house with Shai. She offered to make her a cup of tea. Shai told her she would try the tea instead of the Ginger Ale. When Marci returned to Shai, she had laid down on the couch. She was sleep. Marci turned on the television and waited for Mitch.

Chapter 2

"Ms. Mince, follow me please."

Shai got up from her seat in the waiting room and followed the nurse.

"The doctor will be in to see you. Please take off your clothes and put on the gown on the table. There's a cup there for your urine sample. When you're done place the cup through that little window on the right side of the counter."

"Thank you."

Shai hadn't told Rell she was going to the doctor. She made the appointment after she had missed her period twice. She was too scared to take the EPT at home. If she was pregnant she wanted to know how far along she was. Shai went into the bathroom and followed the nurse's instructions.

Rell walked into Mitch's office laughing with Byron.

"Man, Mitch didn't even give us a chance to change our mind. He just said he had things to do. We knew Marci had him under her control."

Mitch started smiling. He was sitting behind his desk. He looked up.

"Y'all got jokes. I miss one Sunday and you jump right on it. Marci had made plans that I didn't know about. It happens."

"She got you man."

"Byron, who got who?"

5

"Man that's Rell talking. You didn't hear me saying a word. I know I get caught up sometime. So I know the feeling."

"Oh, Byron, you taking sides?"

"No, man, I'm just saying I get caught doing things at the last minute too. Wait Rell you do too."

"Not lately man. I haven't missed any of our outings."

"No, Rell, it works fine for you. You set the dates."

They all laughed. The intercom caused them to be silenced.

"Yes, Ms. Berry."

"I'm looking for Mr. Mince."

"Yes, Ms. Berry, I'm here. What's up?"

"You have a phone call. Ms. Mince says it's urgent?"

"Transfer the call here please."

"Rell?"

"Shai, what's up?"

"Call me on your cell please."

"Alright, are you on your cell?"

"Yes, please call me right back."

"Okay. Hang up the line."

"What's wrong Rell?" Mitch was concerned. Marci told Mitch Shai wasn't feeling much better, and it had been three days.

"I'm not sure. Hello, Shai?"

"Rell what time are you getting off?"

"I can get off now. What's the problem?"

"I'll meet you at the house."

"Mine or yours? Shai what is wrong?"

"Yours. I want to tell you then."

Rell hung up the phone. "Mitch man I'll call you guys back. I don't know what's wrong."

Rell drove home thinking something had happened to Derek or Tonya. He couldn't imagine what, just that something had happened to them. *"Shai should have been at work. Maybe someone found out about us, and she's upset about it."*

Tonya had not been back to the office since her visit two weeks prior. Mitch told her the name of the holding company and escorted her to the front of the offices. Mr. Simpson told Rell she should be calling him within a week to complain. *"Maybe Tonya complained to Shai."*

Rell pulled into his driveway. Shai's car was in the garage. He used that entrance to inspect her car, just in case she had been in an accident. Shai was sitting on the couch with tissue on the table and in her hand. She had been crying. When Rell walked in the room she looked up at him, she had been crying a long time. Her eyes were bloodshot.

"Baby, what's wrong?"

"Rell, I didn't think this would happen. I don't know what we're going to do. Say you love me Rell.

"Alright Shai, you're making me mad now. You know I love you. What is wrong?"

"I went to the doctor today. I hadn't been feeling well for about a week or two. I was sick in the stomach and dizzy and just sick."

"What did the doctor say Shai?"

"I'm five months pregnant. I thought everything was fine. I've had my period." Shai lied about the last two months. She thought if anything she would be three months pregnant, and she would have an abortion.

"Five months Shai? Your period came last month?"

"Yes, the doctor said that is possible. I had a little blood today. She said that is just because I am a little upset."

"You should have told him you were a lot upset. We can't have children Shai. How are we going to put this over on anyone? Damn, what about the baby? Will it be healthy?"

"Rell, there's something else. She said I am fine and so are they."

"They, they who?"

"They're twins, Rell. I'm pregnant with twins."

"Shai, oh no. Baby what did he say about an abortion? I mean you can't want to go through this with their health being questionable."

"Rell, he said I was too far along for it to be safe to have an abortion. It's not safe for the babies or me."

"What about their health Shai? You know they say they could be born with deformities or mental problems when siblings are the parents."

Shai started crying again. Rell was pacing the floor.

"Baby, how are we going to do this? My own kids are going to call me uncle 'because they can't call me daddy?"

"Rell, do you love me?"

"Shai you know I love you. Loving you got us into this shit. But, yes baby, I love you."

"I love you too. I love you and we'll get through this."

"Twins?"

"Twins."

Rell sat next to Shai on the couch. He kissed her and pulled her into his chest as he sat back on the couch.

CPSIA information can be obtained at www.ICGtesting.com
Printed in the USA
BVOW08s2213251015

423981BV00001B/1/P